MW01503354

# Marek Torčík

# Memory Burn

Translated by Graeme and Suzanne Dibble

CEEOL Press
2025

Originally published in Czech Rozložíš paměť by Paseka in 2023

Translated by Graeme and Suzanne Dibble
English translation © 2025 Graeme and Suzanne Dibble

Published in 2024 by CEEOLPRESS,
Frankfurt am Main, Germany

This publication was supported by
the Ministry of Culture of the Czech Republic.

Copy editing: Linda Turner
Typesetting: CEEOL GmbH, CEEOL Press
Layout: Alexander Neroslavsky

ISBN: 978-3-949607-76-9
E-ISBN: 978-3-949607-77-6

"Who has not asked himself at some time or other:
am I a monster or is this what it means to be a person?"

– Clarice Lispector

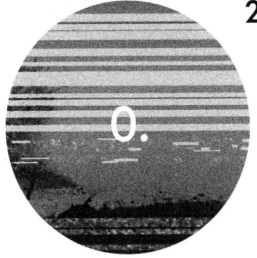

At 3.37 a.m., you're woken by the phone.

Your mother's voice is quiet and yet you can hear every syllable clearly.

"Marek, your grandad's dead."

You fail to detect anything unusual or urgent in this sentence, so you don't manage to come to your senses quickly enough. Your mother hangs up before you can say anything. You sit up and rub your eyes.

For a while, the darkness on the walls seems uniform but, gradually, you discover places punctuated by twisted bands of golden light from the street. Patches you can't focus on.

It occurs to you that there are things you haven't told anyone about yet. For instance, in the eighth year at school,

3

Filip didn't really throw you down the stairs. It was your own stupid fault that you fell, and when you came to, you wanted to use the situation to your advantage. Surprisingly, it all went pretty smoothly. Just a couple of weeks later, you were sitting in the headmaster's office in a new school, listening to a greying man with a glint in his eye. He was shouting: "I will not tolerate any bullying here, mark my words!"

You'd been given a second chance, at least according to your mother.

"Try not to stand out too much, OK?" she urged you as the two of you walked along the corridor towards the classroom. You were determined to fit in. Not to be different, not to talk to anyone about what was on your mind. Not to give any sign of who you were. You had learnt to watch your every step, not to sway your pelvis too much, not to stare at others for too long. Before you went into the room, you cleared your throat and tried out a new – deeper – voice, and since then no-one has known the real you. Whenever the guys started talking about girls, you kept your head down. You'd laugh and pretend to go along with it, and then, later, you copied them by having a naked woman as the wallpaper on your mobile.

But the truth is, you couldn't bear to look at her. Whereas you remember Grandad snatching the mobile out of your hand a few days later. You were visiting him at the psychiatric hospital in Kroměříž when he reached out and grabbed the phone, nearly falling out of bed in the process. He looked at the screen for a long time, nodding appreciatively.

Why didn't you tell anyone about that?

Grandad's dead, but time marches on. Time flows and, in the streams of light from the street, you search for a memory, for something that'll take you back. In the darkness, you can hear another body breathing; Jakub grunts in his sleep and rolls over onto his other side. It's nighttime but the city still echoes with lots of noises. Through the open window come the sounds of cars, a group of men shouting in the street as they leave the pub at closing time. Occasionally, you catch snippets of a foreign language, laughter. You can't seem to sense any sadness in all of this. For a while, you wait for something to change, sitting with your head slightly bowed, your fingers absent-mindedly tapping on the screen of your mobile.

What's missing around you is also missing within you. Instead of sadness, what you discover is a silent, wordless space. You find it slightly odd that suddenly you can't picture Grandad's face. Instead of his actual appearance, all you see is the faces from old photographs.

You try to picture him again. There's absolutely nothing left of him.

You dial your mum's number because you realize you didn't even ask her how she was.

She answers the phone so quickly you barely have time to put it to your ear.

"I was supposed to go and see him in the morning."

The device transmits her voice into the gloom, where it bounces off the walls and comes back to you faintly from across the room.

"I had a bag all packed for him with all the stuff he asked for."

And yet you remember other things quite well. Other faces and feelings. Other stories.

It's probably because your grandad's story was passed on to you by your mother. Your own memories are relegated to the background, like characters who are not involved in the plot. Characters who have seemingly played their part and are now waiting, locked in rooms that are lost in memory. He became the grandad you know – knew – because of her.

With only a few exceptions, he spent the final years of his life in a psychiatric hospital. One day, he simply went mad, started seeing things no-one else could see. The doctors at the hospital in Kroměříž put it down to his illness, and too much alcohol and smoking. *And those lungs too.* Ruined, coated in tar. They could no longer support his memory, and it began to disintegrate along with him.

Your mother talked about him a lot. When you were young, she told you what it meant to grow up with someone like that, what alcohol had done to Grandad, how many times she and Gran had spent hours waiting patiently outside the pub just so they didn't have to go in after him.

It usually came back to one night in particular. The night that changed everything. She kept returning to it, equally shaken and confused each time, as though it might open up another path, the door to a room that had been locked up until then, and she'd understand something that had escaped her before.

Your first memory of Grandad is shrouded in a peculiar haze; sometimes, you feel as if you must have made it up. You weren't even five years old, and the two of you were standing on the hill above Hotel Jana in Přerov, watching the river Bečva, which had burst its banks and spilled out over the school playground as far as the car park. You held your grandad's hand while the frothy brown water below you lapped at the walls of the tower blocks. Grandad watched all of this in silence, then suddenly pointed to a flock of birds circling in the sky and said: "See them? They're confused cos they've got nowhere to land. Normally, they have no trouble flying over water. They're smart cookies – they manage to come back to exactly the same place year after year." You stared at him open-mouthed, hanging on his every word. "Just imagine what it's like for a swallow – suddenly everything below it is different. You see, nature's kitted them out with their very own compass, a tiny bit of metal right here in their beak, and that means they can cover huge distances even when they're flying blind. But they've still got to be able to see to land." He moved his finger towards a black blur that was swooping down at regular intervals, letting out a long desperate cry. "There, look. They're definitely trying to find the place where they usually land."

You swallow, your throat dry. The reverberation of this memory is something you perceive differently today – more sharply. You're pretty sure it hadn't occurred to either of you back then that everything Grandad said could be applied to people as well: we too are always trying to get back to ourselves, back to places that haven't been the same for a long time.

You're ten years old. Apart from the number of books you've read and the fact you don't really talk to anyone, there's nothing strange about you. However, you can't say the same for Marián, a boy who joined your class halfway through the school year. Marián was quiet, wore strangely tapered jeans and had long dark hair. In fact, you immediately came to associate him with a description of Professor Snape. *With greasy black hair, a hooked nose, and sallow skin.* But instead of being sallow, Marián's skin was dark and flecked with tiny white spots. He sat with his legs crossed and spent all his time at school alone. He had a strange perfumey smell and, from your desk, his long neck looked like a girl's. So, at this point, the whole class's attention was focused on Marián. The other boys would regularly empty the contents of the bin into his schoolbag, deliberately barge into him in gym class. Later, in the changing room, you'd notice bruises all over his body. He was a poof and a faggot and walked like a spaz and was a black cunt. "You're worse than a girl," they shouted at him at breaktime, while

8

the teachers headed to the staff room, pretending not to hear anything. You bandied the same words around, hoping no-one would notice your crossed legs, your glances at the sweaty bodies in the changing rooms. Because you still remembered. You still knew what it was like to be on the other side. Until recently, you too had been the target of similar words. You too had been a *poof. A swot*. And lots of other things. You too had returned home with the strap of your schoolbag torn off, your T-shirt ruined.

Within this memory, you're sitting at your desk, staring absent-mindedly out of the window. Marián is walking back from the blackboard, where the teacher had probably been testing him for way too long. The strong scent of fabric softener from his clothes still lingers in your memory. He's about to sit down when Filip, who sits behind him, pulls the chair out from under him. Time doesn't stop. Time speeds up. Marián flings his arms up in the air and hits his head against the edge of the desk. The hollow thud is followed by the clatter of the chair. A muffled thump. Silence. Everything happened too fast for your brain to process. It's the sequence of sounds you remember more than the movement itself. More than the others' reaction, you remember the pool of blood oozing out of the boy's body. A fragile body that deviated from the norm, just like yours.

You're ashamed of yourself. These are images you return to reluctantly, only when you're surrounded by silence and darkness and have no choice. Were you aware at the time how much the whole thing affected you?

9

Grandad used to be fond of saying that the only thing Hitler did right was to put the gypsies and poofs in concentration camps. In his world, words had no impact on the bodies he directed them at; it was just about him finally being able to speak the *truth* out loud. "It's a free fucking country, isn't it?!" he would yell angrily at the TV whenever he didn't like something. He always did this the second someone objected. He was oblivious to the pain caused by language, an impact comparable to a blow to the head. Words couldn't make life unbearable or leave scars in the memory. "He's just sounding off," Mum would say, mostly to reassure herself. Grandad never once connected the things he said with the fist in his grandson's face.

These days, you know that violence can replace language just as easily as words can become weapons. A fist is often just a sentence that is intelligible to everyone.

Back then, Marián was taken away in an ambulance and the whole class was left in a state of shock. No-one spoke, no-one dared move from their seat. But the next day everything went on at the usual pace. You didn't even pause by the empty desk, pretended not to hear the shouting from the headmaster's office, where the boy's mother wanted an explanation of what exactly had happened.

A few months after that, Filip – who by some miracle had managed to get off scot-free – knocked the wind out of you in PE. Marián was back by then; at first, everyone tiptoed around him, and Filip was raging. The class teacher had deliberately sat him at the desk beside Marián. "You have to learn to respect one another," she'd said, refusing to discuss the matter any further. Filip needed to find another outlet for his pent-up anger and the frustration born of boredom. You were all doing the long jump, it was your turn, you started running, counting the steps, three more, two, you stretched out your arms – and, just before you took off, Filip tripped you up. The blood from your split lip was the same colour as the blood freshly stored in your memory. There was less of it and yet your body still vibrates with its aftertaste to this day.

You remember the summer when it all fell apart. The darkness behind the window of someone else's flat, the fall shortly before that; the way some things are related to each other, even though you might not see it yourself. Everything is interconnected. Even Grandad's seizure and Mum's angry, miserable face. You remember the days before and the days after, and once again it occurs to you: there are things you haven't told anyone about yet.

You've never trusted stories that rely on a single point of view. If I'd asked you yesterday, you would've answered that nothing good could come out of memories of your grandad – there are simply too many things you have no idea about. There's so much you don't remember. And, anyway, it's not all about him. Missing memories, gaps in the memory. But what if the answer lies elsewhere? What if the key actually lies in those gaps, and all you need to do is insert unrelated images into them to show that even seemingly disconnected stories are all interwoven.

It was your mother who made Grandad human again. She was the only one in the family who was willing to take care of him. To accept that people can change. To give him a second chance. The same one you were given back then, the same one you've been given so many times and will be given so many more times in your life. She sacrificed a part of herself for the two of you, and you still can't understand why.

In the morning, you wake up tired and confused with a single question, a single sentence in your head. You no longer recall where you read it. *What am I to myself that must be remembered, insisted upon so often?* You open your eyes and the space in front of you is a white wall – solid, with no shadows, lacking dimensions and depth. You close your eyes. *Something other than this*, you reply quietly and open them again. The sounds from the street are already battering against the windowpane. Somewhere below you, the city is ticking along – there are always cars stopping at junctions, trams running constantly and the sound of the traffic lights. Their intermittent rhythm disrupts the pounding of your heart, something you've had a problem with since you were a child – suddenly, the contractions are irregular, the intervals between beats get longer. Jakub says you should see a doctor about it.

At night, the traffic lights are silent, but their sound carries on in the memory.

You reach for your mobile on the bedside table and call your mum. In the gaps that follow the words, you can hear the noise of the workshop.

"They won't let me go home till the afternoon," she whispers, her voice cracking slightly.

You can picture your mother's face. Grandad tormented her most of her life; she rarely remembered anything positive about her childhood.

"I've got stuff I need to finish anyway. I know the world doesn't stop because of him."

You sit up and turn on the lamp, even though it's already light outside. This early in the morning, the language you think with isn't reminiscent of a restless, dangerous instrument. Of something you can use to deal out blows, let alone something you could use to describe the feeling that Grandad is gone and you are unable to say what he meant to you, just as sometimes you are unable to express who you are or describe the presence of another body beside you, the warm glow from that strange certainty that this body will be here for some time to come.

A breath out, a breath in, the creak of the bed frame.

That certainty spills over into the images and sounds around you. It's similar to the way the rhythm of the traffic lights affects your heartbeat and the regular pattern of shouts from the street interrupts the flow of your thoughts. If the things you can't utter can only be hinted at, their presence guessed at behind the cover of words, is it even possible to express a thing in a way that doesn't make it seem different, broken up into fragments?

You look around the room to convince yourself of this. To get closer to the truth. But all you do is trigger another series of memories. They appear suddenly, disjointedly, some only vaguely linked to your grandad, others not at all.

You're five years old, and your dad has taken you out on a pedalo on the pond below Plumlov Castle. You see the whole scene from a distance; you're standing on the bank, watching the child version of yourself gliding over the water.

The you-child is hypnotized by the sight of a giant shark hanging from the roof of the pedalo hire shop. In the darkness, two figures set off across the motionless expanse of water in the middle of the reservoir. The you-child watches the shark disappear, while the images in your mind conjure up other sharks. They swim below the surface and, each time the pedalo judders, the you-child imagines their snouts ramming its hull. Your father stretches out his arm to point at the silhouette of the nearby castle and his watch flies off his wrist. Its trajectory leads directly beneath the darkened surface of the water into the realm of imaginary sharks where, after a few miles, it will come to rest on the sandy bottom. The scene where the Heart of the Ocean stirs up the marine sediment. Cut to Rose's face, cut to the team of archaeologists, cut to your father with a fanatical expression as he strips off his T-shirt and, with the words *stay here*, jumps into the water.

14

When your father resurfaced, he didn't have the watch. Your mother has told you this story so many times that you can no longer recall how the whole thing happened, and perhaps that's why you can't see this memory with your own eyes. Over time, her version has become the model for the real events and you have effectively stopped differentiating between your mother's story and the original situation.

You often come back to this scene. You remember the panic, feel the waves of anger coursing through your body even after all the time that's elapsed. It felt as though your dad had been underwater for hours. Days passed, whole centuries passed, you imagined all kinds of scenarios: a shark with a man's leg in its jaws; your father's motionless face sinking into the darkness. But your father managed to claw his way up from the depths and back onto the pedalo, where he found you, your face purple with anger and tears.

The strange thing about this memory is how many different versions exist. You're the only one who remembers the shark on the roof of the hire shop, the only one who stood on the pedalo in the middle of that mass of water with all the weight of a child's world bearing down on his shoulders. Your father denies there ever was a watch; instead, he dived in after a phone, a wallet, whatever he considers the most essential commodity in a person's life at that particular moment in time. He's not sure if it was a pedalo or a rowing boat. And, in the end, perhaps it really is your mother – who got the whole thing second-hand – who is closest to the original version. Her account has only been eroded by the flow of time, plucked out of memory because, for her, the whole thing never actually happened.

What are memories but stories? I bring them up again in the belief that they belong to the same person you once were. You spin them into a web, sit within them as though they were the things keeping you afloat. But the truth is that with each retelling they turn into something different, something distant.

A few months after the scene on the pedalo, another fragment. You're with your dad in the hotel where he used to work. Dad's in the shower while you're watching the Cartoon Network. You don't have this channel at home, so you can't take your eyes off the screen. There's a terrible smell in the room. Dad comes out of the bathroom, and you shout at him that it stinks in here, could you please wash your feet again. You remember that, afterwards, he had to go off somewhere and you kept on watching TV until the picture gave way to grainy static. But the boundaries of this memory are no more real than the intersection between all the other versions you have stored away – you know it more as a script that you recite aloud, altering the individual scenes, minor and bigger details, according to who your audience is.

You immediately recall another one: You're standing with your dad beside the sink – you on a stool, he with his feet firmly on the floor. You both have white foam on your faces and you scrape it off in long strips with your razors. Yours doesn't have a blade, but that doesn't stop you from copying the careful movements of the man beside you. Once you're finished, you rinse the foam off in the sink and Dad wipes your face with a towel. Then he puts your razor in the cup next to his. The whole ritual fills you with happiness.

The problem arises when you fast-forward a few years and, in a pile of photos your anxious self takes with you when you go away to university, you find the scene by the sink faithfully captured.

Whatever the photo is supposed to show, what you see is a memory.

Now you're trying to work out when it was that someone – most likely Mum – took the photo, and you can no longer remember anything else. What led up to it? At most, you can still sense the movement of the plastic across your smooth face, the foam in the sink diluted by the water. The condensation on the mirror.

Somehow, that photo became the model for reality, the template for a memory playing tricks on you. You first saw it when you were a bit older; someone must have shown it to you, or maybe you sneaked into the wardrobe and secretly carried stacks of albums through to your room. Aren't you remembering it all wrong? All warped? Perhaps your father was right and you've joined several memories together. The end result doesn't make sense to anyone else.

Even before you moved to Prague, finished university and then severed all ties with the place where you grew up and with your family, you thought you had nothing in common with your mother. *We've got nothing to say to each other.* You roll that sentence around on your tongue, invoke it like an incantation so you can tear yourself away – from the pain, the shame, everything you're still afraid of even now.

You stand up, grab your T-shirt off the floor and pull it over your head. In the kitchen you start making coffee, and while you're waiting for at least enough for a cup to drip through into the pot, you sit on the wooden ledge by the window and lean against the wall. You're facing the backyard: a large inner courtyard divided into a grid of gardens and concrete parking spaces. From here, you can see the tips of the church spires and, above all, more and more windows.

When you were young, every window, every reflection in the glass, even the reflection of your own window in the window of the building opposite, represented a new opportunity for escape. Looking inside meant looking into the lives of strangers and not thinking about your own life, at least for a while. Now you know that if you look closely enough, somewhere inside every story and every window, you'll always find a distorted and twisted reflection of yourself. You think something doesn't involve you, and yet there's always at least your shadow rising up towards you from behind the glass.

You remember how one summer's day in 2007 an ambulance took Grandad away from his flat on the top floor of a workers' hostel in Přerov for the first time, and you looked out of the window into someone else's darkened kitchen, and in the reflection of the light from the streetlamps you studied your own face. It didn't even occur to you that the events of the previous weeks had led up to this very point, and that the noises bouncing off the walls that reached you through the open window and a series of open doors could convey something more than just sound.

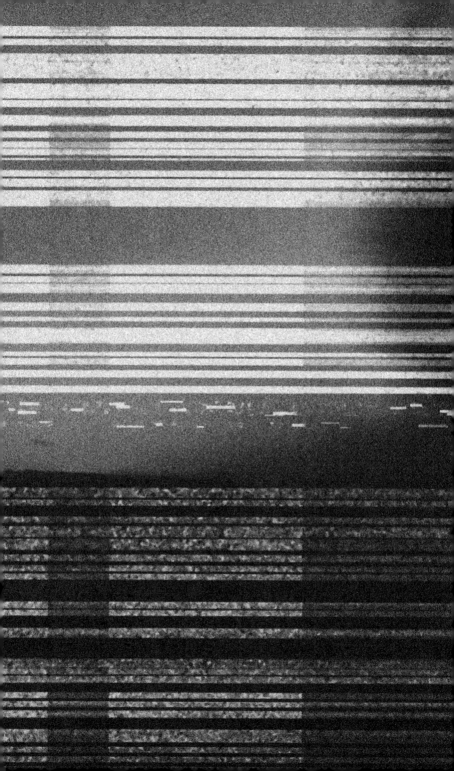

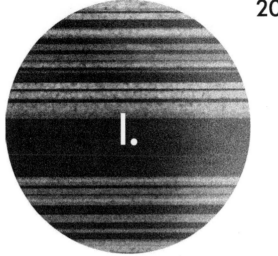

Mum told you about those few days in the summer of 2007, not once but twice.

The first time, she launched straight into it, her voice shaky with anger, in the kitchen of the old flat on Dvořákova street, sitting bolt upright on the edge of the padded bench with the stuffing coming out of its faded upholstery. She was upset because you hadn't been there for her and because of a lot of other things as well.

The second time she talked about it wasn't that long ago. You'd come home for Christmas, one of the few occasions when she still forced herself to take a drink. She brought a bottle of wine up from the cellar – probably one she'd been given at work a while back – and placed it in the middle of a table flanked by similar benches in a similar flat in the same street, very close to the place where you grew up. You could actually see your old flat from this new kitchen, with the occasional flicker of a shadow behind the glass of what were now someone else's windows. That evening she laid out a completely different version before you. You listened to her voice, just as steady as if she were reading the words aloud from a prepared script, and they finally made everything fall into place.

Both versions began exactly the same way: with a description of a space, the kind she operates in every day. Eight hours plus a lunch break. Every day the same depersonalized, pristine surfaces – floor, ceiling, four walls. A place where artificial light does not permit the existence of shadows, carving everything up into sharply defined edges.

She can still recall the day she first set foot in there. You were just a little kid, and in the beginning, she was afraid, didn't know what to do, couldn't concentrate.

"You're lucky," the others tried to convince her. "Dana, be thankful they found a job for you at all."

And yet, the first two months, she couldn't sleep. To cope with it all, she would muster the last of her strength, leaving you at home with Gran in the morning and coming back in the afternoon absolutely knackered, shattered, longing to do nothing but crawl into bed, curl up into a ball and go back to sleep till morning. But then came what she called the second shift, round two. Time to cook, tidy the room, hang up the washing. For her, the working day didn't usually end till after nine, when you finally went to sleep and she would collapse on the sofa in Gran's room, unable to think of anything other than the endless succession of similar days to follow.

She still wonders how she managed. Left alone with a young child, left alone to pay off the debts that Pavel, your father, ran up before he walked out on you. She concentrated all her energy on one thing: getting by until next pay day. She crossed off one day after another on the calendar as if her life depended on it – and quite possibly it did. "It was as if I was hopping on the edge of an abyss," was how she described it then, sitting in the kitchen and demonstrating walking on the edge of the tabletop with her fingers. Desperately trying to keep her balance, she would take a step back and find herself even closer to falling. "I don't wanna make a big song and dance about it, but I was seriously expecting you and me to go plummeting down any minute, to get swept away."

You often wonder why we tell others in that patronizing way that they should bounce back once they hit rock bottom. As if the bottom represented certainty, something to push off. But anyone who really has reached rock bottom will never forget that immense weight pressing down on them, the feeling of the mass of water above them. Mum had managed to break free; she had bounced back and risen right up to the surface but, in the meantime, the current had carried her too far from the shore. If Gran hadn't offered the two of you a room in her flat back then, "I don't even want to imagine where we'd have ended up".

That place has always fascinated you. The space she enters every day: her gaze slides over the uniform walls but finds nothing to latch onto apart from the endless rows of shelves, and so it carries on aimlessly around the room, over the immaculate, spotlessly clean expanse, until it comes up against a giant stainless-steel table with disassembled units on it. Metal plates and tubes create a maze of reflections, prisms pointing at each other at various angles. On the left, a computer with a program open on it. Next to it, she used to have a photo of you: a young kid in a baggy T-shirt with a faded hat jammed onto his head. Now she isn't allowed to have anything on the table. The regulations prohibit any deviation from optimum cleanliness and demand a depersonalized, empty workspace. She can't wear anything other than a set of white overalls, with her feet encased in shoe covers, her head hidden beneath a hood and safety goggles covering her eyes. Everything pulled tight, carefully sealed; the marks they leave on her skin are still visible in the evening.

Most of her life has been spent in spaces like this one. To you it seems that they are just a blind spot, no more than the backdrop to a bigger story. And yet it is within this spot that a person senses the smallest of changes permeating their body. The surrounding cleanliness only serves to emphasize the futility of trying to resist the flow of time. Within this flow, the body doesn't stop but keeps on growing, everything transforming, new cells replacing

24

the old ones. Each morning, the body wakes up a little bit different, a little bit alien. It discards used parts, littering the room with superfluous quantities of worn-out material in the form of tiny specks of dust. But dust has no place in a clean room. Not a single flake of skin, a single decommissioned eyelash is allowed to come into contact with the lens system spread out on the table. Every cubic metre of air passes through a set of filters – even Mum's breath is an unwelcome burden. It stirs up particles, its moisture threatening the thin protective coating on the lenses. And yet she spends every day in this space. All the rhythmic repetition of breaths in and breaths out, the beats and contractions of the body go on inexorably. No-one cares if she's tired; the performance tables relentlessly drive her on, setting the pace – if she works quickly, she can be sure that the number of units she needs to get through will soon go up too. All she has to do is meet the quota and next time they expect twice as much of her.

The factory is her world, she often repeats, and you know she's mainly trying to convince herself. When she was at the trade school, her whole class came here for work experience. On the factory floor, they taught her at the age of sixteen to grind tubes, clean optical components and align finished units exactly as required.

Gran had enrolled her at that school. She knew it would make it easier for her to get a job in the factory afterwards and, anyway, Mum didn't have a clue what else she might want to do.

"It was better to be standing at a lathe than in front of the blackboard. Just imagine, at school you've either got the class teacher feeling you up or that cow the English teacher making fun of you."

Even if she *had* wanted to study, there was no time for school. One evening in September, when she was in first year, Gran finally plucked up the courage to walk out on Grandad. She'd been talking about it for some time, and everyone was half expecting it. Grandad had been coming home in an increasingly sorry state – in the evening, they would find him in various stages of decline. And then she really did leave. "She blew her top, jacked it all in, grabbed Mum's brother and sister and simply took off." But your mother stayed – someone had to take care of him – and that was why she went to work in the factory right after leaving school.

The factory is her family. Before she went on maternity leave, Mum used to bump into Gran in the corridors, they would go to lunch together and they would smoke just a few yards away from each other during their breaks, each in their own circle of friends. She hardly knows anyone who hasn't worked in the factory for at least a while.

Every day, she has to readapt to the artificial environment. After a few minutes, the filtered air stops smelling of technology, her eyes get used to the blue light, and her hearing gradually learns to ignore the constant hum of the air-conditioning. Her body performs mechanical actions. Raise the arm, bend it, lower the arm. Her thumb adapts to a particular instrument, tightens a screw, repositions one part so her hand can insert another part into it. She sends concentrated beams through the polished lenses, and they pass through a series of predetermined points, a maze constructed with a margin of error of hundredths of a second. Aspherical lenses alternate with concave mirrors, and mirrors with prisms, which in turn give way to mechanical parts. The entire device is linked up to a computer your mother uses to monitor deviations. The only defects are those introduced by the human hand.

Because the machine doesn't make mistakes. The machine is flawless. The body lifts up the object and adjusts the angle slightly. It tightens a screw to undo what it has messed up – its own shortcomings. Mum turns to the monitor, moulding her legs along the curve of the chair, crosses her calves over, reaches out her hand and taps the mouse with her fingers.

It's still not right. The small red crosses marking the various centres of curvature refuse to line up on the monitor, to slot into the correct, designated places. As your mum traces the lines of the optical axes with her fingers, she shakes her head in dissatisfaction.

You don't understand any of the stuff she's describing to you, so you at least imagine the look on your mother's face.

She frowns. Sticks out the tip of her tongue, bites her lip. Tries to figure out where she went wrong. In the bar at the bottom right of her monitor, she checks how much time is left till the end of her shift. Each minute evaporates into the ether, into the network of pipes leading out of the building complex. Time is counter-motion. Day after day, it drags her body along with it. From a rested state to aching, swollen limbs. The worn-out material throws her axes out of alignment, pushes her spine askew, colours her eyes red with tiredness. Cigarette smoke suffuses her hair during the breaks and by the end of every shift it's totally dishevelled. After she comes home, she tries to brush it, watching it get thinner year after year. She observes her reflection in the mirror and her fingers trace a new, changing form in the features of her own face.

Time is a counter-current. It is life, which vanishes inexorably in this space.

It vaporizes out of it like ether-acetone from a badly sealed jar. Sometimes she inhales it in gulps. It makes her pupils dilate, her mind grow calm. Then she drifts along in a stupor, following her body from one space to another. The gatehouse, the corridors, the kitchen area, the locker room, the main workshop with the two vacuum furnaces, two dryers and storeroom full of nitrogen boxes, the adjustment room. The list of places and things wends its way further along the long white walls. In the artificial light, these have a deathly, blueish tinge. Places where lenses, tubes and machines matter more than her life.

28

Even back then, there was talk of a crisis, and it made Mum nervous every time. Not long afterwards, in 2008 and 2009, around five hundred people from the factory were laid off. *To keep the company afloat* – you read that phrase in an interview with the owner at the time – *redundancies were necessary – otherwise, we wouldn't have survived.* You could sense fear from your mother. She knew that most of the savings were made on manpower, that it might be her turn next and that no-one was going to keep *her* from going under. She would have to manage that all by herself. So she would sit hunched over the magnifying glass at the big table until evening, the last to leave the workshop.

She often struggled to get to grips with the ever-changing procedures. Almost every month, she had to learn new things, and she was dogged by the feeling that she couldn't keep up, that time was running away from her. "These days, everything's different," she would say, giving you a significant look. All her life, she'd been told to stick to what she knew, to make a good job of that. What scared her most was uncertainty – she hadn't even experienced the good old days they were so fond of talking about on television and now there were worse times around the corner. "These days, it's not enough to be good at one thing. You've got to be able to do a bit of everything, learn new stuff all the time, keep changing things about yourself. And I'm getting too old for all that."

"Someone who knows how to do something and does it well will go a long way. You need to find something *you're* good at," your gran had impressed on you too, and so you spent a large part of your childhood finding more and more things you definitely weren't good at.

You learned to eavesdrop on your mum and gran. You'd think the world was about to end, life was going to collapse in on itself, it would be the end of you too and you'd open a door only to find a series of others, and you'd keep on opening them until one day you finally hit a wall. If you turn round today, all you see behind you is the crisis. It's on TV, on the radio, there's nowhere to hide from it. The strangers' voices coming out of the sets are always going on about the good times being over, about the need to tighten belts, be more frugal, not waste money on fripperies.

Unlike you, Grandad had it all figured out. "We've spent too long at the trough and ended up in a whole heap of shit." At the psychiatric hospital, he watched TV nonstop and then lectured Mum about his discoveries. "That's what we get for harbouring all kinds of vermin here for years."

Mum took his words to heart before he even uttered them. She took them and recast them into a new order. In the evenings, she would sit with the calendar, doing sums on a piece of cardboard over and over again to work out what else she could save on. She had already cut down on cigarettes, but she couldn't cut them out completely because then what would she have left? On the other hand, she could skip lunch at work, not buy you winter boots – if she went to Grandad's place by bike instead of taking the bus, if she saved at least fifty crowns a week, then maybe, just maybe, she could make ends meet.

Before you were born, your mother assembled rifle scopes in another workshop. The pace was faster there. She had to turn out several units every day, whereas here, in this clean cell, barely three a month passed through her hands, and most of them were different. When she converted her new wages into hours, breaking it all down into numbers on the calendar, she discovered that, for the first time in her life, she could see an end to repaying the debts Dad had landed her with. She no longer woke up terrified in the night, dreading the fact that another day lay ahead and it was only halfway through the month.

"I like this job," she repeats to herself every morning before she even sets foot outside the flat. You can still hear her today, because some things don't change. The job saved her. The surrounding cleanliness and absence of dust offer a respite from the old, cramped flat. A respite from you, from Gran. She feels safe in there, undisturbed by the outside world.

You see her bending over the monitor, nervously tapping her foot. Normally she's been on the go since early morning – she has to get the packed lunches ready before work; when it wasn't the holidays, she would check your schoolbag. She still couldn't shake the old habits, even though you were quite independent for your age; she had a compulsive need to keep an eye on you all the time. Then straighten her hair, rub cream on her dry skin, close the windows, put on the washing machine, lock up. The same routine every morning. It takes her a moment to force open the permanently jammed front door. From the block of flats at the end of Dvořákova, a street on the very edge of town, she only has a short walk to work. She's still got it good. Jana, a friend from the optics factory, has to get up at three so she can get to work on time from her small village between Přerov and Olomouc. Mum just dashes across the road and clocks in, thoroughly out of breath, at five to six. Sometimes she walks through the factory complex, the drone of machinery coming from the surrounding workshops, and repeats to herself: *I've still got it good.* Admittedly, to enter the clean cell, she has to climb into a set of overalls and pull a hood over her head but, unlike the others, she gets to work sitting down. All she can hear is the hum of the air-conditioning. The fumes from the adhesive are sucked away by the extractor and she breathes deeply, free from care, not having to worry that in a few years they'll find a tumour in her breast, the way they did with Gran.

Just before her lunch break, the phone in the pocket of her overalls rings. She pulls away from the table and furtively checks the small text on the screen. When she reads Grandad's name, she lets out a long, drawn-out, desperate sound. She doesn't want to talk to him. Strictly speaking, she's not allowed to bring her phone into the workshop, but the foreman usually overlooks it. She's even caught him with one hand to his ear while he casually drilled in a screw with the other. She hesitates for a moment, but in the end she races through the workshop, phone in hand, to the gowning room, where she pushes the green button and puts the device to her ear.

Grandad wastes no time, launching straight into it in a shaky voice.

"You'd better get here right away." Every other word is interspersed with a lengthy pause as he draws breath. "It's totally dead, not moving at all. What the hell am I supposed to do now?"

She rolls her eyes. A gesture she learned as a child. Her father hated it and once slapped her so hard for it that she fell, banged into the radiator and lost consciousness.

"I'm at work." The words slip out in a harsher tone than she'd intended. "I can't come running just because your TV's on the blink." She speaks to him as if she were speaking to a child, carefully releasing each syllable into the flow of the conversation so as not to accidentally wind him up.

The only sound from the device is Grandad's dry, rasping cough.

"All right," says Mum in resignation, and a shiver runs down her spine. Or was it just a blast of cold air from the fan above her head? She's afraid Grandad might have another attack, stop breathing, crash to the floor.

She tells him to listen, just to calm down. You've been home for almost a week, it's the holidays, so she promises him you'll stop by.

"You'll just have to tough it out for a little while."

Another coughing fit almost takes her ear off. As soon as it's over, Grandad begins muttering incoherently.

"Now, Grandad, Grandad, just you listen to me. I'll text him and he'll pop over to see you and together I'm sure you'll manage to fix it."

She tries to shout over him; he's still talking, and she can hear the rattle of his ragged, heavy breathing. When he's finally calmed down a bit, Grandad says in a slightly more conciliatory tone: "All right then. But be sure to text him. Understand, Dana?" He pauses and waits for her to confirm it. "And tell him to get me some tobacco at the newsagent's. You know the place – the woman knows him there."

Just once, she would like to be able to say no to Grandad. But in the end, he always gets his way.

From time to time, various scenarios go through her head in which she turns the tables on her father, stands up to him. She hangs up and puts her head in her hands so the world only reaches her dimly through the lattice of her fingers. She exhales slowly.

He ruined her life. Four words that seethe inside her every time she trots off to get the shopping in for him. He ruined her life. She's repeated them to you so often that you imagine precisely those words echoing through your mother's head. His TV's broken, the place needs cleaning, he's run out of tobacco. There was no end to his demands. It didn't really matter what exactly it was about. Again and again, he forced her to climb up to the top floor of the old workers' hostel, while he never so much as bothered to get out of the armchair – he could at least have opened the door for her.

And yet she was always there for him. Of the three children, your mother was the only one still willing to speak to him at all.

Grandad needed her. She was with him when, after several check-ups, an X-ray and a week of observation in a small hospital room with a view of tree branches, the doctor diagnosed him with COPD. She stood beside him, holding his hand and feeling the coughing fits convulse him. His lungs were only partially working. She was sure, knew for certain – that the drink had played a major role in his condition. What the alcohol hadn't managed to destroy had been finished off by years of work in the Přerov chemical plant. The rest she put down to an average of thirty cigarettes a day. He smelled of smoke, the whites of his eyes were tinged yellow, his fingertips stained brown from the tobacco, and his skin was blotchy.

"It's like I've taken in water, Dana," was how Grandad described it on the way back from the hospital, "like I'm swimming in my own juices or my lungs are holding me under the surface – there's this terrible weight bearing down on me, and it might be the only reason I'm still stuck here, just cos of that weight. It's the last thing keeping me here." She was only half listening to him, still hoping the illness would finally change Grandad's mind. She had a plan. She wanted to get him to apply for a place in a nursing home. "What you need is some proper help," she launched in as soon as she had laboriously manoeuvred him onto the bus using both hands. "I can't be with you all the time, I'm tired out. Just take a look at the place." She settled him into a seat by the window and spent the whole journey trying to reason with him. But Grandad refused to so much as consider it. She couldn't help thinking he didn't want to deprive himself of this last opportunity to control her life.

She used to make fun of him – he refused to be talked round, didn't even want to go to the dentist's and preferred to let his teeth rot. When they thought you weren't looking, Mum and Gran would pull their faces into an exaggerated scowl and put on his voice. "I haven't been to the doctor's in thirty years – thirty, you hear. I'm a real man, so I've got to tough it out."

Day by day, he was changing in front of your eyes. Your mother was beginning to sense something was different; suddenly, his grousing didn't make sense, and the whole business with the television was just the latest in a long line of things that worried her. She was noticing odd gaps in his memory; suddenly, his own memories had started to betray him, resurfacing all tangled up into new, embellished versions.

"Do you remember how me and your mum took the three of you to Plumlov for a week?" he blurted out one day as she was unloading the shopping onto the sticky worktop at his place. She looked up and caught Grandad gazing dreamily out of the window. "You didn't want to go swimming at all – neither did your mum, the silly tart. Turning your nose up at everything, that was your way. Nothing was ever good enough for you prisses." The corner of his mouth twitched and he paused for a long beat, waiting for her to confirm his words. "All the same, we had a nice time."

Mum remembers the long bus journey. She felt sick and was crying because her older sister kept pinching her thigh. The first night in the tattered little tent, she barely slept at all. In the morning, she got up to find Gran sprawled on top of a blanket, sipping coffee out of a tin mug. When asked where Grandad was, Gran just waved her hand in the direction of the dingy pub building.

For a full two days, nobody saw him. "Dad's three sheets to the wind again," was a phrase Gran often said; your mother and her sister repeated it after her in a whisper, hoping that one day they would learn to laugh at it.

That time he'd come back in the middle of the night. At first, she mistook the sound of drops on the side of the tent for rain. After taking a leak, he flung open the entrance and flopped down right in the middle, in the very place where Mum was sleeping.

"We had a nice time," he repeated and, for a moment, she glimpsed a hint of sadness in his eyes. Perhaps he was trying to convince himself of something he knew full well wasn't true.

That was when the thought had first occurred to her: One day, sometime soon, it's coming. She would open the door to his flat and Grandad would be lying there dead. Amid clumps of dust, in a haze of cigarette smoke. There was nothing she could do about it.

As she got older, Mum learned to love him again. "After all, he's still my dad." Sure, he annoyed her. Yet, somewhere beneath the surface, she knew that he loved her and she loved him. She had no doubt about that, even when she was trudging up the stairs to his flat, lugging the shopping and trying not to think about the day when she would see him for the last time. In moments of weakness, when she longed to have a break from him, she asked herself the question everyone probably asks themselves at least once in their life. *What will happen when he's no longer here?*

She used to hate him. She didn't understand why her mother had put up with him for so long. Almost every evening, he came home blind drunk, and every time he would crash into the shoe cabinet in the hall and remain lying there. Occasionally, he would crawl as far as the living room, where he managed to half climb up onto the sofa. Your mum and her sister had to drag him off to bed while Gran was holed up in the kitchen with an ashtray in front of her, breaking her own rule, lighting one cigarette off another until the smoke filled the entire room and began to force its way out through cracks in the door into every corner of the flat. She only got up when Mum's younger brother Jakub woke up.

One time, Mum had ended up alone with Grandad in the bedroom. She and her sister had deposited him on the bed and she'd come back to put some water on the bedside table for him. She was worried about him; he was shaking all over and his nose was smeared with blood and vomit. Perhaps he'd got into a fight or perhaps he'd just fallen over on the way home. "My little Dana –" he said, grabbing her hand and pulling her towards him. She tried to break free but he was holding her too tightly. There were little bubbles popping by his nose and he grunted with every breath. She couldn't have been more than eight, wearing nothing but a nightie, her long brown hair tied back in a ponytail. "My little Dana, you're my angel." The words that flowed out of him congealed in the air before she had a chance to grasp their meaning. Those slimy, grubby words reached right out to the polka-dot fabric of her nightshirt. Again, she jerked away and he gripped her even more tightly. Her resistance pleased him. He grinned.

"You might be stupid, but at least you won't be fat like your mother."

She no longer has any idea if he said those words to her that same evening or on one of the others carefully stored away in her memory. She doesn't know when he started drinking so much; she's seen him drunk for as long as she can remember.

When she needed him to explain something for school – say, if she was stuck with chemistry or maths – he didn't have time for her, didn't help her, left all the work to Gran – "after all, that's what the woman's here for." As for him, he would just mock her from the corner of the kitchen as he watched her struggling with her homework. He sat there with his mug of tea and slurped from it, thinking they weren't paying attention, that they didn't see him pouring something into his mug from a small silver hip flask and then slipping it back in his pocket.

She has a similar scene in front of her right now: exercise books spread out on the kitchen table and him sitting on a chair below the window, rolling a cigarette and shaking his head in dissatisfaction. "She's stupid anyway," he remarks, licking the paper. "There's no point." As he says it, he isn't looking at Mum but at Gran. "Nada, that girl of ours is totally thick. How can she be *my* flesh and blood and still not get it," he says, shoving the exercise book under their noses – first Gran's and then Mum's, but their puzzled expressions only anger him all the more and he chucks the exercise book at Gran and bangs his fist on the table. "I mean, it's perfectly obvious!"

She remembers another evening as well. She'd been given a bad mark and needed to get her report card signed. She handed it to Gran who just glanced at it and slid it over to Grandad without a single word. He looked right through her as if she were nothing but air. He couldn't act disappointed because he hadn't expected anything of her.

"I told you she was stupid."

The phrases you hear over and over again get under your skin, often working their way so deep that they become a part of you. For many years, Mum believed Grandad's words, longing the whole time to show him she had triumphed over him. She wanted to prove to him that what really matters in life is not who's smarter – the important thing is whether you can see it through to the bitter end. She had endured everything. You just had to grit your teeth, to get the better of that counter-current called time and make it to the shore.

*sad*

It doesn't surprise you at all that, one day, Gran finally snapped. She packed her things, grabbed little Jakub, and neither they or your mother's sister Kristýna ever set foot in their old flat on U Tenisu street again. She wanted to take Mum with her as well – she wasn't even eighteen yet – and she threw together a bag of clothes for her and went out into the hall. You see Mum at the other end, her arms dangling helplessly by her sides. "What about him?" she asks, pointing down the hallway to the closed bedroom door. Behind it is Grandad in a pool of his own urine, his

41

shrieks audible all the way up to the second floor. "We can't just leave him here. I..." The weight of the words makes them stick in her throat. She swallows, plucks up the courage and starts again. "I'll stay here with him."

She doesn't understand why she didn't leave Grandad too. It didn't make sense to her; she had so many chances, so many reasons, and yet she stayed. Perhaps her sister was right and it was her way of trying to prove to them that she was a better person. That she would always be there for her father, just as he had never managed to be there for his daughter.

It opened up a gulf between Mum and the rest of the family, with Gran and your aunt and uncle standing on the other side. Each of them mostly looks out for number one, in an attempt to make up for the years when they had to cower quietly before Grandad.

Soon after Gran left, Grandad got fired from the chemical plant. Three of his colleagues dragged him home from work and left him slumped by the front door unconscious. Mum couldn't cover the whole of the rent by herself — she had just started at the factory, was on the lowest pay grade and could barely make it to the end of the month. Through a friend from the trade school, she managed to get Grandad a job in a hospital. So, for a few years, he delivered hospital meals in an old Avia van and things looked quite hopeful at times, but he always went back to the drink in the end.

When you were born, something shifted in Grandad. He stopped drinking gradually, as if he was making his way through an unfamiliar space, step by step. He came back from rehab a second time and was pretty much a new man. Or at least a man capable of leading a normal life. At first, your mother was afraid to leave you alone with him and it took time for her to learn to trust him.

"You know, Dana," Gran once declared to her, "when it comes to your da', the booze was maybe the easiest part to deal with. Even without it, he's still a moron. The worst thing about him is that macho pride of his. Whenever he laid off the booze for a bit, he had to fill that void with something else."

All those times you and Mum had to sit and listen to his lectures. He never let anyone else get a word in – you've inherited that bad habit from him. He shouted everyone down and there was no stopping him. But Mum developed the ability to reply without thinking, to switch off completely, letting whole sentences drift by and only latching onto what was essential. She pictured herself as a lens that only let in part of the light spectrum.

She had this trick of lifting her gaze, nodding and lowering her gaze again.

And on no account letting on what she was really thinking.

But he had his lighter moments too – sometimes she even had a laugh with him. It made her happy if he praised her for something, if he looked at her and she knew he was proud of her. And when your father left the two of you, Grandad was the only one who listened to your mother. She could tell him anything and he would just sit there, grunting in agreement and otherwise saying nothing. The chances are he was oblivious to her, perhaps thinking about something else, quite possibly drunk, but it was good enough for Mum.

By that summer, it was all over, though, and what remained of him was a mere shadow of his former self. Just a memory of him. He spent whole days ensconced in the old armchair, and the contents of TV channels formed his only contact with the outside world. They affected him so deeply that he could no longer distinguish between what was real and what wasn't. Then he would call Mum at work to share his discoveries with her, enthusiastically recounting or grumbling about something to her – once again, she found it impossible to interrupt him. One time, he had to go into hospital for a few days, and he made you record all his favourite shows so he wouldn't miss a thing. As soon as he started on about something, she would set down the phone without any qualms. There was no need to respond; Grandad was totally self-sufficient. Meanwhile, Mum had plenty of time to do the ironing and leaf through the discount flyers, picking up the phone from time to time to make sure he was still on the other end, then putting it down again and carrying on with what she was doing.

But a few days before the broken TV, a few weeks before everything fell apart, he woke her up in the middle of the night and Mum just stared at the phone in confusion.

"They're coming for me!" Grandad's voice frightened her. She had no idea what was going on. "They'll be here any minute and they'll take the lot."

Irritation gave way to fear, which coloured every thought. Through the closed blinds, a thin strip of light from a streetlamp fell on her. More yellow bars cut across the duvet. She sat up and rubbed her eyes with her free hand.

"Who, Grandad?" Through her own voice, she heard the incoherent stream of his words. "Who's coming? It's late, you know, everyone's asleep."

"Them. The bailiffs. The folk from the government. I don't know. But they're coming for me."

He started coughing so hard that she had to pull the phone away from her ear. As soon as the coughing had abated, he was off again.

"They're almost here. They're here, Dana. Someone's ratted me out." With certain words, Grandad's voice sounded weaker, more urgent. "They've definitely ratted me out and now I'm gonna lose everything."

Something relaxed in her face, a muscle she hadn't even known was there. She felt a wave of heat pass across her face – a mixture of amusement, anger and, above all, helplessness.

"Now just hang on a second. It's all in your head. After all, I pay all the bills for you."

She had been looking after his money for years, even carried his bank card in her own purse. Every spring, she went over the utility bills with him, and he was capable of calling her three times a day about it; he wanted her to check, to confirm to him that he really had paid everything. She would reassure him and then the next day he would call again. He was forgetting more and more. He slipped Mum an envelope of money she had left on the table for him the day before. He forgot when she was supposed to take him to the doctor's – then she would open the door to his flat and Grandad would look at her in surprise, grumpy and stubbornly maintaining that they had been to the doctor's the day before. His memory had failed him before, but that night she understood – something was different. He had never rambled like this before. She wanted to reach out her hand, grab hold of him and pull him out of the darkness she'd seen him plunge into that night. Deposit him on the bed and keep him safe until the sun came up.

But the chances are she would just have woken into another nightmare. She knew she could no longer cope on her own. It was her, not Grandad, who was standing on the edge of the impenetrable darkness, trying to find him in the surrounding emptiness with a dying flashlight. She was standing on the brink of something terrible and was sure she had to step back. She had to move, and fast. And yet each time her legs refused to obey her.

The next morning, she decided she'd better go and see him to make sure he was OK. She was afraid to park her bike in front of the hostel. Chemik, as the building was called (back in the day, it was mainly workers from the nearby chemical plant who'd lived there), stood beside the main road. The paint was peeling off the metal panels below the windows. She glanced up on the off chance she could see Grandad at the window. Normally she left her bike chained to the traffic sign next to the bins or to a tree and prayed the whole time that nobody would steal it.

On a bench in front of the entrance, she noticed a couple of suspicious-looking men.

"Both dark-skinned, yeah, and about a head taller than me – no doubt they'd been rummaging through the recycling again," was how she described them to you at dinner that same day.

She stopped in front of the entrance and started hunting for the key in the bottom of her rucksack. As she did so, she refused to take her eyes off the men. She tried to extricate the shopping from the rack on her bike. The bag wedged into the metal frame was heavy, with several days' worth of food in it. She'd wound bungee cords around the handles of the bag and now she couldn't get the knot undone. One of the ties catapulted towards her and, before she had a chance to dodge it, cut her finger.

The bike would have fallen on top of her if one of the men hadn't leapt towards her and caught it in time.

"Here, Mrs, let me give you a hand with that."

The pungent smell of aftershave filled her nose. She gripped the keys in the palm of her hand. The men spoke again and she flinched a little. When she told you about it that evening, she still looked taken aback, surprised that her preconceptions hadn't been borne out.

All she'd managed to come out with was: "Just leave it, I can manage by myself."

The man took a step back and sized her up, but then his hand shot upwards.

"You're going up, right? We'll take it there for you."

Before she could even open her mouth, the first of the men was carrying the bag up the steps to the door. He pulled out his own keys, unlocked the door, stepped into the corridor and held the door open. She turned back, thinking she'd at least chain up her bike, but her path was blocked by the second man, who bundled himself and Mum into the lift.

"Where to, Mrs?"

She quickly reached forward and pressed the button for the eighth floor, taking care not to accidentally brush against the dirty, graffitied wall. The two of them looked at her in amazement, and there might have been total silence inside the lift if it hadn't screeched loudly as it moved. Every jolt startled her, and she had her hands bunched into fists, braced for action.

Once, you overheard her complaining to a friend on the phone: "As if it wasn't bad enough that I have to trek all the way across town for him, he has to go and live in Gypsyville."

The lift gave one last desperate jerk, and the doors opened onto a desolate grey corridor. Mum kept her eyes on the ground, cautiously backing up the few steps towards the door of Grandad's flat. "This is it," she said with relief.

She could feel the eyes of the two men on her and was determined not to turn her back on them. After watching the closed lift doors for a while longer, she turned round, stuck the key in the lock, and only then did it dawn on her: she had left her bike unlocked down below.

In the space of a few seconds, the whole gamut of emotions flashed across her face – first fear, followed by anger, and last of all shame.

She wondered how long it would take to run down there. Then she checked herself. She was hardly going to be able to overpower two men. In resignation, she turned round, unlocked the door and went into the flat, bag in hand.

Grandad was sitting in the armchair, smiling at her from ear to ear. He had no memory of the late-night phone

49

call. "I must have bats in the belfry. I don't even remember being up during the night. Are you sure it wasn't just a dream?" He scratched his chin in confusion. All he had on was his boxers and an old T-shirt with cigarette burns in it.

Maybe it really was her who was losing her mind. Because when she eventually took the lift back down, prepared to make the long journey home on foot, the bike was right there where she had left it.

Another gust of icy air finally rouses her from her memories. She still has her head buried in her hands; for a moment, she completely forgot she was at work. From behind the door comes a loud crash and a shout from someone in the workshop.

She pulls herself together and sends you a text. You turned fourteen in April and are due to go into eighth year at school after the holidays, and she's worried about you. Apart from the bouts of anger that take hold of you from time to time, apart from the occasional mood swings and various tics, she's never had any trouble with you. But neither of you will ever forget how she came back from the last parents' evening white with rage. That's how she would describe it: *I was white with rage*, but to you it seemed as if the whiteness had erased the slightest trace of emotion from her face. She came into your room with a wooden spoon and an absent, white expression.

She once said to you: "You always were an odd one, never got on very well with the other kids. That's why I let you spend most of your time at home leafing through those books of yours." Her sister Kristýna had been the same: she was capable of spending whole days alone and shouted at Mum if she disturbed her solitude, so for a long time she thought nothing of it. "But something happened to you, I could tell."

After the parents' evening, she stood in the middle of the room with the wooden spoon in her hand and white fury on her face; you had been laid out before her, and she had to rebuild your image again. For several days, you refused to talk to her, took refuge in your gran's room or just smiled and nodded foolishly, even though there was nothing to smile and nod at, your eyes burning holes in the wall. To her, it seemed as if you had been replaced with a cheap copy, a mindless machine that just raised its arms and replied breathlessly to questions. "I know he's going through puberty," she whispered to Gran, thinking you couldn't hear her, "but do you remember me being like this?" At the same time, Gran told you about Mum's tearful nights, about shouting at her when she refused to do the washing-up after dinner. Back then, Mum couldn't care less either. They fought a lot. She would come home late and drag Grandad down the hall to bed, and only then would Gran give Mum a talking-to because she'd seen her in town with a bunch of strangers.

By her own admission, your world had long been a mystery to Mum. A world closed in on itself. You feel as if each of you is speaking a different language.

She'd always wanted a daughter. "I'd even come up with a name. I wanted to call you Maruška." She'd planned to dress you up in long skirts and brush your hair. But saying it out loud now, she feels stupid and starts to laugh at her own foolish notions. "When you grew up, we'd tell each other everything." She'd know what to do, she'd understand you, she wouldn't constantly be trying to figure out what might be going on in your head.

She was scared by the thought of the man you would grow into, the man she would share a flat with.

Sometimes she got the feeling you'd stopped being a child long ago.

Like a few days earlier, when you came home late in the evening. You didn't say a word, just slipped past her and got undressed in the bathroom without even bothering to close the door. Standing on tiptoe, you inspected yourself naked in the mirror while Mum inspected you. On your body, she saw several small, dark bruises, a fresh one on your stomach that was bigger. She cleared her throat, and you turned your head in her direction and rolled your eyes. At that moment, it was as if she herself was looking in the mirror. Since that day, you've been locking the bathroom door behind you. Mum finds the whole thing a bit strange. After all, she's seen you naked so many times – it wasn't so long ago that she was bathing in the tub with you, and now you're acting all prudish.

Did she ever stop to wonder where you got those bruises? That evening, she sat you down in the kitchen and started telling you about your uncle Jakub's torn clothes when he was a kid. On the way home from school, he'd pull stolen bits of chalk out of his pockets, throw them at people or at Mum, grab her by the hair and stuff tufts of grass into her mouth. Gran often got called in to the headteacher's office because of him, and she would come home white with fury, grab Kuba by the arm and drag him down the stairs to the basement, where he was left alone in the dark for several hours. He got into fights at school, after school, at home with Gran and with his sisters, with everyone around him. He'd come home with his shirt ripped and his jumper smeared with dirt. She'd never had that kind of trouble with you. Much to your father's disappointment, you weren't the kind of kid that ran around the playground screaming and shoving the others out of the way. Mum recalls scenes from the sandpit: children throwing clumps of wet sand at each other and you standing in the middle with your arms outstretched, not knowing what to do with them. But Mum's memories skip forward, the images flashing by; no-one could miss them... She isn't able to hang on to them for more than a few seconds, so she can't see that you're not her brother and you never will be. All you can hear is her saying to you: "I mean, it wasn't that long ago that you could barely reach the bathroom mirror, that you were clutching my hand in terror on the escalator in Prior, so why the fuck are you getting into fights now?!" #


A loud beep from the nearby vacuum furnace warns Mum she has to get back to work, back to the screwdriver and the table, where the unit she's working on occupies the surface as far as the eye can see. Inside the machine, all the optics fit snugly together, and with each movement she becomes more afraid something might crack. Even the smallest component costs more than she could ever pay back, and the system of mirrors reflects light with absolute certainty. To get to the right part, she has to walk round the device mounted in the white frame; the space between the housing and the optics is filled with wires and all kinds of tubes. It would only take a little bit too much pressure, a slip of the hand, and she would have to start all over again. When she was first putting a unit together, she was constantly checking the tiniest details against the diagram, but now she secures the actual lenses mechanically. With a practised hand, she performs the movement unconsciously, from memory. Turns round slightly in her chair, crosses her legs. Frowns at the monitor, at the unit she's assembling, back at the monitor. Before she left for work in the morning, she stopped in the doorway and watched your face for a few minutes as you slept. Something about you really reminds her of a piece of her, even though you have your father's face. Your arms were wrapped around your knees, your nose wrinkled, and you lay curled up the way she also tended to.

When you're asleep, you look vulnerable and fragile.

She stood there wondering why you couldn't stay like that forever.

On the doctor's advice, you were sent to a spa at age six instead of starting first year at school. The whole thing was paid for by the insurance company, which involved your mother spending months filling in forms and phoning round doctors to find a place for you. You were often sick, always choking and coughing, so she didn't really have much choice. When she finally worked up the courage to tell your father about it, he yelled at her on the phone, shouting that she must have taken leave of her senses and he wasn't about to throw money away on nonsense like that. She slammed the phone down on him and didn't talk to him for several months.

One scene indelibly etched into both your memories took place outside the Radun children's clinic in the spa town of Luhačovice, an austere grey building at the edge of the woods. You're standing in front of it, refusing to let go of your mother. Her hand is slipping away and you're begging her not to leave, tears streaming down your face, squeezing her tightly and trembling all over. Because of this, Gran and Mum called you "bunny rabbit": your skin was appropriately pale and soft, you were quiet-spoken, and you even did a decent job of wiggling your ears. You remember the phone calls, while your mother remembers the visits. As soon as you saw her, you clung to her neck and wouldn't get off her. She remembers the pictures, the letters written by one of the nurses; for a long time, she kept them stashed inside the kitchen bench, under a pile of old calendars and papers from the courts and the banks.

Curled up under the duvet, you look helpless – younger and more defenceless. "In the end, I only made it because of you. We always got through everything together," she once admitted. She was never quite sure which one of you needed the other more.

There isn't much space around your bed. Next to it is a battered desk with a rubber mat decorated with faded pictures of giraffes in the savannah. Mum's divan bed is pushed up against the heater under the window. Apart from that, all that fits in the room is a cupboard, an armchair and a small side table. Outside, it's still dark, the impenetrable wall disturbed from time to time by the lit windows of the flats in the block opposite. Now and then, there's the flicker of a shadowy figure in them; one window goes dark and another one lights up. Mum could observe other people's lives like this after dark and none of them would be any the wiser.

Before she turned around, she reached out to you. She wanted to stretch her arms out wide and hug you, or open up her hand and stroke your hair. But, as always, she froze, stuck mid-motion, unable to take the next step. She straightened her back.

She's always mapping the traces of your dad in you, that memory imprinted onto your face. You have the same eyebrows and lips, a similar jawline. "You got your chin from him, and your eyes too, I reckon," Gran commented as she looked at one of the few photos left at home. She took it out of the album, sized you up, nodded and tucked it away again. But the end result couldn't have been more different, because you have your mum's nose – a button in the middle of your face – skinny arms and legs, the same high-pitched voice. From time to time, your mother will recognize his gestures in you, his familiar movements, his way of walking. The faces he pulls. Then she stands there open-mouthed, watching you and wondering how it is possible – the two of you are separated by time, by two different continents, and yet you move the same way.

According to Dad, everything she did was wrong; they were capable of fighting over the stupidest things. They argued about what *their* boy would grow up to be; your father had his own ideas about how to bring you up, how to make you into a *real man*. She tried to explain it to him, but in the end, words failed her; with distance they lost their force and probably never even reached your father at all. She let him go on yelling at her as she crouched on the kitchen floor, the cord from the old landline receiver wrapped around her hand. By the time he hung up, she was shaking all over.

She wished he had been with you the time he made you take up football. It was his idea. He announced it to her on the phone: he'd managed to arrange the first training session with an old friend for the very next day. "So you don't back out of it again."

She wished he'd seen it with his own eyes – all the coach had to do was raise his voice at you and you burst into tears.

"How am I supposed to tell him that boy's happiest sitting in a corner somewhere," she complained to Gran in desperation, "that he'd rather be reading or drawing – he's just not made that way." Gran was standing at the sink, washing something and probably not really listening to Mum's agitated voice. "If he wants the kid to be different, then he should've stayed, should've been there for him, taken him in hand and done all those things he wants me to do with him. I'm not doing it *for* him, no way."

Mum and Dad had met just out of school. Sometime near the start of the summer, they were with a group of friends after work at the Lagoon, or maybe by the Bečva – she can no longer say exactly where, whereas she remembers various unimportant details. She was sitting with her back against a tree trunk, a short distance away from the fire; she didn't want the smoke blowing on her. Pavel was clutching a beer bottle, though she hadn't seen him take a drink all evening. While the others were passing out and rolling around drunk on the ground, Dad sat in the same spot, just laughing occasionally at someone else's joke.

Mum was hardly drinking either. She put the bottle to her lips, tried to postpone each swig for as long as possible, swallowed just a little, gingerly, gave a shudder, tilted her head back. She glanced in his direction and took a good look at him for the first time.

"He's weird," Mum's friend Karolína remarked the next day. Even back then, they discussed almost everything. "I mean, look at the way he walks. Like some kind of prima donna."

That evening, he walked her home. He waved his arms around wildly; it was a wonder he didn't wallop her with every step he took.

They made fun of him because of his walk too. They made fun of him because he didn't drink, because he was skinny, and Mum heard what they whispered about him at work – he was working at the gatehouse at the time and knew virtually everybody. He was quite a bit shorter than her, so she had a view of his thinning fair hair and the sunburnt skin beneath it.

Gran only talked to you about your dad when Mum wasn't home. "He was always a bit of a sissy himself. You should've seen the way he used to strut about in front of the mirror." Your own memories of your father are fragmented; you mostly know him from letters, as a voice on the phone. "One time he complimented me on my hair, can you believe it, an old biddy like me, and he compliments me on my hair. What kind of man compliments you on your hair? I don't mean you, Marek, you're my grandson, that doesn't count. And those shirts of his!"

Soon your mother began noticing changes. She had been living alone with Grandad for several years when Dad moved into her room. During the first week, while cleaning under the bed, she discovered a box stuffed full of fitness magazines. Oiled-up bodies with bulging muscles covered in swollen veins. Later, just around the time you were due to be born, your father started taking pills, knocking them back several times a day and then examining himself in the mirror, his fists clenched as he contorted himself into various positions, holding the magazine in front of him as a template. He began to check every move he made and comment on everyone else's. He stopped waving his arms around as he walked; he straightened up and made a point of walking down the middle of the pavement, giving way to no-one. He took up all the space next to Mum. She couldn't help thinking that maybe he'd always been this way and she just hadn't noticed it before.

You often visualize the things she tells you about him, as if you'd been there – you see his reflection in the mirror, peering out of windowpanes. It's as if you could remember some of it. The three of you out for the first time. It's just stopped raining and your father's pushing the pram along the wet, cracked pavement, trying to avoid the biggest potholes as well as the trees. The water's still dripping from the tops of the spreading mulberries and occasionally it splashes onto your forehead. The air's chilly and the pram lurches from side to side. Some guy you can't see – you don't need to see him – smiles at Mum. "I could break that little pipsqueak in two," your father blurts out. Glancing back, he inadvertently swerves the pram to the left, almost steering it onto the road.

"Well, I'll never understand what you saw in him." Karolína didn't like your father. She and your mum were in the same boat and your mother could describe every scene to her, complain that he hadn't sent money again, without Karolína interrupting. "Let's just hope the boy doesn't take after him."

The best she could muster was a feeble response.

"One thing I always liked about Pavel was that at least he never drank."

Did she know even then that that was far from being enough?

But if you think about it, everything about your father's behaviour makes sense.

Like her, your father had been born into a family with no money but plenty of problems. His parents were pub cooks and, throughout his childhood, they kept moving from place to place, wherever his father could find work. Every year, it was a different town, a different village; they had nothing at home so they could pack up again as quickly as possible. For the most part, they lived directly above the pub. Just before the Velvet Revolution in 1989, they ended up on the ground floor of a high-rise block of flats in a housing estate in Předmostí, as close as possible to their latest gig in a newly opened non-stop bar.

With the fall of the former regime, your father succumbed to the same misconception as lots of other people: that freedom primarily meant money, a battle where it was every man for himself – and so he too entered the fray. He quit his job in the factory, probably figuring he could earn a lot more on his own for the same amount of work. Like so many others, he borrowed money and set up his own security firm, though he still did most of the work himself. He started hanging around with people Mum couldn't stand. By then, her belly had grown big and she could barely move and yet, every day, she had to lug bags of shopping all by herself. Your father was always at work – or so she thought, until one morning, instead of a pram, he brought an expensive hi-fi system into the flat and put on a cassette. "You won't find a state-of-the-art stereo like this in the whole building," he said, and she replied that she had a headache. Dad paused, thought for a moment and then, with a smile, turned the volume up.

The thought of making and spending money kept him up at night. He constantly saw it in front of him, within his reach. He never used to have any and now he was making it quickly and spending it even more quickly – he couldn't hold on to a single crown. It was as if the bank-notes dissolved when he touched them; the temptation was too great. He didn't see why he couldn't indulge himself, why he couldn't finally have everything he had longed for.

The first time Mum ran away to Gran's, it was just for a week, shortly before you were born. By then, she could no longer cope with shouldering the weight of everything by herself. She'd wanted Dad to go with her to the house of some woman from work to pick up a cot. The woman's child had outgrown it and she was going to let her have it for free. But, on the appointed day, Dad didn't show up to get her, whereas he did come home with a new television. She thought she wouldn't be able to restrain herself, that she would kill him on the spot. She packed up her things, squeezed past him with difficulty and disappeared.

The whole time they were together, she only once summoned up the courage to ask where he'd been getting the money for all this. He observed her silently and shrugged. It was only later she found out the truth. He had been borrowing from friends, from the bank, and in her name as well.

She didn't understand it, didn't even need to. After all, it was about *her* – after he upped and ran off to America, it was Mum who had to stand with her head lowered, handing envelopes of money to strangers out of her own pay cheque. At least he'd managed to get her out of Grandad's place. This is a memory she prefers to tread carefully, lightly, around; she doesn't want to think about it. She gives herself a shake and fixes her attention on something else.

One day, your father simply vanished.

You weren't even four years old when he left the two of you. After one particularly bad fight, he started sleeping in the hotel where he was working as a security guard, a different room every night. One time, Mum came back from a walk and opened the door to find the flat cleaned out. She thought they'd been robbed. For the second time in quick succession, she grabbed you, moved in with her mother on Dvořákova street and never went back to him again.

A few months later, he was standing under the window, pleading with your mother to let him hold you one last time. "I'm leaving for America tomorrow," he declared so matter-of-factly that it left her open-mouthed. "I'm not coming back, Dana." You picture the scene as if it was something out of a movie. Your father standing on the pavement and Gran shouting at him through the kitchen window to leave them alone. Through the folds of your memory, your father's angry voice reaches you, even though you can't possibly remember it. But why did she let him in in the end?

The next day, Mum woke up to find the other half of the bed empty. Just an indentation and a crumpled pillow.

Your father never told her what he was planning. In the letter that was sitting on the kitchen worktop, he assured her: *I'll take care of you both.* Did she know he wouldn't? After all, she knew him only too well; she can't have had any illusions. For over a year, you heard nothing from him.

What she hadn't expected, though, were the reasons why he'd left. They were first shouted at her by a complete stranger in the street. She remained rooted to the spot, open-mouthed. "I'm going to smash your face in," he called to her. "Kindly pass that message on to Pavel." She still didn't understand what was going on. She picked you up and set off in the opposite direction. She forgot about the whole incident until the door of the flat was kicked in by a guy who must have been at least three feet taller than Mum. He barged in, turned the whole flat upside down and finally seized hold of the TV and threw it out of the window. He turned round, took a step towards her, grabbed her by the waist and pressed her up against the wall.

His breath is something she can't get out of her head. That musty, hot stench still stings Mum's nostrils. He threw her down on the ground and continued searching until he found the envelope where she kept all her savings.

Did she want to run away then too? Pack up her things and head somewhere far away? For a long time, she didn't feel safe in that room; she couldn't get to sleep because that would mean leaving her body at the mercy of outside threats for several hours. From then on, she locked the door and checked the windows several times an evening;

she would wake up frightened in the night and kick the covers off furiously.

The moment that guy had left, she'd collapsed on the floor and remained lying there until you and Gran found her in that position. The two of you squeezed through the door, which was hanging from just one of the hinges, and cautiously examined the surrounding chaos as you made your way to the bedroom. You leant down towards Mum and eyed her warily.

That was probably the day she stopped believing in a life that might still turn out OK in the end.

Since your dad was no longer in the country and wasn't communicating with Mum, the divorce took several years. For several years, she was ashamed to show her face in the town and went to sleep with a knife under her pillow. Again and again, she had to open the door to debt collectors and men who always pushed their way in and carried things off from a flat your father had never lived in. Some of them came with official papers and stuck yellow stickers on pieces of furniture, while others didn't trouble themselves with permits. They didn't even care who the things belonged to. On top of that, they deducted money from Mum's pay cheque every month. She would come home exhausted and have to use the last remnants of her strength to keep it together.

If it hadn't been for Gran, you wouldn't have had money for food. Mum regularly had to ask her to pay for the shopping – not even a week had gone by since payday and there was no money left for anything. She borrowed from Dad's sister to get things for nursery school, and, in the meantime, Gran secretly made the rounds of Dad's acquaintances. "Someone's got to knock some sense into their skulls."

The first time your father called, it didn't take long before he and Mum were yelling at each other. In the end, she flung the receiver down in anger and it fell off the hook and hung down from the kitchen counter. You vaguely recall picking it up, carefully putting it to your ear and listening for the sound of your father's voice through the rapid intermittent tones.

Nothing can give Mum back that time, that counter-current, the murky river she's still wading through today in an effort to reach the shore. It's only by exerting all her strength that she's kept herself from going under. She observed the world around her and the current carried her inexorably forward. The sight of her reflection in the mirror often fills her with astonishment – she's still here. Looking back, she sees time slipping through her fingers until she made it here, to this moment. A current that only relents as it comes to a bend – for a brief moment, there is finally stillness and time slows down.

She took one last look around the room. A photograph of Dad in Central Park, crouching down and laughing. Photographs beside the White House, Mount Rushmore, in front of Niagara Falls. Postcards from Colorado, Texas, Harvard – you'd pinned them all to a cork board above the desk, right next to an American flag. They printed it out for you at her work on thick card and, for a long time, she claimed it had come in a parcel for your birthday.

Her gaze drifted from the flag back to your face. She felt trapped, alone; she was trying to send out a distress signal, a call for help. No-one asked her how she felt. No-one listened to her. You were just a little kid, and Gran wasn't really there for her – not when she needed to talk to her, confide in her. She stood alone in the room, letting all the feelings burrow deep into her memory. They distorted the individual images until suddenly she wasn't sure of anything. Later, even in the workshop, they all come rushing back to her at once, the individual flashes competing for attention, and she has trouble concentrating on her work – it's as if the space she's operating in doesn't have four walls. As if she's completely lost her footing and tumbled deep inside her own head.

It's half past two when she downs tools. Inside the gowning room. she slowly peels off her overalls. The process reminds her of a snake: she too is shedding an old skin that's no longer needed. The one beneath it is all creased with sweat and her fingers are pruney from the latex gloves. She struggles a bit to open her locker; she's absolutely done in, and it takes her a while to get changed. In the mirror, she slowly fixes her hair and rubs some cream on her face.

She steps out of the factory into a hot summer's day, a clear sky overhead. It's only interrupted by a single cloud, drifting along slowly and calmly above the heads of the pedestrians, who are in no hurry to go anywhere. Mum digs a packet of cigarettes out of her handbag, pulls one out and lights it. It's muggy and she has to force the mixture of air and smoke into her lungs; it's hard going. Inside the factory, inside the air-conditioned rooms, she almost forgets, burying thoughts of the outside world within her. That makes it hit her with all the more force afterwards – the scents of the bushes, their colours, the shapes all around her. She takes a drag on her cigarette and sets out in the direction of Hypernova hypermarket.

She's walked this way so many times that her movements are purely automatic: from Kabelíkova she turns onto Optiky; the sweltering street is cooled by the shade provided by trees of various heights. Her mind is blank, conscious of nothing but the mechanical movement of her hand towards her mouth, a breath in followed by a breath out and the vague sensation of the smoke billowing in her lungs. She looks both ways, crosses the road, takes a left and, after passing the pharmacy, comes out into a grassy area between tower blocks.

On a small, trampled-down patch of ground near the pavement, she catches sight of a group of children. They're standing in a rough circle, scuffling and yelling something at each other. There's loud music playing from one of the many open windows, a tune she knows and actually quite

69

likes, so all she hears through the music is disjointed, fragmented scraps of sentences.

Before going into the Koloseum shopping centre, she changes her mind – she *will* stop by to see Grandad later, otherwise she'll get no peace. She does a shop for him too, stacking several tins of goulash in the basket. Grandad likes those, they're easy for him to heat up and don't cost much. She throws in a few instant soups and some bread. At the newsagent's by the exit, she buys two packets of unfiltered Camels as well, then she carefully packs everything into two plastic bags and sets out for home by the same route.

In the meantime, the cluster of children has thinned out a bit, and out of the corner of her eye, she spots a small boy in the middle who is lying on the ground, protecting his head with his hands.

Something about this scene doesn't look right to her, something's off. She hears voices but still can't make out more than a few words. She heads towards them along a path trodden in the grass but stops halfway. She finally understands what's going on.

"You breathe one word of this and we'll kick your face in."

"What the fuck are you wearing?"

A boy in a stripey T-shirt, who can't be more than ten, draws his arm back and chucks a rock at the boy huddled on the ground.

She shifts both bags into one hand and clears her throat quietly. She can't think of anything else to do. Several of the children turn round to look at her, including the boy who just threw the stone. She coughs again, takes a step forward and the crowd slowly disperses, leaving just the boy in the stripey T-shirt standing in front of her. He clenches his fists and looks her defiantly in the eye. She takes another step and the boy runs off. Mum puts the bags down next to each other, crouches beside the curled-up figure and cautiously reaches out a hand to him. The boy's body trembles a little. She leans over and notices a gash on his temple, a thin trickle of blood running down his cheek, dripping off his nose and seeping into the grass.

"You all right?" she asks, producing a tissue from her handbag.

The boy nods almost imperceptibly and slowly clambers to his feet. She gently brushes the dirt and bits of grass off him with her hand.

You imagine her gazing intently at the face framed by dark hair and seeing you in him. Maybe that's why she told you about the whole thing so many times. As if the resemblance between you was supposed to demonstrate something you didn't know yourself yet.

"Run off home," she says to him after a moment.

Without hesitating, the boy dashes off towards the gap between the tower blocks, each stride a different length

71

– this is how you run too – without even turning round, stumbling a few times, and disappears around the corner.

In the space between the buildings, people are walking past, completely unaware of what has just happened so close by. The flat patch of ground is finally empty and quiet. Mum is all alone, surrounded only by houses and flats with open, empty windows. It's hot and humid, the direct sunlight hitting her through the prefab blocks – she can feel it all over her body. Her hair is plastered to the skin on her neck. *I'm standing under a magnifying glass*, she thinks, lifting up a bag of shopping.

The afterimage of this event keeps playing on a loop in front of Mum's eyes for several seconds.

She was barely five years old the first time she saw Grandad strike Gran. He launched himself at her in the kitchen. Knocked the table over. Mum can no longer remember the reason for their fight; nor does she even care that much. In the doorway, she froze mid-motion; she had come to fetch Gran, probably to show her something, reached up on tiptoe for the handle and opened the door just as Grandad lunged forward. She saw the table hit the floor, saw the outstretched fist and Gran's hands protecting her face. She opened her mouth to say something, but a waft of alcohol sealed her lips again. She turned and fled to her room, quickly crawled into the gap under the bed and, curled up into a ball in the narrow space, covered her ears and pretended none of the sounds could reach her – neither the shouting nor the smashing of dishes nor the pounding of feet. She fell asleep and didn't wake up until late at night, nothing but dense darkness around her. At first, the confined space terrified her. Unable to straighten her legs, she kicked out and felt a searing pain in her knee. She bit her lip, wanting to cry out, but fear wouldn't let her make the slightest sound.

You read somewhere that pain can awaken the animal in people. It strips us of our humanity, leaving a person to scent the air around them warily, anticipating the next blow. "I don't even feel like a human being any more," Mum told you on the phone not so long ago, "but what can I do, I just have to get on with it." Now you know that all you have to do is spread out all the pain in front of you, take a look around you, and you'll discover that it's the ability to feel it that keeps you human.

In the meantime, she applied her theory to others.

"Gran's made of different stuff; she's got nerves of steel. Just think what Grandad must have put her through."

She often saw Gran in the corridors of the factory, always surrounded by a bunch of women, laughing – these days she barely even recognized her new voice.

She saw her seated behind a long table with lenses ready for inspection. In one eye, she always wore a watchmaker's loupe – she didn't even take it off when she was going for lunch. She was always talking to someone. Mum would never have admitted it, but she was jealous of her. She had quickly managed to escape from Grandad's shadow, to shake him off, while every day Mum had to go back to him, open the door, kick aside the stinking pile of laundry, drag his limp body off to bed and set to work for the second time that day.

She remembers her father bringing a wardrobe down on top of her mother. Holding a knife in his hands and waving it around. The memories come in waves; they form one big loop and she can tell exactly which one will come next.

She's in the U Tenisu flat; it's summer, late evening.

Your dad's in the corridor, pounding with his fists on the locked door, while a stranger attacks your mother. Your grandad let him in, invited him over, and she didn't even have a chance to shut herself in the bedroom with you.

When she eventually tells you this, she will force the words out through clenched teeth. You will draw them out of her gradually, and it's only once she gives in and admits the whole truth to you that you will understand why she never wants to relive that laughter or the sweaty hands of that stranger again. Why she refuses to open the door to locked rooms, rooms full of things she mustn't think about. All it takes is a hint of that memory and she's back there again.

She walks through town with the bags, concentrating on nothing but the weight of the shopping, the uneven pavement she's making her way along. Meanwhile, clouds are gathering overhead and gliding across the sky, growing bigger and darker before her eyes. Mum makes a turn, passes the building with the convenience store, runs her eyes over the peeling signs and the contorted ochre statue of a woman with a loaf of bread. Once, when she was still at trade school, she and Karolína had wrapped it up in toilet paper. That was a tradition of theirs – they selected a different place each time and covered their target from head to toe. Even the loaf got the same treatment, and they took the greatest care over the stone woman's breasts. They stepped back to inspect the shapeless wad of grey paper. If their timing was right and the rain came on, the sodden mass would slowly ooze down the statue, leaving slimy trails over it.

"With that little stunt of yours, the two of you have defiled everything that statue celebrates. Workers, especially female workers, women, your mothers."

They sat in the headmaster's office at the trade school with their heads bowed but felt no particular sense of shame. The headmaster had summoned them the very next day. He folded his hands in his lap, tapping his foot until the glass in the display cabinet behind him shook.

"You're lucky that statue is so ugly, otherwise I might have to punish you."

Beside her, Karolína almost burst out laughing.

If only she could choose what to remember. Keep a collection of memories and throw the rest away. She could pretend to recall the others, agree – yes, that's the way it was, that really was how it happened – while thinking about something else. Instead, she ended up with these fuzzy grey impressions that begged for attention in fits and starts. All her life, Mum has been betrayed by her mind. She forgets names, forgets whatever she doesn't write down on a piece of paper or mark on the calendar. Sometimes it seems to her that she's got nothing left of the good memories at all. Nothing but mere reflections.

But those don't offer much solace.

The truth is, she only finds that in the safety of mechanical, machine-like movements. When she thinks of the disassembled units, of the clean, unpeopled room, the artificial and unchanging light. She doesn't even smell the fumes from the cotton buds soaked in acetone. When she breathes in, her head no longer hurts; it's quiet and calm. She cleans the lenses with a circular motion and then fits them into the body of the device, loosens a screw, secures it. In the workshop, she manages to put the memories aside; they fade into the background until she hardly notices them any more.

At the end of the street, she turns onto Dvořákova. The main road is lined with mulberry trees on one side and birches on the other. So the street acts as a partition dividing the world into two halves. The left side is a bit brighter, the silver leaves and bark giving off a dim white light, while the right-hand side, the one closer to the factory, is plunged into shadow. She crosses over into the light and, outside the front door, she digs out the keys from the bottom of her handbag. The building is the same as eight others arranged in a grid one behind the other, five floors and four entrances. Your flat is on the ground floor, and sometimes she is grateful for that, while at other times she feels like running away. At least she doesn't have to lug the shopping all the way upstairs through the dingy corridor. The door to the flat, forced open so many times, is barely holding together. To close it, she has to lean against it and give it a kick.

At home, she gets changed for the third time that day. She unpacks the shopping and stacks the things for Grandad on the table. After she's rested for a bit, she'll head to his place. She arranges her own half of the shopping on the shelves, carefully piling packets of rice on top of each other. She's been layering and stockpiling for as long as she can remember; she builds stacks on the shelves out of packs of flour wrapped up in plastic bags. In summer, the air in the flat doesn't stir at all and there's a slight smell from the warmed-up lino in the hallway, even though she opened all the windows as soon as she got back. She puts the kettle on, sits down on the couch in Gran's room with a mug of coffee, turns on the TV and is asleep within five minutes.

You burst through the door, waking your mother up. The impact makes the walls vibrate, and she gives a start and nearly tips over the mug wedged between her legs. It's a reflex you're familiar with: she wakes up in the night and throws her arms around, kicks out, occasionally talks in her sleep, just like you. Now she's drenched in sweat from the heat and can feel her heart pounding in her chest. She's all stiff and can't move. She takes a sip of cold coffee from the mug and closes her eyes again.

In the flat, you can hear everything. You take off your shoes and slam another door shut behind you, this time the one to your shared room.

That was the summer Gran started sleeping at the allotment more and more often. She had secured the small plot right in the middle of the allotments on the other side of the Lagoon back when she was still working. She paid less than three hundred crowns a year for it; apart from a well with a pump and a couple of vegetable patches, the only thing on the land was a small toolshed with a pointy roof, more of a box with no windows and a door from an old freezer. That was where she slept. She had dragged an old mattress and a sleeping bag inside, and at night she kept the door open just a crack so it was possible to breathe in there.

"I need to keep an eye out or the neighbour will strip the lot bare," she explained when Mum asked her about it, even though she knew full well that all the elderly man from the next-door plot did was sit in front of his hut all day long, puffing on his pipe. She knew that, like her, Gran needed time alone, that the flat was getting too small for the three of you.

As for Mum, she could have done with at least a couple of hours to herself every day. She would have liked to stretch out and do nothing. But, in the end, the time she had left each day always went by too fast. Sometimes she longed for it, sensed it almost within her grasp – all you need to do is reach out, Dana, wrap your fingers around it. But when she did have a little bit of time left at the end of the day, unfamiliar territory loomed in front of her, where she walked back and forth aimlessly, opening up the individual rooms. She peered inside. Nothing. She looked out of the window.

Cook, tidy up the room. Vacuum the hall, clean the bathroom and toilet.

Do the washing, the ironing. She was drowning in it, couldn't breathe.

The work kept coming round again: she finally managed to empty the laundry basket, turned her back for a moment and found a dirty sweatshirt or boxer shorts in it. She did the washing-up and, a minute later, a dirty mug mysteriously appeared on the worktop.

She would find herself polishing the bathroom mirror several times a day to get rid of the spatters. And the toilet – she flushed it after the others and, at the same time, wiped the pee off the floor.

She bottled up the anger that took hold of her, storing it in an empty space in her chest. Every time she had to clean drops of urine off the toilet bowl, she fought off flashbacks from her childhood, when she and Gran had knelt on the bathroom floor, scrubbing the tiles with a brush soaked in disinfectant. Images saturated with ammonia, reeking of urine and the stench of vomit. Grandad lying in a pile of it in the bedroom, sprawled in a corner, stinking and snoring loudly.

At times like that, she and Gran didn't speak to each other. They progressed in silence, painstakingly, inch by inch, as if their lives depended on it, as if together with the urine and the stink, they were also washing away the damaged parts of themselves. Mum observed Gran out of the corner of her eye, searching her face for any hint of emotion, tears or at least a flash of anger, and found nothing but an empty shell and hard, resigned eyes staring straight ahead, lost in their own depths.

It was only when you came along that she gradually began to understand Gran.

She hears you running down the hall to the bathroom and sees your shadow, a blur behind the frosted glass door panel. That's followed by another bang, the rattle of the key in the lock. She rolls her eyes and puts the mug down. She gets up from the couch slowly, reluctantly, walks down the hall and knocks on the door. This is how all your arguments begin. You lock yourself in the bathroom and spend an hour in the tub – you have the feeling she can't get to you there. She has no idea what you're doing in there all that time.

Something drops onto the floor. You try to stay quiet. Mum knocks again but doesn't say anything herself.

There's a rattling in the lock, then the door opens, and you stick your head out.

"What?"

She peeks in through the crack. You're naked to the waist. Subconsciously, she runs her gaze over you, pausing at the reddish, bloody mark on your stomach.

"Nothing," she mutters after a moment, shifting her weight from one foot to the other. "But you could at least say hello to me."

You look at her, your mouth hanging open in confusion.

Your mother just shakes her head and closes the door again. The two of you play a similar game every day: she speaks to you, you ignore her. You stare into space or walk away mid-sentence; you don't hear her at all, barely even care about her.

In the kitchen, she takes a board out of one drawer and a knife out of another and starts chopping vegetables. But her mind is elsewhere.

It isn't that long since she was helping you into your pyjamas. You stuck your leg out and she slipped one lint-covered trouser leg over it. You stuck the other one out. She raised your arms and pulled on the top half. She remembers you as a little boy, curled up next to her in the bed; she remembers the mornings when she woke up with your leg wedged in her armpit.

You finally open the bathroom door half an hour later and clouds of steam billow out of it. Your face is all red with a happy, tired expression on it.

"So what about that grandad of yours?" she asks. You lean against the doorframe and run your hand through your wet, dishevelled hair. "Did you go and see him?"

You tell her everything – at least everything she asks about. She nods and occasionally makes a noise to show she's listening to you. You crane your neck in the direction of the chopped vegetables.

"What are we having?"

But she ignores your question, doesn't even turn to face you.

"And what was up with his TV?"

"Nothing."

It makes her nervous when you stand behind her, so she turns round and sits you down in a chair.

"I just walked in, had a look and it came back to life straight away. He could easily have sorted it out himself, but he was totally out of it." You ask her to pour you a glass of water. She sets it down in front of you and you drink it in one gulp before carrying on: "He was totally freaking out. But then the TV came on and he flopped back down in his armchair and forgot all about me."

Grandad only had a few pieces of furniture in his small bedroom. You and Martin had dragged them there on a trolley across the whole of Přerov. That was when Martin was still going out with your mum. There were a few slats missing from the base of Grandad's bed. The armchair was saggy with use, the fabric fraying on the armrests and clumps of yellowish wadding sticking out of it.

"Grandad must have been pleased," replies Mum, trying to wipe away the tears from the onion vapours with her sleeve. "Apart from the TV, he hasn't really got anything else these days."

"You don't say!" you answer in a tone which Mum interprets as amusement. In reality, you are using it to mask your distaste at what's become of Grandad. "He actually seemed annoyed that I was there. Didn't so much as thank me, just gave me this weird look and then practically shoved me out the door."

Mum scatters the onion over a hot pan, stirs it and turns the heat down a bit. Grandad had always been like that: as long as he needed her or somebody else, he had a way of making sure they were there for him. As soon as they'd helped him, he went back to treating them as if they were surplus to requirement, an object left there to be tripped over every time.

Before Mum's younger brother was born, she and your aunt thought the reason Grandad was so horrible to them was because of their sex. Then Kuba came into the world ("A son at last!" he hollered out of the window of the maternity hospital to the whole street), and, for about a month, he paid attention to him and was full of enthusiasm, but gradually even that spark went out and the Grandad they knew so well returned. He never hid his contempt from them – for example, the time when, after six months of pleas and searching, Gran brought your mum and aunt the long-coveted jeans. The two of them were standing in front of the mirror, checking themselves out, and Grandad walked past and gave them a lingering look of disgust. Gran would be explaining something to them and he would butt in mid-sentence. All the attention in their home was focused solely on him. As soon as Gran asked what the children had been doing all day, Grandad interrupted them and ordered the table to be set. They ate dinner in silence and Grandad would get up from the table first and make straight for the TV. It went on like that day after day – he always had to have the last word.

On her first day of school, Mum waited eagerly for him outside the front door, holding her school bag, and Grandad – perhaps he was a tiny bit proud of her, though he gave no sign of it – was supposed to walk her there. He went just far enough to put on a show for the neighbours ("See what a beautiful daughter I have, how smart she is. Look, Pepa, how that new skirt suits her!") and then all it took was for them to pass the nearest pub and Grandad stopped – "you go on ahead", he shouted to her, "I'll catch you up in a minute."

She wipes her nose with the back of her hand and instantly regrets it. The smell of onion sets off the tears again and she steps away from the stove and takes a slow breath in and out again. She adds the rest of the vegetables to the pan, pours in a drop of water, covers the pan with a lid and puts a pot of water on the other ring for the pasta.

"And what have you been doing all day?" she asks, trying not to think of the days when she wished her father would ask her the same question.

Your shoulders slump. There are things you've never told her about. You used to treat it as a game, but you've been playing it for so long that, one morning, you woke up and realized you no longer spoke the same language. Or, at least, not one you could use to talk to her about things and be sure she'd accept them. That's why you now pretend to be pissed off and dodge the issue and your mum circles around you, asking for more and more details and backing you into a corner. In the end, one of you starts to get irritated for real and the other one notices and gets annoyed tool and you don't speak to each other for a while and then the next day it happens all over again.

"In the morning, I was out with a friend," you answer cautiously. "On our bikes, but more like around the Lagoon, just hanging out. Then nothing."

Mum empties a whole packet of pasta into the boiling water, stirs it and puts the lid on the pot. She leans on the worktop and her gaze drifts over to you. Could she have picked up on some of those hints? Ever since the parents' evening, you haven't been sure of anything; you've been trying to avoid your mother, dodge any questions that could lead you onto shaky ground.

"And was it really a friend? It wasn't by any chance a girlfriend?"

"Leave it out, will you?" you snap crossly.

She watches you turn red in the face. You avoid eye contact, clench your fists. As she observes you, you can feel her gaze burning a hole right through you all the way into the wall behind your back. From this angle, your face looks sharp and thin, and she sees more of your father in you than ever before. She turns her head to preserve the image.

"All right, but why –," she drags out the last word, "why couldn't you tell me that? You would tell me if you had a girlfriend, right?"

You can't stand it any more and leap up from the chair.

But she just can't help herself. Her parents never showed that kind of interest in her. Gran did ask from time to time, but probably in an attempt to mask a general fear, a need to protect Mum from the fate that had befallen *her*.

Perhaps that was why she set so much store by the idea that when she had a child of her own, they would be best friends. In her mind, she often pictured the daughter she had dreamed of, trying on her clothes and spinning round till she stumbled. They would lie on the bed together and discuss things she'd never been able to talk about with her own mother.

But then you were born and your mother felt a slight pang inside her. She had to revise all her ideas, reconfigure the angle at which she had planned out her life in advance.

Before you each started speaking a different, foreign language, you'd gone through just about everything together. When she was at her lowest ebb – by then, you were able to read other people's moods – you used to lie together in the corner of her bed. During the night, you'd shuffle over to her, because you'd had a bad dream or you just couldn't sleep, and you'd gently shake her and crawl under the duvet. In the darkness, she touched you with her forehead and, even though she couldn't see it, she imagined you winking at her. She whispered made-up stories in your ear – stories about the soft toys you brought to bed with you and about what your dad might be doing in America, what the two of you would do when you went there for a visit one day soon.

You used to see her crying as well when it all got too much for her. She'd be sitting all alone in the room, and you'd open the door and stare at her for a moment in consternation. You took a step forward and wrapped your arms around her. Not out of pity – it was more that, somewhere inside, you felt her pain. It welled up to the surface of her and the sadness spilled over into you.

Was she hurt when you started showing more interest in Dad? Your father hadn't even wanted you; she once told you about the night she'd revealed to him that she was pregnant. They were heading back from somewhere on a borrowed motorbike and Mum was in a suspiciously good mood, holding onto his waist while her hair was blown about by a fresh breeze. Above them was an inky sky riddled with stars, and in it a single cloud, a single smudge. She craned her neck and, over the roar of the engine, shouted the news into his ear. My father stopped. She waited for him to turn to face her but, instead, he dismounted, threw the motorbike into the ditch and disappeared into the darkness without a single word. She was left alone at the edge of the woods, gradually adjusting to the darkened surroundings.

Back home, they didn't speak to each other for a few days, and if she brought the subject up, he pretended not to hear until, one evening, he asked her if she would consider getting an abortion.

But she kept this part from you: she didn't tell you anything about your father's insistence, about his pleas, about the pamphlet he brought from the hospital. She made up a story about how the very next day after the incident with the motorbike he'd brought home a big cuddly toy crow, which she had actually been given by someone else. You only remember it from a photo where you're sitting on a potty, hugging the crow and beaming. But your father doesn't remember the stuffed toy and finally came out with the truth the night you saw each other for the first time in twenty years.

It was Gran who had put this idea in Mum's head: supposedly, a person is born for a second time into the body of their child. A body that has developed thanks to her but gradually takes on a strange and alien form. "Kids rob you of the last remnants of good sense," was Karolína's take on the subject. "Or turn you into a kid yourself. I mean, you must have heard the way people prattle on, all that baby-talk? I can't stand it."

Once, not that long ago, Mum and Dad were arguing on the phone. You had learned to listen through closed doors, straining your ears to catch more of what they were saying. But you still didn't hear how, just before he hung up, he couldn't resist taking one last dig at Mum.

"I don't want the lad growing up to be what you've always wanted: a mini you but in the form of a boy."

She wasn't born for a second time into that tangle of bedclothes and twisted limbs. In the maternity ward, she spent a long time watching that bundle of connections and nerves and didn't know what to do with it. In the recesses of her mind, other things Gran had said flashed through her head. The moment she saw each of her three children for the first time, she told Mum, she had felt a terrible urge to run away from them. "You were all such shrivelled-up little prunes, she laughed in the reflection of Mum's memory. You were born crumpled, with blueish skin – you didn't look the least bit human. Mum observed you in the maternity hospital with wide eyes. Your ear had grown into your head and, for several weeks, she carefully massaged it until, one day, it came away from the down-covered skull with a quiet pop.

No-one had prepared her, no-one had warned her that with your arrival, fear would creep into her life. She was afraid something would go wrong, that you would slip out of her grasp and smash your head on the ground. When you were a toddler, she would hoist you up in the air, throw you right up to the ceiling, catch you again and bundle you back into her chest. You laughed and snorted so hard you could hardly breathe. Meanwhile, Mum had ridiculously gory visions running through her head. She would drop the child on the ground, accidentally forget him at the council office or in a shop. That made the thought of how blithely unconcerned you were about the world around you frighten her all the more. You would stretch out in the cot, clutch the bars and observe your mum curiously, holding Gran's hand a short distance away and begging her for something. By that time, your father was hardly ever at home and she was struggling to make ends meet again.

It's hard for her to admit you're no longer a child.

She can still see you standing in your dressing gown in the middle of the room, waving your arms helplessly. Your wet hair tumbles over your forehead and she walks up to you, pushes it aside and lifts you into her arms.

These days, she wouldn't be able to pick you up, more like the other way round, and the thought fills her with fear. Soon you'll be taller than her; sitting at the table, you take up more and more space. Just like your father. You are seized with rage. She imagines a more grown-up version of you. Subconsciously, she clenches her hand into a fist and examines you through narrowed eyes.

"Guys are all dicks." Karolína never held back on her. "Every last one of them. Even my two boys." Mum didn't protest, just laughed quietly. "Just you wait – the first time yours calls you a cow because you refuse to put his socks away for him or you won't let him watch TV, it's all down-hill from there." Karolína liked to scare her with stories about her own sons growing up to be smaller versions of their father. "It's in their genes." Their father had left Karolína for a younger woman and only took the boys at the weekend – and only occasionally, when it happened to suit him. He refused to support them financially and Karolína had to beg him every month. "I don't even wanna know what they say about me when I'm not home."

Even so, she couldn't help feeling something wasn't right with you.

"That's not how a normal boy behaves." It was Karolína who had planted that seed of doubt.

That's another reason why you can't tell your mum what's on your mind, can't confide in her. You jump to your feet and make to leave. "Hold on a minute," she stops you, pulling you back. "I was only kidding. Sit back down, we'll be eating in a little while."

Reluctantly, you sit down on the bench. She has her back to you again as she stirs the pasta into the mixture in the pan, so she doesn't see your annoyed expression.

"Gran said we're helping her out at the allotment this evening, that you arranged it with her."

Her shoulders stiffen. Before she answers, she seasons the mixture in the pot, just salt and pepper, sprinkles on grated cheese and mixes it all in again. Only then does she speak.

"We didn't arrange anything. I guess she'll be in touch if she needs something. I don't know anything about it."

She gets two bowls out of the cupboard, divides two generous portions between them, fetches a bottle of ketchup from the fridge and carries the food over to the table.

You eat in silence, the air in the kitchen filled with the clinking of cutlery until, at some point, your phone buzzes in your pocket. You fish it out, gripping your fork between your teeth. But when you read the message, you grin and the fork falls out of your mouth. Mum reaches across the table and smacks you on the head. Recently, she'll be walking by and see you grinning, shielding your phone with your body, and if she gets too close, you'll glare at her sullenly. She doesn't even want to think about how much credit you must be frittering away. Last month, she confiscated your mobile because of it; she had no idea Gran was secretly topping up your credit.

"Can't you put it down for a minute? Why don't you tell me again what you've been doing all day?"

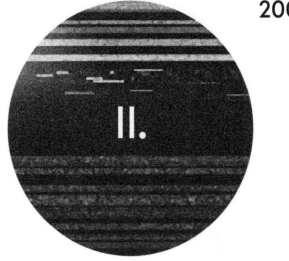

You often wonder whether it's even possible to talk about things that other people can't see or refuse to see. Whether you can talk about something you've lost, about the sadness that resulted from it, without losing it all a second time. You'd love to be able to tell her everything one day.

You go back a few steps, to a little earlier the same day. Once again, you're alone, back in your own company. From the water's surface, only your tired eyes, stretched out into two quivering strings, return your gaze. Reflections of light fall on your face and it's so hot you can hardly think.

Beside you, you can still sense that empty space, and your fingers feel for the indentation in the pebbles, drawn to it once more. You glance back at the path trampled through the grass.

You're sitting by a quiet bend of the Bečva on a section of riverbank strewn with stones, hidden from other people's view. Because this place is all yours. This little corner with the overgrown bushes and clumps of nettles that keep people out. No-one would think of pushing their way through this thick undergrowth when there's easy access to the river just a few feet away. You're ankle-deep in the water and a scab has already formed on your stomach. In the morning, you and Marián slogged your way here and you managed to slip and graze yourself. Losing your footing is something that happens to you a lot – you're capable of tripping up on a flat surface, or you'll be walking along a corridor and bang your shoulder against the wall. You stripped off your T-shirt, soaked it in the river and managed to get some of the blood off it. Now it's drying on the pebbles nearby. You watch the brownish current of the river and try to grasp for the thousandth time why you have to deal with problems like these.

"I've gotta go. See you tomorrow."

A shiver runs down your spine.

You were about eight when you first stopped paying attention at school. Instead of looking at the blackboard, you absent-mindedly gazed at Petr as he drew goofy pictures in his exercise book. There was nothing odd about that. But as time went on, you realized it wasn't the doodles you were interested in. Your eyes were fixed on the movement of his hand as it traced the curves on the paper, the expression his face took on, and the way he always stuck out the tip of his tongue and leaned back slightly to appraise his work. Why were you staring at him like that? You switched your attention to Anička, hunched on the chair next to his, and looked at her dark, wavy hair for a while. Shouldn't you be watching her instead?

Gradually, the staring began to be accompanied by a strange sensation in your lower abdomen. You were capable of spending hours observing how Filip's hair curled into little loops, covering his ears and coiling over the tanned skin on his neck.

In PE, you learned to avoid the slightest contact with another boy's body like the plague. But it was difficult to take your eyes off the undressed bodies in the changing room. Sometimes you'd catch yourself staring through somebody's half-naked body with gritted teeth.

Your dreams began to contain images of thighs, calves and naked body parts on an endless loop. Instead of a manly slap on the back, Petr wishes you a happy birthday, hugs you and gives you a kiss.

You dreamt of a lot of other things you're still slightly ashamed to think about.

In the morning, you wake up with an unpleasantness moistness in your crotch and, later on, you can't look the others in the eye. It's as if your body has been held prisoner for years and then set free. You walk down the hallway, jaw clenched, praying Mum won't catch you. Then you bury your stained boxers at the very bottom of the laundry basket.

You often think of running away, without realizing that you're living out a scenario lots of other people have gone through before you; that you're just conforming to a pattern when you imagine going somewhere far away where you could find peace of mind and forget about everything.

Earlier, before the others' voices, before the bullying and Marián, it never occurred to you that there might be anything wrong with you. At nursery school, you and Filip would lie beside each other after lunch, when you were often unable to get to sleep, and whisper crazy stories to each other. Some inner voice told you: you should crawl in beside him. Throw the duvet over both of you. Curl up underneath it, without really knowing why. Back then, you didn't understand exactly how these things worked. You lacked the vocabulary, despite the fact that, when it came down to it, words were all that remained.

Meanwhile, the others had you sussed much more quickly. Though you can no longer remember exactly when everything went sideways, the first thing you recall is always the colour red.

In first year, you decided to go to the school fancy-dress party dressed as Harry Potter. Mum made you a hat and cape from an offcut of old curtain material she'd dyed and, at work, she got them to make you a pair of frames without lenses. You refused to take off the oversized glasses and spent several days practising spells in front of the mirror. A stick in place of a wand and a cape made of shiny fabric that flowed over your shoulders and clung to your body slightly. Before the party, Mum drew a scar on your forehead with lipstick, combed your hair and positioned your hat on top.

The gym had been decorated with crepe paper chains stuck to the walls with sellotape; they were even hanging from the gymnastics rings and the basketball hoop.

In the crowd, you sought out Filip, Petr and Martin, your friends from the estate. Up until then, you'd been an inseparable gang. After school, you'd weave your way between the metal frames of the washing lines, whacking sticks against them while making noises like light sabres. The poles still remind you of electricity pylons; every autumn, birds would sit on the wires stretched out between them, and in winter ice formed on them. Other times, you'd crawl into the fallout shelters in the cellars. That was something Mum particularly disliked, and she forbade you from jumping on the concrete blocks with the air vents as they were the only thing that would allow the people hiding down below to breathe. You thought there really were people down there, so you'd deliberately stamp around every vent and shout down the opening through the build-up of rubbish, cigarette butts and dust.

The younger kids were a bit afraid of you all. One time, Filip stole a pack of Pokémon cards from someone in the next building and then divided them out evenly among you. It would never have occurred to you that one day you'd find yourself on the other side.

In the gym, you went and stood beside the others and Filip immediately gave you a shove and sent you flying.

"What on earth are you wearing?" he said, his voice cracking with anger while, next to him, Petr and Martin burst out laughing.

"I mean, it looks like a dress."

"He looks like some kinda witch. Look how tight it is!"

You managed to get back on your feet and dust off your knees. You checked your appearance: the cloak was clinging to your hips and, every time you moved, there was the crackling of static. You couldn't pull the material away from you: it sprung back like a boomerang. By then Filip had noticed the scar on your forehead.

"And what's that meant to be? Is that lipstick? Did you steal that off your mum?"

You bit your tongue so hard your mouth was filled with a horrible metallic taste.

"It's a scar."

You didn't know what else to say. At the first opportune moment, when all three had their backs to you, you wiped the lipstick off your forehead with the hem of the cloak.

Two days after that, Filip knocked your front teeth out on the bench in front of the flats. He claimed it was an ac cident. He really hadn't meant to shove you, not that hard; he'd just lost his balance and sent you sprawling onto the curb by mistake. Even through your closed lips, the blood streamed from your mouth and wouldn't stop. Individual drops fell to the ground, forming red splotches on the paving stones.

You remember those red drops being absolutely everywhere – on your skin, your T-shirt, the pages of your textbooks. The colour red keeps coming back to you again and again. You and Filip didn't need to know the exact words to grasp something – his blows spoke more eloquently. For practically the whole of first year, you lay low at your desk, terrified of every loud noise. You didn't tell anyone about the bullying, not even when it all got too much for you and the pain went beyond the limits of what you could bear.

Mum didn't know what to do with you. She couldn't understand it. You kept coming home from school late, covered in bruises, your clothes torn, and you didn't speak to anyone. If Mum asked you a question, you denied everything. You were afraid because she knew most of the parents or, at least, worked alongside them.

At that time, you'd have done anything to get out of going to school. At night, you were kept awake by the vision of another day spent at your desk. You learned to fake illness – you had a sore stomach, a headache. You'd squeeze the thermometer under your arm until the mercury rose at least two lines above 37. At this point, Grandad was functioning fairly normally. He was drinking a bit, but because

Mum and Gran had to go out to work every day, they let him look after you. Whenever he made you strong black tea, he'd take a bottle out of a tattered plastic bag, turn his back to you, fiddle about with it for a moment, and then present with you a mug filled to the brim.

You sniffed it suspiciously.

"Drink up. Come on now, it's the best thing for men like us."

He stood over you the whole time, his arms across his chest, tapping his foot impatiently. You sipped it cautiously and a warm sensation spread through your belly. You took another drink and now Grandad was beaming from ear to ear.

"See? You can do it."

He made the same tea for himself, only he poured in a lot more from the bottle. He sat down at the table, spread out some old advertising leaflets in front of him – he'd read them all ages ago – and took out a box stuffed full of tobacco. The two of you slowly slurped your tea while he rolled a cigarette one-handed. Your eyes followed his every movement, and there was a slight tingling in your head. He was licking another paper when he suddenly paused, looked you up and down, and winked conspiratorially.

"Don't even think about telling your mum. She wouldn't understand, d'you hear? This has to stay between us."

Gradually, this became your ritual, your little secret. He would make you a second mug, then a third. After drinking Grandad's tea, the whole world crumbled into tiny pieces, helping you to forget. In the afternoon, you'd both lie on Gran's couch, Grandad would turn on the TV and tune into some sport and, within a couple of minutes, you'd both be asleep.

When Marián appeared in the class halfway through fourth year, the others lost interest in you, at least for a while. You became an empty space beside a desk. To them, Marián represented everything you had been before and more besides. No-one liked him – not even the teachers could stomach having a Romani in their class, especially one who looked like him. He began to take the flak instead of you, and you saw no reason to alter anything about that situation.

You made up a list of rules for yourself: watch the way you move; stay silent at all costs; don't stand out; answer questions and then fall silent again; don't speak to anyone. Your body drifted along from one day to the next like a ghost, going through the motions like a robot. It got up in the morning and went to bed in the evening. The time in between was just a blur. You stood in the middle of the current, trying to hold your ground. From the back of your mind, your own voice spoke to you, whispering strange, terrifying things, and, as a result, you stopped eating and couldn't look at your own reflection in the mirror.

The first time you cut yourself was with nail scissors. Maybe you wanted the colour red to come back again, this time on your terms. You stood naked in the bathtub and a kind of river started roaring in your ears, its current rocking you and carrying you away to safety. It whispered something about you still being here, still being alive. It was a good feeling. The flowing colour made spots dance in front of your eyes and, for a moment, the whole world stopped. You did it the next time too, watching the shallow furrows of the wounds pumping out more and more blood.

You managed to conceal the scabs from everyone except Gran. She never mentioned them to Mum. One weekend, you were helping her in the allotment. As you swung the hoe, your shorts rode up just as she happened to be looking in your direction. She took you by the hand and sat you down on the first step by the shed.

For a long while, she silently gazed into your eyes.

"Why do you do it?"

You shook your head and whispered that you didn't want to talk about it.

"It's crazy what you're doing. Your body's a gift. You have to look after it."

But, to you, your body didn't seem like a gift – more like an empty space. You couldn't find anything inside it, any feeling that didn't stir up pain. At that time, you hadn't been able to write about it yet, so you'd learned to destroy the body in a different way.

"If you feel bad, just take a look around you."

You looked around and saw a dilapidated toolshed, a rusty fence. She stroked your hair with a dirt-covered hand.

"You'll never be alone cos your mum and I will always be there for you. And we're alive too, you hear?" She took your hand and placed it on her chest. There was something missing beside her left breast – you had never noticed it before. You ran the palm of your hand over the curved protrusion and felt your gran's ribs through the dry material of her top. The last time you'd been this close to her, you must have been about five. Every summer, you used to go a cottage in Velké Karlovice – it belonged to the factory and they rented it out to employees for next to nothing. It wasn't that big and there was no running water, so you had to fetch it in basins from an octagonal wooden washhouse. The spiderwebs on the beams used to frighten you, while the glass panels in the washhouse door let in colourful little spots of light, which you'd try in vain to catch every evening. When you were hiking in the surrounding countryside, your feet usually started to hurt right at the halfway point. Mum wouldn't have been able to carry you the whole way, so Gran would give you a piggy-back. Her protruding shoulder blades pressed into your face – they were as sharp as they are today, and yet you always managed to fall asleep on them.

"When your heart beats, it lets the world know it's there. You can't just forget about it – that's impossible.

105

Now yours and mine have very different rhythms, but just concentrate for a bit. Here..." She shifted your hand back to her breast. "Give it time and they'll gradually begin to beat the same way."

You listened to her and heard only the echo of your own pulse. Gran straightened up, leaned against the freezer door and tilted her head.

"Everything in your body is as it should be. Everything. And I know that 'cos you're my flesh and blood. Look at me. Do you think there's anything wrong with me?"

*Not with you*, you wanted to reply. *But there is with me.*

"Don't forget that. And the next time you feel sad, grit your teeth for me and bear it."

How could you forget anything? You hope that one day you'll get it out of your head, but what's happening to you is becoming part of you, taking up space, until gradually you no longer know who you were before.


You're fourteen and you sometimes cry at night. You can't stop dreaming about how much easier it would be if you wanted to touch Klára, Anička, Tereza, or any of the girls in your class, or if you were one of them. You invent absurd scenarios in which you quietly close the door to your flat and set out into the streets; the town is deserted at night, and you see no-one and no-one sees you. You imagine Mum in the morning, staring in confusion at the empty bed before shrugging her shoulders and heading out. At school, all that would be left of you would be an empty chair. No-one would miss you, you say to yourself; all you do is take up space.

Mum often does an impression of an old man who works at the factory. She draws herself up and walks around the room with her hand on her hip, swaying her pelvis and mincing along. She flops down on the sofa and crosses one leg over the other. Meanwhile, you're standing off to one side, trying to appear calm, when she calls to you in a honeyed voice: "Sweetie, do be a love and pass me the remote." That makes her and Gran crack up, and Mum brays with laughter until she ends up coughing. "I swear, I'm gonna choke to death 'cos of that fairy."

They think you're not watching, that it doesn't bother you, but things like that accumulate inside you like dust in your room. Mum cleans it every day, and yet the dust comes back again, making its way in from the main road, from the chimneys of the factories and the hospital, from the fear inside your head.

You'd like to tell them you haven't forgotten – everything is as it should be in your body – but perhaps you've misunderstood, perhaps something is different and something inside you really has slotted into the wrong place.

You watch *Gilmore Girls* together on TV as it's one of the few programmes you can all agree on. You're sitting on the sofa in Gran's room – you don't have a television in yours – and they've both just come back from work and are commenting wearily on Michel's high-pitched voice. "That one's so gay it's unbelievable."

Would they talk about him that way if they knew who was really sitting with them in the room?

"What's up with you?" asks Mum. She noticed you frowning, grinding your teeth. "You know you can tell me anything."

Really? Several things instantly come to mind that you can't bring yourself to talk to her about.

For instance, Jess only has to appear on the screen to send a chill through your body. Mum and Gran love Dean because he's nice and calm and tall. But you've always felt more drawn to the gloomy, taciturn, hurt expression that Jess puts on almost every time the camera's on him. Just like you, he's always messing things up; he never does anything right.

You've had a fair amount of time to think everything through. You imagine holding hands with one of the girls from your class. You'd like to change and be normal, but no matter how hard you try, it just doesn't work. And because Gran was wrong and everything is *not* as it should be inside of you, at night you go to bed and your mind is filled with completely different images.

You always come to this spot by the river whenever you need some time alone, whenever things get too much.

You take your bike, or walk down through the estate from your flat, past the bustling hospital, and continue along the river, crossing the old suspension bridge. It's saggy and rickety, and if there's a gust of wind, it lurches from side to side. You remember how you used to jump up and down on it when you were a young child, stamping on the cracked concrete and taking delight in every response you got from the structure. You turn right and after passing the pub by the Lagoon, you continue on for a few minutes along an overgrown trail until you're finally there. It was at a similar spot not far from here that Mum taught you to swim, but you stumbled upon *this* place by chance. In the winter, you sit on a washed-up tree stump and observe the clouds of steam coming from your mouth. Sometimes you head here straight after school, toss your schoolbag into the bushes and let everything melt away. It's the first week of the holidays, the sun seems to be trying to kill you all, it's roasting all the time and, even in your rolled-up T-shirt and three-quarter-length trousers, you feel as if your brain is about to be fried at any minute. You sit in the shade of the trees and let the lukewarm, murky water trickle through your fingers.

No-one can see you here. Not like at home, where you and Mum are crammed together in a small room, while Gran has the bigger one all to herself. When Dad left you both and strange men kept on pushing their way into your home and demanding money from Mum, it was Gran who stood up to them. She'd stand in the doorway, rolling pin in hand, screaming at them at the top of her lungs. At that time, Mum used to go straight from the factory to her second job, and she'd return late in the evening and repeat over and over again how tired she was, how her head hurt, how she couldn't walk. "Not now," she'd say, pushing you away from her and shutting herself in the kitchen.

You have to listen over and over again to the stories about how you learned to walk in slippers full of holes. You're still unaware of how deep down painful memories can lodge themselves, or how little it takes for them to resurface. You'd happily go on wearing your old, shabby clothes, but Mum insists you have a freshly washed and ironed T-shirt every morning – "We don't have to *look* like beggars as well". She alters second-hand clothes on a sewing machine and shortens old trousers handed down from Karolína's boys. She likes her home to be tidy – everything in the flat has its own specially designated place; everything has to look nice and neat. In the evening, she makes you fold your clothes into a pile on the chair and line up the slippers underneath the bed. "It's a pigsty in here," she'll say if you forget to do something. "It's like living with Gypsies. Clear it up before anyone sees." But hardly anyone ever visits you at home, so you don't see the point. In the morning, you leave white splodges of tooth-paste on the sink and she gets angry because they'll dry up and form grey stains on the shiny surface.

At home, you do your best not to offend her sense of order, but when it comes to things that are truly impor-tant, your mother fails to see them.

Your father, on the other hand, has started to get his act together lately. It's thanks to him that you have a mobile phone and a computer. He and Mum argued about it countless times – she wanted him to send money instead since you needed that much more. In the end, she gave in. A couple of months later, she brought his discarded laptop and old mobile back from the post office, commenting: "I just don't see what you'll do with them." You didn't want to admit that she was right – after all, you didn't even have internet at home. All you cared about was keeping up with the others.

Apart from a few unreliable memories, you can barely recollect your father. In some of your memories, he doesn't have a face, only a voice detached from his body and distorted over the phone. Flat and deep. He draws out each syllable at the end of a word until it merges with the next one. There are still a few photos of him at home and he's sent a few more along with a parcel of presents, books and CDs he's burned, so it's only because of those that you know what he looks like. Once, you got a shabby old baseball cap from him for your birthday. A grey one with an Adidas logo. Since then, it's never been off your head and you've worn it so much that the material on the visor has come away and the colour is mottled and faded from the sun.

It's been almost a year since everything changed. Since your life was shaken to its very foundations and you were torn away from that quiet place out of the spotlight. Up until then, you'd been on the sidelines, only venturing outside on your own, and although that made you sad at times, you were most at ease when no-one could see you. You learned to slip into every nook and crevice where it was impossible to put a foot wrong. No-one picked on you, made fun of how skinny you were, how you waved your arms about comically when you walked. Your marks at school weren't good enough to make you a swot and you didn't like sports. You were afraid of groups of people. You managed to keep your voice lowered and disappear in the middle of every room – in fact, you were never really there.

But last September, you went into the classroom and Petr – you'd been sitting at the desk beside his for the last three years – was now sitting with Filip. He didn't even bother to look up and just gestured in the direction of the first row of desks.

"Sorry, man. There's a free place over there."

Being seated next to Marián was a death sentence. Not that you really had much to lose, but you were still afraid of sinking even deeper. Even after all these years, Filip had managed to remain popular – all he had to do was continually demonstrate to the others they should take him seriously. For three years, Marián's exercise books had been mysteriously vanishing only to turn up wet, ripped to shreds and stuffed into his schoolbag with bits of toilet paper and crumbled chalk. Filip would slam into Marián in the corridor with such force that he fell to the floor. The others would form a circle around them, waiting to see what would happen next. They'd laugh whenever Marián spoke in class, and their laughter made Filip even bolder. As time went on, he stepped up the attacks. You kept to yourself, watching the same things the others used to do to you, only this time with greater intensity. You never tried to stop them. Until that day when they pulled the chair out from under Marián, no-one else tried either. You've never managed to get the image of that day out of your head, and you often hear that drawn-out, high-pitched sound and see the blood in front of you, dark and thick and flowing between his fingers.

In your memories, you often feel like a camera, your eye outside the shot, always outside the action. If things aren't happening to you, you can't relate to them.

Back then, Filip got a B for behaviour, but the class still treated him like a hero, patting him on the back. You too raised your hand and did the same; you wanted to be one of them, to belong among them at least this once.

But your body didn't belong anywhere. Marián was beyond reach for a few weeks, so you found yourself back in their sights, the taste of blood in your mouth once more. Back then, you didn't know what you know today: bullying and violence are meant to humiliate you and make you feel small and insignificant, because when you're down on the ground, you can't put up a fight.

When Marián came back one day, you couldn't believe your luck. Once again, you had managed to find that blind spot, that crevice you could slip back into. But the shame still clung to you.

They say Filip's dad praised him. You're not sure how much truth there is in that, but you wouldn't be surprised. One time, he'd visited your place with Filip. It was the odour that lingered in your mind – you could still smell the sour sweat on the armchair the next day. Filip's father walks with a stick and looks down on everyone. Before he injured his knee at the factory, he used to work with Mum in the workshop. During the whole visit, she sat on the edge of the bed, occasionally making a quiet comment, while he did most of the talking.

"Me, I haven't got a bean to my name, you know. I take time off work to do the rounds of the government offices," he said, stretching out his leg and tapping his knee with the stick. "It was almost my turn in the queue when this old Gypsy woman came in."

His big sweaty body was sprawled across the only arm-chair in the room. His laughter and voice filled the entire image, putting even Filip in the shade – he was crouching on the floor to one side, looking at the American flag on the wall with some amusement.

"We all had to move aside sharpish because *a Gypsy* was coming through. I tell you, Dana, we've really fucked things up. Before, we'd have wiped the floor with them. It was better when they used to lock 'em in cages. But now we serve everything up to them on a platter, and God forbid Filip here ever brings one back home."

He slapped his son on the back, signalling to him to straighten up.

"Sit up straight like a man, eh?"

You felt the stranger's eyes resting on you for a fleeting instant before switching back to Mum.

"I don't know what'd be worse. A Gypo or a poof."

You have a pretty clear memory of when you became aware of this word, when a word affected you directly for the very first time.

All of a sudden, the boys from the class started accusing each other of it, shouting it at one another and making exaggeratedly girlish gestures. At other times, for example in PE, one boy would jump on another's back, moaning loudly and miming thrusting movements. You looked up this particular word on the library computer – your head flicking round the whole time to make sure nobody could see you – and you were amazed at how many more words there were for something you had only vaguely begun to recognize as other names for you. The list on Wikipedia said it all – you only had to click on it and any normal person would understand, while the nervous lump in your throat grew even tighter:

synonyms:
poof, poofter, faggot, pansy, homo, (*neutral*) gay man

A list of insults and only a couple of words that could go at least some way to describing who you are. After all, every word is ultimately just a distorting mirror – you see someone's face in it and worry that it could be yours.

That time one year ago, you completely froze. The air in the classroom was thick and stale. When you finally managed to tear your eyes off Petr and Filip, you slowly made your way to the front row. Marián had been sitting in the chair by the window for some time, staring out with an absent, sleepy expression. You slumped onto the free chair as there was no point trying your luck elsewhere. The rest of your classmates were already sitting in pairs or keeping a place for someone else. A couple of the girls shot you pitying looks, while others snorted with laughter. You laid your things out on the desk and used an open exercise book to cover the plywood veneer that had been scratched with a set of compasses.

Marián had on an oversized T-shirt with the Studio Ghibli logo on it. He wore it a lot, and it gave off an overpowering scent of fabric softener that made it hard to breathe. You could feel the other' stares piercing your back. It occurred to you that they might be waiting to see what you'd do, waiting for some show of strength. Any minute now, you were bound to knock his pencil case off the desk or jam your elbow into his stomach.

Before you could made up your mind to take action and rescue the situation, the teacher came into the classroom.

Neither of you spoke the whole day. You sat as far away as possible at the far end of your desk and tried not to so much as glance in his direction. It was better to bore a hole in the blackboard with your eyes.

Eventually, the silence became unbearable. Marián kept stubbornly to his own space, his body angled towards the window, legs crossed. You realized how slight he was – smaller and skinnier than you. He sat curled up at the desk, slouching. The skin on his arms was flecked with a number of light-coloured spots of different sizes, some no bigger than a regular mole and others branching off into long, irregular shapes. He had a crew cut, the hair white in one place where a large mark encroached on it at the nape of his neck.

Light filtered in through the cracks in the dusty blinds, breaking up on Marián's face and creating twisted stripes on his skin. Beneath them, he took up less and less space. He was afraid of you. Perhaps he didn't know what to do either. You'd happily have walked away and taken yourself off somewhere very far away. You could feel the eyes of the whole class on you without even having to even turn around.

In the storage space under one of the benches in the kitchen, you once found some of Dad's bodybuilding magazines with diagrams to show you how to work out properly. He hadn't left much behind for you; for a long time, the only things you were aware of were the hi-fi in your room and a couple of horrible satin shirts you wanted to throw out, but Mum kept them in the wardrobe, insisting you'd grow into them one day.

Shortly after your discovery of these magazines, your unsuspecting mother opened the door to the toilet. You didn't know what to do first – cross your legs or hide the magazine. Before you had time to think, you'd chucked it down the toilet and then all you could do was look on as the paper swelled up in the water.

Sitting at the desk beside Marián filled you with a similar dread as that moment when the water in the toilet bowl threatened to overflow and flood the floor. With each passing minute, the tipping point might be reached and a word or someone's laughter would trickle onto you. You waited, but nothing happened. Marián kept on breathing, his shoulders moving up and down; he was silent, and you were silent with him.

When the bell finally rang that first day, the surrounding noises reached you through a defensive wall and made no sense. You shoved everything in your bag and shot off down the corridor. You walked quickly past the ping-pong tables and stopped at an open area with a mosaic in front of the steps. You clenched and unclenched your fists, watching the stream of children from the other classrooms, more and more of them laughing in the corridor as they ran down the stairs. Some girl from the ninth year gave you a look of disgust. The same look you give your own reflection in the mirror each morning.

Your toes slowly start to turn pruney in the water. The white, wrinkled skin tingles slightly, the cool of the river penetrates to your bones, and this feeling, this moment, merges with the rustling of leaves from the surrounding trees. You listen to the birds as they happily flap their wet wings. They swoop down to drink, settle on one of the large rocks, dip their beaks, and then quickly vanish again. They remind you of silly little children – they don't have to try to be anything other than themselves. You envy them that.

You breathe deeply, stretched out on the pebbles on the bank. You used to wish there was someone lying there with you, someone whose hand you could take and who would take yours, and who you would listen to music with on headphones, drowning out the noise of the people talking loudly on a blanket nearby. You'd rather naïvely believed you wouldn't have to worry about anything else – that things would suddenly be different.

Marián's face creeps into your mind.

Marián's face keeps on creeping into your mind.

It's always suspended just in front of you, almost within reach – all you have to do is reach out your hand and you grasp nothing but air. Since that time at the start of October when you had to break the wall of silence built of unspoken words, you have constantly been picturing his thin face, the spot by his lip.

And yet it all began in such a ridiculous way. Your pen had run out during history and you didn't have another one on you. There was no point asking anyone else as you knew what they'd say.

Marián was concentrating hard as he scribbled in his exercise book and had about a dozen pens strewn across his half of the desk. You craned your neck and examined the drawing curiously; it was coming along pretty well. The character in the middle of the page looked like something out of a Japanese cartoon, a boy sitting on a chair with his head buried in his hands.

First the words slipped out and only afterwards did you realize what you were doing.

"You're good at drawing."

You blinked and tried to focus on the blurred cluster of tower blocks outside the window. Someone had left smudges on the glass with their fingers and, like the closed blinds, the world outside was coated in a layer of grey chalk dust.

Marián froze, turned his head towards you and looked at you for an uncomfortably long time, trying to figure out what you were up to – you could do anything, bang on the desk to show you're just like all the others. Cut from the same cloth as them. Fists and blood. But you remain as you are, unable to make the slightest movement.

He nodded ever so slightly, cautiously, and went back to his exercise book.

The screeching of chalk brought you to your senses again. In the other classrooms, they'd long since switched to whiteboards, but not in yours. It was hard to make out anything on the mottled surface through all the layers of writing from previous lessons. To make things worse, Mrs Coufalová didn't know how to write on it properly: she seemed determined to carve the words into the green surface, setting everyone's nerves on edge throughout the lesson. She might as well have been dragging her nails across the blackboard – she would still have managed to finish telling you about the wedding of Břetislav and Jitka in her boring, monotonous voice. About how the handsome prince couldn't control himself and abducted his future wife. You imagined Filip in his place – he wouldn't be able to control himself either and would do whatever he wanted.

Pulling yourself together, you asked Marián for a pen. He casually tossed one in your direction and turned back to his sketch.

At breaktime, you edged closer to him and whispered: "That really is good."

The corner of his mouth twitched. He had another drawing on the next page: a concrete throne with a small boy on it. The throne was broken at the top with lines running down it – or perhaps they were crooked sun beams. The boy sat wrapped in a long cloak, which twisted round his legs and trailed off beyond the edge of the page.

"This is Akira and that's Shinji," explained Marián, pointing first to the boy seated on the throne and then to the one on the chair.

Neither of those names meant anything to you, but you felt drawn to Marián. His face was tense and the skin on his nose and between his eyebrows was furrowed into two shallow creases. You stopped paying attention to anything else until the maths teacher threw a piece of chalk at you. You'd never been able to produce anything worthwhile on paper. In the hallway at home, your mum had hung up a picture of a camel with five legs – the kind of picture that wouldn't have raised an eyebrow if it had been drawn by a little kid. Except the camel's fifth leg was supposed to be its tail and you were already nine years old.

On the way home from school that day, you stopped by the steps of Hotel Fit and watched from the pavement as parents and children climbed over the fence into the garden of the nearby nursery school. Some of them stood a little off to the side, while others, knee-deep in grass and leaves, gathered fallen chestnuts and put them in their pockets. In the first year of primary school, you and Mum would have been there too. Together, you'd have climbed over the fence; Mum would have helped you up and you would have assisted her on the way down. You'd have thrown handfuls of leaves at each other, and then, at home, you'd have put the chestnuts on the table and wiped them clean with a handkerchief, ready to take them to the collection point in the morning.

They're always collecting something at your school. Orange peel, chestnuts, paper, plastic bottle tops. Usually, someone will organize a competition to go along with it as well – for example, in the first year, the class that collected the most paper could win a trip to Prague. At that time, Grandad was still delivering hospital lunches in an old Avia van and, on the way home, he'd always cadge some flyers. He drove all over Přerov for your sake, lugging grubby bundles tied up with blue string to the cab and cramming them in among the empty, sticky thermos flasks. One time, he took you with him and locked you in the back of the van, which was covered with posters of naked women and filled with plastic food containers. You sat in a narrow gap at the side, your face pressed up against a picture of naked breasts, and the only light to reach you came from a small hole in the roof. It seemed to you that this time you were bound to win.

In the end, though, the winning class was always the one Honza – the son of a town councillor – was in.

"You can't do anything about it. That's just the way these things work," Mum consoled you. "Maybe it'll be your turn next time."

You're still waiting for all those next times she spoke about; they're always just around the corner and you wonder when your turn will finally come.

Recently, you've been bumping into Honza a lot near the two hotels. He's surrounded by a bunch of guys, and they hang out together by the garages or down near the entrance to the fallout shelter. All around them is a haze of cigarette smoke and a fleeting, sweetish smell. There's nothing better to do round there anyway. There's nowhere to go; it's all just empty car parks, tennis courts and half-empty pubs. The group can't be seen from any of the places where people normally walk past. If anyone does happen to notice them, they just glance over at them and then quickly look away.

Only someone who was also lost would know about their gang.

One day about two years ago, they called you over. You wondered what they were up to – they were bigger and more mature – and you ran through the bushes, slipped on some wet leaves and slid down the hill towards them. Rap was blaring out from someone's mobile. The guys were standing in a circle, swaying to the rhythm, and the music was so loud it blocked out the rest of the world. All that was left were decomposing plastic bags, broken glass and used condoms, tins of paint thinner. Someone's phlegm landed on your shoe, but you were too scared to wipe away the gooey mess. You looked up and saw one of the guys standing right above you, wearing a dirty brown hoodie. He wiped his mouth with the edge of his sleeve, scratched his crotch with the same hand, then helped you up.

You looked around nervously.

"So, man, d'you wanna take a hit with us?"

Honza laughed loudly. He was a good bit younger than the others, stood slightly apart and didn't really seem to fit in with this crowd. He had clean new clothes and neat hair. In one hand, he was clutching a plastic bag, which he quickly hid behind his back when he caught your eye.

"Mate, he's no idea what you're on about."

"He's kinda weird, isn't he? What age is he anyway?"

"Give him a ciggie first and we'll see."

Someone stuck a cigarette in your hand just as a car was going past on the road a few dozen yards from you. You took fright and dropped it on the ground.

"What the fuck are you doing? No-one can see you here." The boy in the brown hoodie picked up the cigarette, blew the dirt off it, and took a long drag. As he did so, he didn't take his eyes off you for a second. "We can do whatever we like here. This is freedom." He leaned over and blew smoke straight into your face. Someone changed the tune and the guy pulled the hood up over his head and began spitting words into your face.

*Listen up, no-one's playing games here.*

You watched him flailing his arms, motioning as if he wanted to punch someone you couldn't see, even though he was standing in front of you. His hands went up and down while the ash fell from his cigarette. That sweetish smell around him. You remember the blurred grey edges of his pupils. His chapped lips. You were transfixed by them. He was standing so close that you could see thin purple veins around his nose and a mole under his left eye. He winked at you, took another drag.

And when he blew in your direction again, you inhaled deeply.

You're pretty sure they were standing there that time on your way back from school, but you couldn't hear them over the kids screaming. You walk the same route day after day and they're always there. The colours of the leaves change, the rust spreads on the gate of the bunker and dark patches appear on the façades of the surrounding houses. Everything changes except that crew. Even when you don't see them, you can sense they're nearby. You wanted to join them again. You were haunted by the way that guy looked at you – it was as if someone was looking at you for the very first time. But they never called you over again. The next time you headed in their direction, one of them spat and another one shouted something. You pretended not to hear their insults but, after that, you chose to cross over to the other side of the road, where their shouts merged with the laughter of the children gathering chestnuts. Unless they suddenly start smashing things up, no-one in the neighbourhood will give them a second glance.

They could easily go on standing there until the world comes to an end. For them – and the same applies to you – there's no place left in it anyway.

But there's something that's been bugging you. If *this* is *freedom*, if you are only free when no-one can see you or reach out to you, how do you know you even exist? If you are alone, you have nowhere to go, no place to move on to, never mind anyone to lean on.

In the past, you would have stubbornly insisted that you could see everything. But you were wrong – you too refused to see Marián the whole time. In your memories, he stood apart, merging with the surface of the water, and not even the largest wave could push him forward. Until suddenly you were walking up the stairs one day and he was all you could think about. There was the sound of an ambulance, a television blaring from the open windows of the nearest flat. You pictured his expression as he concentrated, the pencil tracing a line on the paper, the tightly clenched muscles of his face.

The next day, Mr Koníček let you play dodgeball for the last half hour of PE. You didn't want to play because the boys in the class threw the ball really hard, and Filip and Petr always ganged up so that one or the other of them would win in the end. What was the point of even trying; you might as well just wait for somebody to get you.

It wasn't the first time you'd been knocked out first. Even Marián stayed in the game a good five minutes longer.

Defeated, you shuffled over to an alcove with exercise mats piled up on top of each other. You climbed up to the top and watched the others from above. One by one, they went off to the side, far away from you, where they sat down on a bench alongside the wall.

Marián stood like a statue in the corner of the gym, not moving a muscle. The only thing you need to do in dodge-ball is to watch what's happening around you and duck behind someone else at the right moment. However, Marián didn't seem to realize this, judging by his erratic movements and the way he flinched at every loud noise. When Petr eventually hit him in the back, he walked across the gym and actually looked quite pleased. He spotted you, the corner of his mouth twitched and he headed in your direction, where he leaned against the tower of mats. Your legs were dangling just above his head, your eyes darting between him and the game.

The ball landed barely a yard away from you. Filip leapt towards it, not even looking at you, then pushed off, the squeak of his sole cutting through the air.

Marián thrust his hands in his pockets and nervously tapped his foot, which got on your nerves slightly. You tried to ignore the sound and focus on the whistling and shouting but, once again, your attention was drawn back to the regular drumming of his foot on the floor. You took a breath in and suddenly you'd had enough of the silence.

"I don't actually know who Akira is. Or the other one."

Marián looked up at you, obviously confused. Then it dawned on him what you were talking about and his face lit up.

"They're characters."

"OK."

"They're my two favourite mangas. Especially Akira. Evangelion is a good series, but the books aren't all that great."

You didn't really get what he was on about. Marián frowned, turned his whole body towards you and slapped a mat just a few inches from your leg.

"I guess you don't read a lot of comics."

You shook your head.

"Do you watch any anime? Say, like Mononoke?"

You looked around cautiously. There were only three players left in the game. The class was yelling at them from the bench by the wall and no-one was looking in your direction.

"Yeah," you lowered your gaze towards Marián again, "I know that one." You don't let on that you never got to see the whole film because Mum didn't like it and made you change the channel.

Marián looked pleased. He braced his hands against the mats and jumped up.

"There you go. Well, this is something similar. Maybe a bit more horror."

"OK."

He was sitting very close. You subconsciously turned your head towards the others.

"Akira's this young boy and he has… powers. But it isn't really about him."

Just like this PE lesson wasn't about you. Filip had won. You raised your head just as he was enthusiastically doing a

129

victory lap, waving his arms while the others clapped. He came to a stop and, after making sure Mr Koníček had his back to him, went over to the pommel horse.

"Yeah, stick it in her!" shouted Petr, leaping towards the horse from the other side, and they both began thrusting. "Give her a good seeing-to, man!"

By then, even Mr Koníček had spotted them. He laughed and threw the ball to Filip. "Maybe play another round instead?"

Marián gave you an amused look and rolled his eyes.

A couple of minutes later, the two of you were sitting in the same place again. This time, he'd got knocked out first, and when you headed over to the mats, he was already waiting there.

"I can't stand this game," he muttered as soon as you'd jumped up beside him.

"It's the lamest thing in the world."

Like you, Marián braced his hands against the edge but, at the same time, he kicked with his legs until the whole stack of mats started to wobble dangerously.

"So, who is it about? That comic?"

His face gave away too many things all at once. You could almost see the struggle going on beneath his skin.

"It's all about a boy who has telekinetic powers and almost destroys the world. Because everyone's abandoned him and he's felt useless all his life and, suddenly, he can do things the others can't even dream of. Like crushing a baddie's head just by looking at him."

While he was speaking, the smell of fabric conditioner wafted over to you. Compared to the stink of the mats, the rubber soles and the gym, it no longer seemed so bad.

"OK, but I guess that isn't the kid you drew."

He chuckled, instantly making you feel foolish.

"No, that's Tetsuo. Akira is a child who blows up the whole of Tokyo at the start of this comic. They'd carried out some experiments on him."

Marián probably noticed how confused you were as he thought for a moment and then added: "I can lend you the comics. I've got them at home, but they're in English."

"That's no problem," you blurted out, straightening your back. "My dad's in America, so English is my second language." This wasn't entirely true. In reality, you could manage to read a few pages, but you didn't understand most of the vocabulary and it was hard for you to follow the plot.

"So I heard." He screwed up his face. "You talk about it quite a lot."

You were struck by the realization that someone had been listening to what you said.

"Yeah, and then there's Shinji. He's the other one. Those two characters are quite similar – everyone does what they want to them. Shinji is more of an outsider. He reminds me of me." He was silent for a moment, sizing you up, and then he added in a whisper, as though you weren't actually supposed to hear: "And a bit of you too, but that's probably the hair."

Marián bent over and scratched his calf, and there was the flash of his skin from under his T-shirt. You quickly turned away and looked up at the ceiling.

"I really like how it's brutal and different and yet dead funny at the same time. The characters are great." A roar resounded through the gym and you both jumped. You nervously scanned your surroundings while Marián continued. "They're loners and yet they're not victims. You get the feeling they're completely out of sync with the rest of the world, and yet they're all a bit awkward at the same time. Akira's a kid, obviously, I'm thinking more of the others. Instead of just waiting like idiots for things to blow up in their faces, they decide not to put up with any shit. If that makes sense."

None of it made any sense to you; you didn't understand why he was telling you these things. He was about to say something else when Petr crashed into the mats from down below. He was dodging the ball and had failed to turn in time.

You would have fallen if you hadn't caught hold of the edge at the last minute.

Petr sprang back to his feet and ran off again. You recovered your wits, blinked and then realized your hand had been on Marián's the whole time.

In horror, you jerked back. You stretched out and curled up your fingers several times before finally putting your hand in your pocket.

By the time you realized what you were doing, it was too late. Marián lowered his gaze to the ground. You could still make out the impression on the surface of the mat where he'd touched it. It remembered the touch, preserving a barely visible trace of it.

The bell rang and you silently shuffled off to the changing room, images racing through your mind. You have no idea how long it took you to get changed, but you were the last one left in the room, standing there with your sweatshirt inside out, staring at the wall.

You bit your tongue and swallowed.

Later that night, you heard Mum tossing and turning in bed and talking in her sleep. You couldn't get to sleep, your hand tingling as you clenched your fist over and over again, imagining what the boys in the class would do if they could see inside your head. As things were, their laughter rang in your ears every night. You turned onto your side and saw Marián's face on the wall in front of you.

At breaktime on Friday morning, he placed a book with a red cover on the desk and pushed it towards you.

Just then, you happened to be holding your mid-morning snack. The bread was wrapped in a paper napkin, and trying to disentangle it was an almost superhuman task.

The moist napkin had stuck to the sandwich and you had to carefully peel it off bit by bit.

"Thanks," you blurted out in surprise. Meanwhile, he reached over and tapped the cover.

"It's the first part. Give it a try; you might not even like it."

You put down the bread, picked up the book carefully, leafed through it, then stuck it in your schoolbag.

"It starts to get really good in the second half." Marián moved back to his place and took out his exercise books from the shelf under the desk. "I still don't have the last part yet, but if you want, I can lend you all the ones I've got."

You soon forgot all about the book stashed in your schoolbag. While you were waiting in the lunch queue, Filip barged into you. He pushed past, plastic tray in one hand, forging a way with the other. You lost your balance and went crashing into the cutlery stand with your full weight, cutlery clattering all across the floor. Before you could figure out what had happened, one of the cooks was standing over you, shaking her fist. You saw Filip out the corner of your eye. From the food hatch, he was happily surveying the chaos he'd caused, giving you the finger at the same time. You had to spend almost the whole break clearing up the cutlery and then stand in the queue again to get some grey meat with a thick vein running through it, some sauce and a little rice. Your nose wrinkled involuntarily. The meat was always impossible to cut and stuck in your throat until you'd washed it down with a sickly-sweet coloured glass of juice from an urn. You poured a little into a glass and, on the way to an empty table at the far end of the canteen, you passed Marián – he was sitting alone, concentrating so hard on his own tray that he didn't see you.

You spent all of Saturday morning cleaning with Mum.

The cooperative flats on Dvořákova rotated cleaning duties each week and, by some miracle, you were always assigned the entire corridor. You had to mop the stairs, clean the shoe scrapers and wash the front door. Marián's Akira was on your mind the whole time. You still hadn't taken the book out of your schoolbag. You finally got a chance after lunch. Mum fell asleep – as always with her mouth open and her coffee wedged between her legs – and only then could you sit over beside Gran and read in peace.

The black-and-white panels presented a scenario you were familiar with – characters largely unseen by others, who others are only interested in when they have something to offer them. When they can use them. At school, you felt like an outcast, while in these books you floated like a ghost. Empty and shapeless. In every story, you've been running away from the rules – this is how you have to move and speak; this is the only right course of action. In books, things were also predetermined, but at least you could be someone else for a while. You recall days spent in the Přerov library, squatting down by the lowest shelves, reading for hours while hidden in a corner. If you happened to look up from the pages, you met the reflection of your window in the darkened window opposite, and you knew that every window and every book was just another way out. You brought books home by the bagful and learned to escape into their pages.

When you were finally done with Akira's story and re-surfaced into the room, Gran was sitting with her head forward, snoring, while gunfire was coming from the television. It was strange and sad – you still have this feeling even today when you finish a book. With it, you're also leaving behind a previous life. You can no longer return to it. You watched the gunfight on the screen for a while until an advert woke Gran up and she chased you out of her room.

You immediately returned the book to Marián on Monday.

"So?"

"Yeah, it's really great."

"Yeah?"

His face relaxed. He leant against the wall down by the lockers and looked at you curiously.

"Cool. I wouldn't have guessed, but that's brilliant. So do you want more?"

You quickly checked to see if anyone was watching you.

"Definitely."

And so, after school you walked Marián home so you could borrow the next part straight away. You first passed a group of kids from the years below you – they were standing behind the bins beside the loading ramp for the canteen, passing a cigarette around. Marián skipped along in silence, swaying comically with every step. The boys in the class made fun of him for this, copying the movements which even Gran and Mum found funny. You thought he looked more like a young kid, jumping about to the music in his head.

When you reached the blocks of flats on Kozlovská street, Marián's face suddenly lit up, a sparkle dancing in his eyes.

"And would you like to see the film sometime too?"

You had to consider your next step carefully.

"I can't bring anyone home."

In reality, this was just an excuse, as you knew Mum would never let anyone like him in the house.

"No problem. Neither can I. Not that I've got anyone to bring home, but Mum doesn't allow it. But she goes to work in the afternoon, sometimes even at night, so it wouldn't matter anyway."

It's only later on that you find out his mother works in the same factory as yours. Since then, you've been keeping a list of the things you have in common. Marián grew up without a father too, even though, at first, he refused to say why. "They say I have his eyes," he said, shrugging his shoulders. One time, a photo of his dad fell out one of his sketch books. You picked it up and held it to the light. "Otherwise, I just look like my mum." As if you were listening to yourself speaking. You remembered your own father and how he'd comment on everything he thought was wrong with you. The last time you and Mum sent him a photograph of you, he couldn't resist making a snide remark over the phone:

"You're awfully skinny. Tell your mum you should start doing more sport again."

He was referring to the day when, after six months of nagging, Mum had finally given in and signed you up for football. All it took was one training session and you were in tears. Dad was furious and wanted you to pass the phone over to Mum. "What's going to become of you if all it takes is a bit of rough stuff and you start bawling?" She was standing in the gap between the kitchen units and the freezer, shaking her head at you. "You have to learn to grit your teeth and tough it out." A week later, Dad sent you a pair of old football boots through one of his pals. You unwrapped them and chunks of dried mud fell onto the table. Maybe that was why Mum grabbed the box and, without saying a word, carried it down to the cellar.

Marián's father had died before Marián was even born. He seldom mentioned him and his indifference rubbed off on you too. He made jokes and you laughed, allowing yourself to believe that it was better for Marián this way – unlike your father, his can't order him about. He'll never pull him up for the way he dresses, what his interests are, or lecture him on how to talk properly. This role might have been taken on by other family members, but you didn't know much about them. Only once did Marián let slip that his gran lived in a different town and would have him over a few times each year.

You were quiet on the way to his place and let him do all the talking. From Kozlovská street, he continued past the dried-up fountain below the town walls, leading you along the Bečva, where he stopped at a crossing and you could watch the current and the leaves on the surface. You crossed the main road and then stopped at one of the side streets behind the embankment, not far from Grandad's place.

The building he lived in wasn't the dilapidated ruin his classmates teased him about. You'd expected the kind you found on Škodovka, all broken windows and squalor, as you'd seen on TV. Instead of that, what you saw in front of you was a very ordinary building, slightly dingy, with a crooked pavement and slabs overgrown with weeds – quite similar, in fact, to the houses on Dvořákova.

You pointed in surprise towards a school just a few yards away.

Marián shrugged. "They wouldn't take me anywhere else," he said, before disappearing through the front door, leaving you alone in front of the building, where you kicked at the kerb until your foot began to tingle. He was only gone for a couple of minutes, and when he returned, he was carrying another three books.

At school, it became increasingly difficult to feign distance. You froze with your mouth open, swallowed your words at the last moment and turned your head away. You never even really considered why it mattered so much to you if someone saw you talking to him.

It was almost as if Grandad's surname had something to do with it. Even your dad used to make fun of you. "Daněk[1] – you're one of those timid animals that's scared all the time. Nice to look at, but it's better to give you a wide berth." And yet it wasn't as if your father's name was much better. In first year at school, your mum took you to a sweet shop to celebrate your report card. For a few minutes, you looked at the cakes laid out in the window display, and then Mum leaned over to you and whispered: "Do you know that your surname means 'little cake' in Polish?" You turned to her a little puzzled, thinking she was teasing you. "Really – that's why you're such a wee sweetie. You're half deer and half cake."

The Daněk side has pretty much always dominated you – you still remembered what happened before and didn't want to draw attention to yourself. Every word you exchanged with Marián threatened to push the boundaries a little further. It could disrupt the natural order of who was

1    Daněk = a fallow deer (translators' note)

on top, who was below, and whose side you were actually on.

Inevitably, what you feared might happen eventually did.

One day, you're sitting at your desk at breaktime and Marián is talking about something. You've got your head buried in your schoolbag, half listening as you try to dig your compasses out of the bottom of it.

"Well, fuck me." Petr sneaks up behind you and punches you in the back.

"So you're going out with Marián now?"

He turns round and shouts to the whole class: "Someone here is having fun with this dirty bastard!" Your face is suddenly on fire.

"Well, aren't you a couple of lovebirds, a couple of poofters." Filip joins him. He's standing by the teacher's desk, hands on his hips.

Marián has his eyes fixed on the floor, pretending not to hear anything.

Filip shoves your chair and you slam into the desk.

The whole scene plays out in front of you: Filip is totally out of control. Encouraged by the rest of the class, he towers high above you, arms still on his hips. "So now you're going to be little buddies, eh?" He turns for a round of applause, and when he's finally had enough, he focuses on you again. "Or are you going to get straight down to it, eh? You thought I'd forgotten about you?" He pushes you again and you slip from the chair and fall to the ground. The whole room erupts with laughter.

"Little fuckers like you make me sick."

More than anything, you want to kick him squarely in the crotch.

Or at least run away, but your legs won't obey you. You lie there sprawled on the floor, wishing you could at least summon up some courage. Your legs are shaking. Anger flows through your body with the blood. Everything else freezes.

And then Marián gets up from his chair and offers you his hand.

You dust off your knees and let yourself be pulled into the corridor.

"Mind he doesn't nick something off you, ya poof! And mind your arse!"

The shouting trails off behind you. In the corridor, it's drowned out by the noise of the other children. As though all that hatred stayed in the classroom and the corridor was neutral territory. It also helps that there's a monitor there – one of the first-year teachers is marching back and forth, wearing headphones and sunglasses for no apparent reason.

Marián walks a few steps in front of you, basically dragging you behind him. He passes several doors until he reaches a staircase. On your floor of the building, near an open area with a red sofa, a table and armchairs, is an old mosaic on the wall.

A background of blue and red with two identical boys wearing wreaths on their heads. Two doves are fluttering below them.

Marián catches you looking at him and grins. "I swear, *this* is the gayest thing in the world."

The two boys are stretching their arms out towards each other, and a halo surrounds the spot where they are about to touch.

Up until then, you'd walked past the mosaic every day like the rest of them. So many people pass this way without even glancing at the wall. From now on, though, you can't take your eyes off it. Finally, you really see it, and you imagine that when the boys actually touch each other, the whole school will explode into a rainbow.

Marián pushes his way through the group of first years and continues down the stairs.

On the ground floor by the lockers, he turns off down a small dark corridor. You'd only been there a couple of times – in winter, people brought stuff here for the collections. Someone has stuck a piece of paper on the glass door with a note saying: *Students unaccompanied by a teacher are not permitted in this area.*

"Are we allowed to be here at all?"

Without stopping, he beckons you with his free hand and pulls you inside.

You pass by lots more doors and only stop once you've gone down another set of stairs, though no-one uses these much. There's a smell of linoleum and burnt dust, while time is measured by the loud thuds of a clock right above you. A dirty brownish light occasionally filters its way through the windows.

Marián pulls you into an alcove below the stairs and sits down on a peeling bench. Someone must have brought it down from the gym. "You can also get here straight down these stairs, but then they'd discover this place." You sit down beside him and notice the silence – only the dull thud of feet from the upper floors reaches you. "I come here when things get too much. No-one really knows about it, except the janitor. But he's cool. I think he comes here for a smoke when it's cold outside. At least judging by the smell."

You gradually calm down, your anger replaced by a tingling sensation in your body. Like when a storm eventually subsides in summertime and you remain standing by the window, watching the storm slowly turn to heavy rain. Marián is sitting close to you. You can almost touch him.

From then on, you spent almost every break there below the stairs. Sometimes, Marián lent you his headphones; other times, he'd draw and leave you in peace to leaf through the books.

Occasionally, you'd both just sit there, leaning against a different part of the wall, counting down till the end of the school day and almost not hearing the bell.

Time either dragged or flew by – always the opposite of what you wanted. The breaks went past in a flash, while the lessons seemed never-ending. You didn't feel that time was passing. Instead, it trudged along at whatever pace it wanted.

All you really wanted was your place beneath the stairs and some peace and quiet.

Of course, it didn't escape the attention of the boys in the class that you were always away somewhere, spending more and more time together. They shouted at you and threw things at you during lessons. The only one to defend you was Klára, who you used to be friends with. She stood in front of you and said something in a low voice, but you doubt anyone heard her apart from you.

All of the times you'd looked away and refused to help Marián kept coming back to you. You hadn't wanted to be part of it because it was none of your business. It didn't take long to discover how thin the line can be between outside and inside, between *me* and the others. For so long, you thought that nothing could touch you, that you'd been through the worst. *This has nothing to do with me.* You kept your head down and stayed quiet. But then you made one wrong move and your body, which sometimes weighs nothing and is merely a reflection in the nearest window, that very body is swept away by the current again.

Marián was much better at handling things. He barely flinched when they took his sketch books and ripped them up in front of him. He just picked the pieces up off the floor and put them in the bin. On the same day, Filip stabbed you in the back with a fork when you were standing in the lunch queue. You tried not to make a sound. You just bit your tongue and then tasted blood in your mouth for the rest of the day. You hoped that if you didn't act like a wimp – just kept hanging on in there – they would soon get tired of it. You just have to hang on in there and one day you'll forget everything.

In reality, you put on a mask and eventually lost yourself in it.

This was why you refused to talk to your mum for almost a week after the parents' meeting.

"You have to stop hanging out with him," she came out with that same evening. You were sitting at the table and the spoon slipped out of your hand, hit the plate with a loud clink and splashed soup onto the tablecloth.

"What?"

"You heard me. You're not to hang around with someone who's no good for you."

But you hadn't said a word about Marián at home. You didn't stand up to your mother, though you weren't about to change anything about yourself either. How could she know that Marián had saved you? She had no idea who had given you all those bruises. You were aware she knew about them – the huge mark under your left shoulder blade and other smaller ones on your ribs. That time in the bathroom, she'd said nothing. She put the towel in the washing machine and closed the door. Later in the evening, she sat at the other end of the table, frowning.

"Is someone hurting you?"

You didn't know how to answer questions like that yet.

"Marek, you know you can tell me anything."

You said nothing, just trod carefully around her, trying not to alarm her.

From the greasy film on the surface of the soup, your reflection stared up at you, twisted and inverted – this is how she sees you, you thought, trying to maintain a calm expression just for her sake. You eventually managed to throw Mum off the scent, making certain she suspected nothing about life on the other side.

On the other side, you're sitting on the old town walls by the river, your legs dangling down towards the people and cars, watching the shoulders of two elongated shadows slowly touch each other.

On the other side, you talk in your sleep. You know you had your first dream about Marián sometime in November. There wasn't anything strange about your dreams yet. In this particular one, you were both sitting under the stairs when he lay his head down in your lap, gazing up at your face. You awoke sweaty and confused and stared at the ceiling for a long time.

The next night, your mind let go of all its inhibitions.

Your memory is unforgiving and brings back images. Somewhere in the back of your mind, it projects the shattered fragments of the day onto a screen. You could almost swear Marián was thinking about the same things, there on the bench beside you. After all, he knows what they say about you, just as you remember the day when you swore at him so as not to stand out from the others.

Soon, you'll come up against a wall of things you don't know how to talk about, things you don't want to talk about yet.

But these unsaid words tear at your vocal cords. You should have known all that pressure could only lead to trouble. Then, just before the summer holidays and the last PE class, you forget yourself.

You were in the changing rooms, putting your school clothes back on, and didn't even realize you were standing there, staring in his direction.

Above the elastic of his boxers is a thin line of hair, and there's a lighter area where one large mark encroaches on it. He bends over and pulls up his trousers. The two of you are alone and not alone in the room. The bumps of his spine protrude from his body, reminding you of small hills

148

lined up in a row. As if in a dream, you reach out to touch him, to place your fingers in the curves of his spine.

"Spotty here'll give you one, don't worry about that."

The words jolt you back to reality. You turn round to find yourself staring straight at Filip. He's grinning.

"You could at least get a room for that disgusting filth, eh lads?"

"Too right," adds Petr, turning his nose up in disgust. "No-one here wants to see your homo shit."

Filip draws back a little, straightens up slowly, checks to make sure all eyes in the room are on him, then runs his hand over his crotch, cupping it, keeping his eyes on you the whole time.

"You'd like that, eh? You're so hot for it, you can't wait to take it up the arse."

He takes a step forward and then slaps your ear with all of his strength, sighs, and then draws back again.

"But don't worry, Spotty here will be happy to stick it in balls-deep, won't you, *more*[2]?" Your head is spinning. Marián, standing in the corner of the room, starts to merge with the wall. He's not looking at you, more through you. You don't understand how Filip guessed, but at that moment you so wanted to call Marián the same thing, whisper that word in his ear, take it, take their weapon and turn it into your own secret language.

---

2   Romani for young man (translators' note)

Before you even realize what you're doing, you raise your arms and give Filip a shove. You want to say something but then decide against it, turn your back to him and slowly put your clothes in your bag.

"You've really fucked up big-time."

You feel a heavy blow to your back. Then another. It doesn't even hurt much.

You fall down and your head hits the floor. Later, you'll return to every fall and the stories behind them, searching desperately for some meaning in them. Your nose is bleeding. Someone's kicking you in the stomach and nose; someone else is punching you in places where you feel nothing. You cover your face with your hands, and the world draws a veil over you. You remain alone inside an empty place, blocking out all the surrounding noises till you're left with just your own ragged breathing.

The reason you return to this scene isn't because the memory of it is particularly painful – it was far from being the worst thing that happened to you, and you can get used to the pain, which will soon come to seem everyday and commonplace. You return to it as someone might turn to a piece of evidence to strengthen their own convictions. You have two similar memories, since no event ever happens just once. Even violence has its own echo, amplifying every time it bounces off a surface. Sooner or later, the initial impulse will give rise to a copy, and so everything around you happens at least twice. You fall down twice and pick yourself up from the floor twice. The memories of both falls will wake you from your sleep. One day, they'll begin to make sense, you tell yourself, but before you've really understood them, you'll spend years trying to forget them, or at least put them off until later.

Later, you have to get up, because your mobile's vibrating in your pocket.

*Go and see Grandad. His telly isn't working and he's in a bad way. Kisses, M.*

You read your mum's text and hesitate about whether to reply. You don't feel like going anywhere, but you know what'll happen if you don't: Mum will blow up at you. You wait, arms folded, fists clenched, phone held far away from your body, just slightly nearer than the water, and then you stretch out your legs to meet the incoming wave.

You remember how one time, before you'd even started school, you came home from the sandpit between the blocks of flats having learned a new word. You had no idea what it meant, but you knew it was imperative you use this word. In the evening, you were standing in the middle of the room when Mum told you to pick up your crumpled tracksuit from the floor, but instead of doing that, you angrily hurled this new word at her.

She froze mid-motion and looked at you for a long time before going to the kitchen and returning with the wooden spoon.

When she had finished, you remained lying on the floor, pyjama bottoms around your knees, your bottom so red you couldn't even move. You can vividly recall her hand as an echo, as a current whose fury rebounds from one place to another. The source of that current can be traced to Grandad.

"If I ever hear you swear again, I'll rip you apart like a frog."

You yanked your finger to help you imagine the pain. An image came to mind of a frog pulled in two – slime oozing from its legs – and you began to cry.

A little later, when you were creeping off to the toilet, you paused at the door to Gran's room and heard Mum whisper wearily: "I would never have got away with that with you two. I only ever remember yelling at you that one time and Dad gave me such a thrashing, it still hurts when I think about it."

You used to think Mum's stories about Grandad and the things she told you about him were just another way of demonstrating to you how much better off you were.

"What I wouldn't have given for this," she says, setting a plate with horseradish sauce down in front of you. "When I was the same age as you, we didn't have anything like this."

But you have different memories of Grandad from a period when he probably wasn't drinking so much, when he was capable of leaving his flat and spending time with you. He was still a bit scary. He was the one who taught you how to pretend, to endure the pain and act as though nothing unusual were happening. Back then, Mum and Gran got you a bike – the same one that's now lying on the grass nearby. They'd both saved up for more than a year for it, and when they finally had enough money, Gran took you to the Koloseum and let you choose between the two cheapest bikes. You were so enthusiastic that the very next day you'd managed to wear out the brakes.

Grandad took you to the repair shop since neither Mum nor Gran knew anything about bikes. You were silent the whole way to the shop, worried about what would happen if they couldn't fix the bike. Grandad smoked one cigarette after another and cursed, "You should be able to sort this out yourself, Marek. You're a big boy now!" On the way back, he stopped off at the petrol station for tobacco, no doubt for his nerves, disappearing inside and leaving you to wait outside.

On a patch of ground beneath a billboard advertising cheap loans, you entertained yourself by kicking the tufts of grass that were growing round the floodlights. Even though it was daylight, they were switched on. You suddenly had an idea and bent down to see if they were hot by putting your hand on one of them. The tears came first and it was only afterwards that you felt the pain. You swore just as the automatic door opened and Grandad appeared. You quickly dried your eyes, gritted your teeth and stuck your burnt hand in your pocket. Grandad smoked all the way home too, talking to you about something, but his words reached you through a thick veil and you couldn't understand him. You had to exert all your strength to stop yourself collapsing from the pain. You knew you couldn't do that in front of him. For once, you wanted to be what he wanted of you.

And you were scared too. You remembered Mum's words – if Grandad found out, he might rip you apart like a frog.

Back home, first, you put your bike away in the cellar and by the time Mum told you to take your hands out of your pockets, the palm had already swollen up and the skin had turned purple with swollen white sores in the middle. Your fingers throbbed and you felt dizzy.

Naturally, your mum and gran blamed Grandad for the whole thing. He should have been looking out for you to make sure nothing happened to you. They shouted at him, but Grandad just looked at you the whole time. Before he left, he patted you on the head with his wizened hand.

After procrastinating for ten minutes or so, you get up and pull your T-shirt over your head. You drag your bike out of the bushes and steer it onto the path. You check one last time to make sure you've got everything, throw your leg over the bar, put your backpack on and start pedalling. The air is still hot, and you don't feel like cycling halfway across town just for him. You sometimes get the feeling Grandad doesn't even like you. You can sense it from him, even through the stench of cigarettes. When you speak, Grandad looks away as though wishing you weren't there in his flat.

You race across town at such a speed that you have to pull your cap down lower. That way, the air is slightly cooler. The landscape is an indistinct smudge, a coloured line.

You stop just in front of the building and lay your bike down on the grass among the peeled-off strips of paint from the façade.

Recently, you and Mum got your own set of keys, so you go into the corridor and, unlike your mum, take the stairs, ignoring the permanently faulty lift – more than once, you've been trapped in it and had to endure several hours in a dirty cabin smelling of urine until someone let you out. However, on the top floor, you like looking out the windows down towards the main road. You and Grandad used to watch the trucks pass by below the window, and he'd gauge the time of day by them – a traffic jam meant either time for food or time for medicine. If you stand at the window and lean out, you can feel the vibrations of the passing cars rumbling up through the panels towards you. Standing on tiptoe, you can make out the winding Bečva and the roofs of the tower blocks until the town disappears from view. On one side is the tower of the castle and the Hotel Strojař; on the other is the Kazeta building and the brick chimneys of the old power station. From here, the people below look tiny and insignificant, and you imagine what it would be like to fall from here– how long it would take and how painful the impact would be. Heights can slow down time, pulling you out of a specific space – you stand in your own bubble and the town hums, the sound coming in waves, one crashing against another, against the embankment, against the foundations of the building, rising up the walls all the way to the roof.

Gradually, you begin to drown in the noise. On the way to Grandad's, you focus on each stair, but, even so, Marián still emerges from the cracks between each step.

Like that time in the changing rooms after PE, when he bends down, offers you his hand and helps you back on your feet. Now you lift them up all by yourself and with each step you wade deeper into your memory. Its image gradually forces out the present until what you see in front of you is a slightly different scene.

There's a ringing in your ears, and it takes a while for you to recover. The space in the background gradually takes shape, with wall after wall being built over the present. The two of you were alone in the school changing room. Marián looked worried. There were small furrows across his brow, and you wanted to tell him it was all right. You took a breath, but not a sound came out. You got to your feet, but they were like jelly, and you moved gingerly over to the bench.

In the corridor outside the changing room, you felt a bit better. You shuffled over to your locker, threw your sweaty clothes inside and grabbed your schoolbag. There was a sharp pain whenever you moved your left leg. You closed the locker and noticed Filip out of the corner of your eye. He was standing with the others by the entrance, pointing in your direction.

It was muggy outside. You headed home silently, your mind a complete blank. It took you a few minutes to realize that Marián had been walking beside you the whole time. Like you, he was staring straight ahead.


In the meantime, you're climbing the stairs to Grandad's floor. He's left the door open, and in the corridor you can smell the smoke from inside, which lingers in the flat even after it's been aired. You screw up your nose. The smell clings to everything and is impossible to get rid of. It seeps into your clothes, Mum's plastic food containers, the books he's borrowed. You go inside.

Grandad has practically no furniture in his flat. There's a dark bathroom with a kitchen stuck next to it, and a small bedroom. A yellow film covers everything, and all you can smell is dust and smoke. Even the originally white walls have a murky, dirty tinge to them. You just have to touch any surface and your fingers will stick to it.

Grandad's standing beside the kitchen window, leaning on the windowsill. Even from the door, you can see he's shaking all over. On the floor beside him is an overturned ashtray – cigarette butts and ash everywhere.

"So, what's up with the TV, Grandad?"

You bend down, pick up the cigarette butts and flush them down the toilet.

He doesn't seem to have noticed you. You put the ashtray back on the table and Grandad moves, finally registering that someone else is in the room.

"She really sent you?"

He slowly turns round to face you, exhaling in disbelief.

"This way."

You follow him to the next room, where he leans in the doorway, pointing with trembling fingers at the black screen. "I really have no idea what's up with it."

The TV's not even that old. He got it from Gran when she and Mum clubbed together for a new one last Christmas. However, to tune in any channels, you had to connect it up to another two plastic boxes first.

"I was sitting there," he says, pointing at the armchair, "and the news was on, and that idiot was talking, you know the one, what's his name…" He searches for the name while you try to find the remote among a pile of leaflets on the armchair. "It doesn't matter. They're all bastards." If Grandad gets started on politics, what pours out of him is mainly bitterness, the anger that has built up over years of failure when they forgot about *people like me*, when new generations of politicians promised change *but*

158

*things are still the same, or maybe even fucking worse than I remember.* He coughs. You try pressing a few buttons on the remote, but nothing happens.

"Jesus Christ," he says to no-one in particular, "I've got no idea what I'm gonna do. What am I gonna do if it doesn't work? I need to get it working by this evening. There's the match with..." The sentence is cut short by another bout of coughing. You gesture to him to sit down, and Grandad just waves his hand, his other one clutching the door handle. The angle he's standing at reminds you of the times he used to come to your house drunk, staggering up the steps, and Mum would slam the door in his face. On the rare occasions she'd let him in, he'd lean against the doorframe, swaying back and forth in an alarming manner. Today, you just feel sorry for him.

You cross the room to the TV. The casing isn't hot, and you wipe away a layer of dust with your hand, revealing some yellow droplets. You find them throughout the flat, on the walls and even on the doors. Mum says it's nicotine from the smoke. She tried scraping them off with a knife a couple of times. The two of you scrubbed the windows with the abrasive side of a sponge, but the droplets wouldn't budge.

"I... I can't manage without it," he says, his words punctuated by ragged breaths. His voice rasps as he exhales and white foam collects in the corners of his mouth.

"What the hell am I going to do? What am I going to do now?"

He slumps into the armchair and wipes his nose. He repeats the same sentence once, twice, its meaning escaping you. Grandad is absolutely filthy, with a stain on his T-shirt – probably from coffee – and cigarette burns in several places. He seems oblivious to you; you doubt he even sees you. He just opens his mouth, bubbles forming in the corners.

You reach behind the TV set, where all the cables are fine except for one loose one. It puts up a bit of a struggle, slipping out of your grasp, but eventually you push it back in.

The screen crackles and a blueish light illuminates your face.

"How did you do that?" asks Grandad, scrambling to his feet. You rush over to him and stick the remote in his hand to calm him down a bit. He wraps his frail fingers around it. They're more like bones covered in shrivelled brown skin with blackened, frayed nails. Up close, they smell of cigarettes with a hint of urine.

You take a step back. The television's blaring once more – whenever you come here, you're greeted by a barrage of noise. It provides him with company. It's the only thing that will talk to him and not judge him. Without it, he'd have nothing to fill the void – the same silence you sometimes fear too. It descends whenever you're alone for a while. And, like Grandad, you at least play some music or escape into a book to fill the emptiness a little.

You leave Grandad in his armchair. He looks happy, he's completely stopped coughing and his hands are no longer shaking so much. He's probably already forgotten all about you. In the kitchen, you bring out a dustpan and brush from beneath the sink and clean up a bit. You sweep the floor and put the cigarette butts in an empty plastic bag you find lying on a chair. One of the handles is ripped, so you carry it from underneath and take it to the front door.

The memory of that second day creeps back into your mind – you're climbing up the steps between the hotels behind the school. As always, you can hear the reverberation of shouts from the children in the nursery school playground along with music from the bushes at the foot of the hill. You stare ahead of you, trying not to look at Marián, left foot, right foot, carrying you further on past the garages. Normally, you'd turn for home, but now you're walking without exactly knowing where to, while Marián says nothing the whole time.

The same places over and over again. Every day, you pass a row of flats, then another, then the hospital grounds. They blend together in your mind until you can't distinguish between them and they all merge into one. But, this time, you change direction. You turn left, go down the hill, past a neglected basketball court – you'll soon be back here to take another fall – and Marián's still walking alongside you, still saying nothing. You continue across the road and along a narrow path, plunging into the gloom of the forest. You turn right, leaving the hospital behind you, and soon you come out onto a path trampled in the grass by the Bečva. One image overtakes another. The river is flowing along on the left side. On the right, you can see some fairly well-tended allotments. Cottages alternate with trees, trees with bushes. Occasionally, you spot someone in the gardens – it could be a woman in a bikini, digging in a flower bed with a trowel, or a child waving his arms above his head, running along beside the fence only to trip and fall, bursting into tears. A woman rushes over to him and brushes the grass off him. All of these images seem foreign and distant to you. Soon you won't be able to tell them apart from your dreams. Anger wells up inside you and then subsides. The allotments suddenly come to an end, but the trail continues across a small meadow and rows of adjacent trees. You stop. So does Marián. You find a path leading through the grass to the water and set off along it. The pebbled bank isn't as sheltered as your spot on the other side of the river but, right now, it seems just as comforting to you. You flop down on the ground and breathe deeply.

Marián sits down beside you, close beside you. You can smell the fragrance of his clothes. You look at him.

Somewhere in the distance, a dog barks.

You give a start and you're back in Grandad's flat.

"What's that?"

Grandad is saying something but, to you, it seems as though his voice is coming from a great distance away.

"I said leave it." You can't see him from the kitchen but, from the tone of his voice, it's clear he doesn't want you in his flat. You rinse the last mug and put it on the draining board. Through the veil of raindrops, you can see the whole of the town from the window. A truck goes by below and the windowpanes rattle. There isn't a single cloud in the sky, just a milky haze, scattered in patches, stretching into the distance.

"Come here and tell me if you've got yourself a bird yet," shouts Grandad from the other room, making you feel sick. "You can tell me. When I was your age, I was chasing skirt all over town."

You swallow, wipe the worktop and throw the wet dishcloth over the windowsill. You want to be far away from here. Anywhere but here.

"No? Well, you should. A wee bit of fluff, eh? Otherwise, they'll start saying you're one of those pansies."

You catch your own reflection in the window. It seems as if it were moving independently of you. You blink and within the safety of your memory, you're sitting beside Marián on the sun-warmed stones once more. You both sit there motionless for several minutes. He looks over at you, but you're somewhere outside the frame of the image. You have the feeling that at this moment, not even the river or the leaves in the treetops are moving.

All of the memories have been recorded precisely in your mind and you can replay them as though you were experiencing them for the first time.

It's quiet by the river, with only your stomach starting to growl loudly.

Marián reaches over and puts his hand on your cheek. You can still feel it now. You're in two places at once. He's with you in this room as well – the heat, the hand, the light. You blink in surprise, and he leans over towards you.

You recall the sequence of events. Sweaty hair on your forehead, a moist hand on your cheek. Your eyes wide open, Marián's shut. It's hot outside, as though someone had cranked up the brightness and contrast to full, making your head hurt. You open your mouth and his tongue comes up against your teeth. He pulls back and you both laugh. He leans over to you again.

"It's supposed to be modern now. Even they…" Grandad nods towards the TV, "…talk about it all the time. It's all coming over here from fucking America. Before, it was the Communists who used to force all this crap on us, and now they're the ones foisting it on us." He coughs and swallows the accumulated phlegm. "Hopefully, someone will put a stop to it soon. No-one's interested in that kind of thing here. At least, *I hope* no-one's interested in it here. That's all we need."

You hear his words and don't hear them at the same time. You're straddling several places at once – your grandad's, at home in your room, outside. Your body is walking up and down the stairs, riding your bike, lying on the pebbles on the riverbank. You would like to retain a specific part of the memory in front of you for more than a few seconds, but each time it slips through your fingers. You would like to remember just one image and forget everything else.

Grandad's still talking, but you're no longer listening. You say goodbye, pick up the plastic bag with the cigarette butts and then chuck it in the bin downstairs. You get on your bike and leave Grandad in the building behind you, just as you left Marián standing outside your building later that first day. He went home alone and, for a long time, you lay sprawled in bed, staring at the stains created by the layers of old plaster on the bare ceiling.

There's almost half an hour to go before the train leaves, but the platform is already dotted with groups of drowsy people. It's neither noisy nor silent – there's just the hum of cars, strangers' voices and tension – a pressure that will soon disturb the air just above the ground, warming the still cold concrete. This early in the morning, the sky hasn't taken on the right shade yet, and the light breaking through the ragged clouds forms a warm orange coating on the arms of the cranes and the roofs of the buildings, with just an occasional sliver of blue shining through it, as though you'd had your eyes closed for a long time and suddenly squinted cautiously through your eyelashes into the sun to discover the world in a blur of shimmering colour.

You sling your rucksack over your shoulder and dig your mobile out of a pocket. You quickly scroll through some recent messages from your mum, hearing her voice as you read them – *please come* she texted three times in a row. A few days ago, in the middle of the night, you'd had an inkling she'd end up dealing with it all alone. You drag your thumb across the screen until you finally find the time and place of the ceremony.

Lowering your arm, you scan your surroundings and catch a glimpse of your gloomy face reflected on an advertising panel. The glass is dull and dirty, and instead of the poster, what you notice is your own face with strange shapes, dust and new colours projected below it. The reflection changes every now and then, and you see it twice, in two places, different each time. You move your head slightly and the image gives way to a stranger's shadow, swaying from side to side and heading towards you. The figure is clutching a plastic bag. First, a man's voice cuts through the air, followed by the familiar smell of cigarettes. Your grandad – you can see him clearly and vividly standing before you – smelled exactly the same. While he waited for you in front of the school, he'd impatiently walk up and down, dragging a pitiful old plastic bag behind him and chucking away one cigarette butt after another.

You tear your eyes away from the panel and look around – suddenly it's all noise and bustle around you. The man with the plastic bag has momentarily disappeared from view. A little to the left of you is a child of about five with a face mask fluttering around his neck, hopping about dangerously close to the edge of the platform. A train screeches to a halt on a nearby track. Then there's a voice from the Tannoy, the hiss of doors. At each loud noise, the child squeals with delight and jumps forward.

A week before Grandad died, before this flood of memories, you and Jakub had been waiting at a railway station in a suburb of Stockholm at roughly the same time of morning. That train had been delayed too. But how different can two seemingly similar moments be? The air had been damp from the rain, with a harsh, bleached-out light everywhere. Another child had been walking in a similarly careless way even closer to the tracks. You had got up early to go on a trip. You were supposed to change trains twice and then take the ferry to the island of Nåttarö. You'd sent a photo of the two of you to Mum and then to Dad. You'd started tapping your foot. Even Jakub was slightly bored. It wasn't long before the two of you were walking along the edge of the platform as well. You dangled your leg over and almost fell.

"More than twenty thousand crowns, you hear? That's all of my savings."

Mum was on her way back from the florist's when she phoned you yesterday. The day before, she'd been adamant that she didn't want any flowers at the funeral. ("I haven't a clue what I'd do with them. I still don't even know where we're going to put Grandad.") Judging by the noises and curses, she was trying to open the front door with one hand while balancing a funeral arrangement in the other.

"And to cap it all, I read that I'm supposed to sort out the inheritance. But I don't get it. I paid for everything for him anyway. Grandad could never have survived on what he was getting. So now I'm worried he's left debts behind. What inheritance? They don't expect to have to end up dealing with someone like him. And now just imagine all the money I had to shell out on the ceremony – first off, you've got the suit, the shoes, and all the red tape."

You remember all the details of the day you and Mum cleaned out Grandad's flat in the worker's hostel, not long after he'd moved permanently to the nursing home. There was an old gas stove hidden under a pile of clothes in the wardrobe. He'd stashed away dozens of tins of goulash, meat and beans, and then, right at the back, behind all of this junk, you'd found a hidden shoebox overflowing with official papers and other documents. Mum put it on Grandad's bed and left you to divide the contents into two tottering piles – one was to be taken to the dump; the other back home to the cellar, next to the tins and jars. If you subtracted the amount on the rent statement from the number on the pension receipt, there was just over a thousand left. Surprised, you showed it to your mother, but she just waved her hand dismissively. That wasn't news to her. If it hadn't been for her, not even the gas stove would have saved Grandad; no number of tins would have helped him.

"I'll tell you, though, there's one thing that really bloody annoys me. Why is it I have to sort all this out on my own? My brother at least calls, at least promises to help me, but my sister? So I swallowed whatever pride I had left and wrote to her to say Grandad would have wanted her there."

You're not convinced Grandad would actually have cared. Both he and Mum avoided talking about your aunt. They hadn't seen her for years, and even before that, you hardly ever visited her. When you did, she didn't take her eyes off you the whole time, carefully following your every step and even checking your pockets before you left. "She's always been weird, but I'd hoped at least this might bring her round. He was her dad, after all, and she hadn't seen him in ages – so I wrote that to her as well, I thought it might get through to her. And then a wee while ago, she sent me a message.... Hold on a sec. I have to put this down..." Unfamiliar sounds rattled in the receiver. "She wrote to me that *her father* had been dead to her for more than thirty years. Those are her very words. *My father has been dead to me for more than thirty years.*"

Mum had called a few more times since the day Grandad died. In between the complaints and practical questions, she'd pause and be silent for a long time. All you could hear was her breathing and, at the end of it, Mum's voice would repeat: I'll never forgive myself for not doing more for Grandad. She kept on uttering the same words, describing the same memories, as though they contained some hidden meaning.

"I made a mistake," she said in a thin voice, almost transparent enough for you to see through to what she was thinking. "I should never have sent him away. I should have taken him in. I could have coped with it somehow."

"And you'd have wanted that, Mum?" you asked her. "After everything?"

"Marek, you've always spent too much time rooting around in the past. Sometimes it's just... Sometimes it's better to let things lie."

You'd been standing in the street in front of your flat for ten minutes, circling the parked cars with a precisely measured stride. *Let them lie, but where?* You remember a line from one of your favourite poems: *Why hold onto all that? And I said, Where can I put it down?* Even if you do that, sooner or later you'll recall the pain anyway.

"I know what you mean, though – obviously I can't get it out of my head. I hardly sleep at all these days. I just lie there, staring at the ceiling, counting the lorries going by on the road, and even so, as soon I stop, it hits me all over again."

At the end of every call, Mum always tried to talk about nice things, her voice unnaturally high – sometimes it would crack as she tried stubbornly to stick to the topic and not slip back into the past. Before hanging up for the last time, she sighed deeply and added: "He was my dad. I can't pretend any different."

The train finally arrives and you get into the last carriage. You've barely managed to find your seat when the door to the compartment bursts open and the man from the platform squeezes awkwardly inside. He sprawls across the seat opposite and takes out a can of beer from his plastic bag. He opens it, pulls off his face mask with the other hand and stretches out his legs. The tips of his shoes are almost touching you, so you tuck your legs in towards you in response. You can barely see anything through your steamed-up glasses, so you take them off and put them on the small table by the window. The leatherette upholstery is cold and slippery; you lean your elbow on the armrest. The man accompanies each movement with a loud sigh as though marking his newly claimed territory. He sips his beer, pulls out his phone and, without so much as a greeting, starts shouting into it.

"A poof like that deserves to snuff it anyway."

You go rigid at his words. You know them so well, so intimately, and yet they catch you off guard every time. Taken together like this, they don't always have to represent a threat. They're not necessarily aimed at you.

To reinforce his words, the man makes a fist and angrily punches the chair.

"No, I don't know. Or maybe it was about time that bitch of his took off. I'll find her. She won't say no to me."

You don't want to think about who he has in mind, so you focus on the rhythm of the train. As soon as it sets off, the sounds and colours flash by in rapid succession. Your breathing is shallow and fast through the face mask – it could hardly be otherwise in this heat. You brace your knees against the folding table and, with your earphones in, observe the landscape: it changes while you remain the same, a fixed image in the window pinned to other houses, other fields and trees. You check what you're wearing in the reflection, straighten your back and look over at the man opposite again. He notices you and mutters something.

It wasn't so long ago that a message from Filip appeared on your Facebook page. It began with the same insult, which is why you remember it now. For a long time, you refused to open it – the first sentence was enough to give you the gist. *Has anyone kicked this poof's arse yet, or do I have to do it myself?* You suspect Filip's rage was just compensating for something he was afraid of – something he saw in you and recognized in himself. That's why his profile photos were of him in camouflage gear, crouching down as he posed with a gun in his hand. He was smiling.

Gradually, he levelled more and more threats at you. Perhaps the lack of recoil triggered a new barrage of rage in him; perhaps he was just curious to see how you'd react. Because of him, things that had long been submerged in the depths of your memory were resurfacing. Until now, you'd walked around them with your eyes closed, not even recognizing your own face in them. They included the

half-remembered names of people from your class, a series of faces and images. For so many years, you'd tried to
forget them, push the humiliation and shame out of your
mind. You'd created an empty space around the memories,
hoping that maybe one day you'd draw strength from it.

Except trauma never transforms itself into an empty
space. It is an added weight that gradually swells up, growing every year until it eventually takes up more space than
you yourself.

Now, as the man carefully repeats Filip's words, you're
relieved to find that, at least this time, they're not directed
against you. "I say that all the fucking time." He opens
another can with his free hand, leans forward and loudly
slurps the overflowing foam through his chapped lips.
"Everything's gone to shit. Before, you'd just have waited
for him, but now you're afraid to open your mouth."

Once, when you were still at nursery school and Mum
was working late, Grandad was supposed to come and collect you in the afternoon. You waited and waited. In the
end, Filip and one of the teachers – a strict elderly woman
with a purple perm – were the last ones there. She'd fallen
asleep in an armchair beside an overheated radiator and
couldn't see the two of you sprawled out on a camp bed
in the room round the corner, the one where they used to
put on a cassette tape after lunch with the sound of the
sea and the cry of gulls. Most of the beds had long since
been cleared away but, lying on one of the last ones, you
both took your trousers down under the duvet and curi-

ously examined the bodies hidden underneath them. You don't remember whose idea it had been or what was going through your mind. No-one discovered you. After a while, you both pulled up your trousers, got up from the bed and went through to the main room to build a Lego spaceship. As you were saying goodbye, Filip had waved and stuck out his tongue at you.

You'd been surprised when Mum appeared in the corridor beside the cloakroom instead of Grandad. Out of breath and drenched in sweat, she leant against the wall, watching impatiently as you tried unsuccessfully to put on your left shoe. You kept gazing out of the window, forgetting you were holding it in your hand. She soon lost patience, grabbed you and dragged you out into the street with just one shoe on. At home, she thrust a cloth in your hand while she fetched a bucket of water – she wanted you to help her wash the stairs – but no sooner had she bundled you out into the hallway than the tottering figure of Grandad loomed at the front door.

How long had he been pounding on the warped old door? Minutes, hours, days? And how would you describe Mum's expression? She held you close, sitting with her back to the door, flinching with each bang. If she was worried the old door wouldn't hold, she hardly showed it. She had taught you to swallow your anger and save your fear and regret for some other time – and then, above all, project your insecurities onto others. That time, she had shaken it off and waited until the alcohol wore off before taking Grandad home.

Like the other kids on the estate, you'd been told not to go into the woods behind the flats. In spite of that, you secretly kept going there, crawling through the bushes, picking up syringes or skeletons of dead birds or searching for a stick of just the right length. And so Mum made up stories about how the place was haunted by a witch, how a murderer who lured small boys into the woods lived there and what you were bringing home weren't actually the skeletons of birds but the skulls of those boys. From then on, you'd eye the dark gaps between the tree trunks suspiciously and scarper at the slightest rustle of leaves.

You still avoid the place to this day, even though you've known for a long time that there never was a murderer living in the woods.

All your life, you were taught to construct a series of conflicting ideas around yourself. You should trust no-one but yourself; the others are shadows, silent threats whose presence always bodes ill. Any type of difference – if it comes from outside – is supposed to trigger fear and a sense of danger. But if the difference comes from within, and it is you who is different, then fear gives way to loathing, to a sense of shame at your own reflection.

Sometimes, just living, occupying a place in the world day after day, seems like such a risky thing to do. Now you know it takes perseverance and courage to accept your own difference.

You can't remember having heard about anyone *like you* when you were young. And if you had, it would only have been from similar insults. You wouldn't even have noticed you were different if the others hadn't started drawing attention to you. If they hadn't labelled you as a perversion, an ideology, as if all you had on your mind were deranged adult dreams, or as if you even had a choice in the matter. Adults like to delude themselves that they're protecting children like you from sexuality, protecting you from pain. But, in reality, they're just exposing the more vulnerable to more violence.

One day in fourth year, Filip and the others ambushed you in the toilet. You felt something cold and damp against your face, the pressure of a stranger's hands on your neck. They shoved your head into the ceramic toilet bowl. "Never forget this," someone shouted as the water went up your nose. "This is where you belong – amongst the piss and shit." You were gasping for breath, coughing, trying to breathe, but instead you just kept taking in filthy water. Second after second disappeared into darkness. It reeked of urine in the cubicle and you were cold. Finally, they jammed a chair against the door from the other side and ran away. Exhausted, you fell asleep with your head on the toilet seat. You could still hear the sound of water dripping from your wet hair into the bowl. Before closing your eyes, the idea struck you: *Maybe they're right. Maybe I really do belong here.*

During the eight years you've been with Jakub, you've never been able to confide in him about any of this. He doesn't know anything about the bullying or about Marián, and you haven't even told him much about Grandad. You had rather naïvely believed: *I escaped from that a long time ago*, and yet now it's all coming back.

The shame is eating away at you from the inside, seeping through body and mind until it colours one memory after another. The shame is a circle you can't escape from, just as you can't step out of your own shadow. And time is a river – its current keeps flowing through your fingers and you can't turn it back. Why does the shame keep bringing back these memories again and again? Like rain, like waves breaking against driftwood on the shore. You still cling to the hope that these same waves will wash over you until you dissolve in them and become someone other than who you were before.

People first start to distance themselves from others when they realize how different they are. It's inevitable. You're watching TV when suddenly you glimpse yourself in one of the characters. And then the distance grows with understanding: you keep stumbling over a language where it doesn't matter who a person really is – each time, they end up marginalized, consigned to a predetermined place because they don't belong anywhere else.

Long after that time at high school when you told Mum you were gay, she still refused to say the word out loud. If she really had to, her lower lip would tremble and her voice would drop to a barely audible whisper. "You know," she once told you over the phone, "I don't have anything against people *like you*, that's obvious. There's Olda at work, for example – he's my friend and he hasn't got it easy with his partner, but he's really nice. I just don't think people like that should bring up children. That's going too far."

Before the words *like you*, she'll sometimes pause almost imperceptibly and lower her voice. It makes you feel as if the two of you are talking about a really awful, unpleasant thing. You've no idea how to respond, so you just listen.

"It's so unfair on the children. Remember what they did to you. And I think a child needs two parents to be normal. Look how you turned out."

As though you were to blame for everything. And yet she couldn't even have known how you turned out, because you never really talked to her properly about what happened to you or what the others did. You only removed your mask once – during the summer holidays, when you finally came home in the early hours of the morning to find her half-asleep on the kitchen bench.

"You're lucky you were born here and not somewhere in Africa," she blurted out recently. You'd just been looking through some holiday snaps. She grabbed you by the shoulders and looked you straight in the eye. "It's so difficult for people like you over there." You swiped to the next photo. "At least, be a bit grateful."

First, the world teaches you resentment, but as soon as your anger holds up a mirror to the world, as soon as it ceases to suit the world, it tells you to stop being angry.

Whenever you try to argue with her, Mum repeats Grandad's favourite phrase: "That's your opinion and I have mine." Whenever she talks about *other people*, about people *like you*, she adopts a strangely contemptuous tone. "You know…" she'll begin, and it's obvious she doesn't believe you, won't be talked round, not even if you're talking about your own life experience. "These days, it's all just lies anyway. The two of us will never find out the truth of it all."

The train gives a sudden jolt and the man opposite spills beer over himself. The yellow foam runs down his belly onto the grubby fabric of his trousers. "I'm not gonna complain, am I?" he shouts down the phone, shaking the foamy drops off his hand, "But I reckon things aren't what they used to be."

And yet the past is a place we often long to return to, just as often as we hold it up as a warning to others. For instance, the previous regime left people like your parents with an aversion towards the slightest hint of restriction and totalitarianism, but it also left them with a lot of cosy childhood memories where the world seemed safe and orderly. Meanwhile, after the revolution, they gradually lost their certainties, their jobs, their homes, their secure place in the world. Life fragmented into a mosaic they couldn't make sense of. All they could do was lament the old days. The discrepancy in this strange nostalgia is similar to other, no less dangerous gaps in their thinking, and it's from these that their prejudices are born. All you have to believe is that the enemy is, at the same time, strong enough to represent a threat and too weak to rule. And so women are overly sensitive and fragile, Romanies are always aggressive, the poor are too lazy to get themselves out of poverty, and yet all of you are oppressing decent, normal people.

"I know some of them can work, but they're in the minority," declares Mum every time the subject of Romanies comes up. There were quite a few of them in the factory – but everyone knew that Romanies don't work, or they only work so they can claim benefits later or deliberately take jobs away from *our* people. That's how it'd always been; that's how they talked about it on the news, in your neighbourhood, even at home over dinner.

You had even learned to hate *those others*. That was the only way to protect yourself against the bogeyman. Prejudices mark out a space and give us borders within which we can still feel safe.

About two years ago, Mum came to visit you for a few days and, at breakfast, she piped up: "When I went out for a smoke this morning, while you and Jakub were still sleeping, these three women were walking along the street, bundled up in those robes they wear, and they looked just like ghosts. It was like something you'd see on the news, you know, and I just stood there, staring at them open-mouthed until my cigarette went out."

A week later, she was complaining over the phone: "I don't want them here, Marek, cos soon we'll end up like them. And you should be worried too. I mean, they treat poo...homosexuals really badly there."

You wish you could show her what happens when fear is abused by the powerful – those same people who'd been passing her over for so long – in order to divert attention away from the things that really matter. There's nothing easier than pointing the finger at other people, those even lower down the pecking order, and making bogeymen out of them, channelling all that resentment elsewhere.

For as long as you're on the bottom rungs of society, someone will kick you or pass you over until the bodies of those people who are even lower than you become the only things you can exert at least some vestiges of power over. You can still show that their bodies are not quite human, that they lack something. Something you still have. You're not quite at the bottom yet, you can still move forward. And it's those bodies that need to be deprived of the hope of a better life. The boundary of who you are is the boundary of the body, but the boundary of the body will never entirely belong to you. All it takes is for someone in power to start remembering and caring about those below you and to provide them with what they'd been denied for so long, but what/that you had enjoyed. But you can't help yourself – it seems as though the others have stripped you of the last remnants of your pride, taken away the last certainty keeping you afloat until, in the end, you are as invisible as they were before.

You'd be lying to yourself if you said you hadn't used to think the same way. There were lots of similar opinions circulating round your high school. You grew up with them, so holding up a mirror to your own prejudices is even more difficult when your own language and the language of those around you stubbornly keeps repeating them.

Is it the fault of language or is it our own fault when we refuse to acknowledge other people's stories? Sometimes you feel as though we're buried inside our language, buried inside ourselves – we try to send out signals, gestures and sounds without even expecting any response. No-one's listening; instead, we're all just talking.

You know full well Mum doesn't really mean it. In her world, words don't mean anything bad. They can't hurt people *like you*, just as she thinks words never hurt her. You don't know exactly when you both stopped speaking the same language. In the end, you also help create this silence filled with words without meaning. Your words bounce off the gates of a foreign world and only an echo returns.

It's hard to accept that Mum might understand you if only you could manage to put it differently. For so many years, you've tried to run away, only to end up losing touch with your own language and speaking like a foreigner. You hear a different explanation from her every time. She'd heard such-and-such from people at work, read something else on the internet. And what she says also contains phrases from various comments under posts, which she repeats almost verbatim. Is there any point in putting up a fight? Most of the time, you just shake your head and mutter something. It's pointless trying to object; every time, you realize you're speaking that foreign language again, those foreign words that lead nowhere.

As the heat builds, the carriage starts to smell of linoleum, leatherette and the dust that's accumulated behind the window. You can smell it even through your face mask, as it mingles with your own breath. Outside are fields of rapeseed, the boxy shapes of logistics depots and just the occasional glimpse of a house. Warm orange light streams in through the window. You turn to the side, lean against the headrest and stretch your neck until the fragments of the sun's rays fall across your face. You used to do this as a little kid. Your memory of other people's faces is often bound up with the way the light hits them at different angles.

The smell of the carriage reminds you of your summer jobs at the factory, the dark corridors in the buildings with pipes crisscrossing the ceiling, twisting their way along it like inverted railway tracks running from nowhere to nowhere. Every summer for four years while you were at high school, you'd walk beneath them, aimlessly pushing a cart with ether-acetone and half-assembled units. You can remember the heat in the connecting corridors between buildings, the same pungent odour of linoleum and scorched dust. For eight and a half hours, the world outside disappeared, leaving time to tick by inexorably. Occasionally, you'd manage to steal the odd cigarette from Mum's locker, where you kept your things. Hiding behind the skips overflowing with discarded tubes and twisted metal, you'd light up. You never realized how close this was to becoming your life.

"Aren't you ashamed your folks don't even have a high-school diploma?"

At the time, you were taken aback by the question, which had been put to you by a fair-haired guy sitting at the opposite side of the table. He observed you with the hint of a grin. In front of him was an almost empty beer glass, behind him a wall with posters of football players, along with their jerseys and pennants. It wasn't so long ago you'd hardly known anyone whose parents worked outside the factory. You didn't see why you should feel ashamed of something like that; after all, there were other things to be ashamed of. The smoke from the ashtray formed loops that rose towards the single light bulb above the guy's head, their twisted appearance reminding you of the flow of a murky autumn river. You waved your hand and stirred it up.

"And what do they do exactly? I couldn't do that, working with my hands all day for peanuts. Why don't they find something else?"

"What d'you want them to do? I mean, machines do everything nowadays," remarked the guy to his right. You looked at them both and wondered how to reply. "I think someone should teach them to get off their arses and start putting in some hard graft."

It wasn't the first time someone had tried to foist the idea on you that poor people were those who had failed in life. They haven't tried hard enough, so they can't be surprised that there's nothing left for them. They need to live modestly – they say this to the very people who've been doing exactly that their whole lives. They need to work hard, raise themselves up. Get out of their comfort zones. We're the ones who bring all the bad things in life upon ourselves. You hear this phrase a lot too, usually when someone is confiding in others about their own misfortune. But such ideas rarely reflect reality.

There were days when Mum came back so exhausted from her day at the factory that she'd barely sat down on the couch before her eyes closed. She'd come home from work, cook dinner, and then she and Gran would both fall asleep in front of the telly. You had to wake her up. She'd be lying with her neck at an angle and if she'd stayed that way, she wouldn't have been able to move it the next day. She often had a sore head from the fumes and dry air at the workshop. You learned to spot the first signs, interpret her outbursts, her temper and the closed door to her room. You got used to Mum hiding beneath the duvet, the pillow covering her head. If she hadn't made sounds like an injured animal, you'd have thought she was long dead. On bad days, no-one was allowed to speak to her. The slightest noise was all it took and there'd be slippers flying towards your head. When things were at their worst, she'd take a thick woollen hat from a drawer in the hall and pull it over her head. She still has it at home – a hat with a brown pompom, but now it's covered in bobbles and falling apart. She never wore it outside, so you and Gran soon realized that the hat was a symbol, a sign flagging up her pain. If she was wearing it, things were bad. For the rest of the day, she'd lie in your room, the blinds shut, and you made sure to tiptoe around her. But at the same time, she couldn't risk looking for another job. The one she had represented the only certainty she had in life.

And so you felt embarrassed when you wanted something different in life from what she'd planned for you.

Sometime in the spring of 2007, you and Mum sat hunched over a brochure for Přerov grammar school for the first time. "Isn't it too soon?" she asked in surprise as she carefully leafed through it. It was Marián who'd suggested it to you. "One of these days, I'm getting out of here, heading to a bigger city," he kept reminding you. He had been revealing his own plans to you for so long that you took fright and quickly tried to come up with some of your own. But you couldn't tell your mother that, so instead you presented her with the pages they'd printed out for you in the library, which you'd practically memorized on the way home.

"I don't know, Marek. What would you do afterwards? You have to realize I can't go on supporting you forever. What about the technical college?" She had a serious expression on her face. "High school's a waste of time unless you go on to uni after. Do you honestly think you could cope with that?"

You nodded cautiously and moved the pages nearer. You needed to convince Mum you knew exactly what you wanted.

"OK, fine then." She looked at you suspiciously, the doubts still obvious on her face. "And what if you don't get in anywhere? What about accommodation and travel – that all adds up, doesn't it?

"And what is it you want to do anyway? I don't know. Do you have any idea how well the kids from the tech college do at our factory? At college you'd already be getting work experience – in the production hall, for example. The work's not as crazy as it used to be and it's not such a slog. It can be a bit of a pain being on your feet all day, but you get used to it." She seemed enthusiastic about this idea. "After college, you could start in a better position straight away – and I bet they'd pay you more than they do me."

There would be nothing unusual about it. Apart from Grandad, everyone in the family had worked in the factory for at least a short while.

And the factory buildings had always been there for you, waiting in the same place each morning. They towered above you on your way to school and back. On the wall nearest your house, you can still make out a burnt section of the façade, even though it's been ages since a fire broke out there. The flames slowly licked the first row of windows and people just walked past as though the fire didn't even remotely interest them. You waited. Someone would have to stop. Any minute now, one of those people would have to do something. In the end, you phoned the fire brigade yourself from a call box. You hated the thought that Mum might be sad. You stood on tiptoe in the smelly phone box. The telephone rang and the only thing you could think about was that soon she might have nowhere to go to work, nothing to do.

It never occurred to you that you might also be rescuing your own future.

She only took you to work once when you were little – to the open day. You were barely five, and you begged her, pestered her all day, and only stopped when she finally dressed you in your shirt, helped you squeeze into your trousers and put on your shoes, and then took you by the hand and led you out of the house.

Ever since you were a child, you'd wanted to look inside, to cross the blue footbridge between the two buildings just behind your block of flats. To discover what lay within. Every day, Mum disappeared and then reappeared at the gatehouse, but you didn't understand what she was doing there all day. One day, she brought home a broken lens slightly smaller than your hand. You placed it on the table and stared at it for a long time in wonder. You'd often wait for Mum after nursery school, your gaze riveted on the brown rectangles on the building's façade, crushing Gran's hand in your grip. You were afraid – what if one day she never returned from the factory? What if she stayed in there forever? Maybe, one day, she'd decide simply not to return, just like Dad had. You wanted to run to her, stay by her side all day, help with whatever she was doing, just so you wouldn't lose her. As soon as she opened the front door, you flew through the hall, leapt on her and refused to let go.

That day, in a shirt and worn corduroy trousers with the legs rolled up, you happily skipped a few steps ahead of Mum and were the first to run through the open door of the gatehouse. Inside the corridors, you could smell linoleum, dry air and the occasional trace of chemicals. Turpentine, acetone and various adhesives. Right at the start, they led you into the main production hall, where machine tools stood in rows. You felt small beneath them and watched on tiptoe as someone's arm miraculously pulled oddly shaped parts out of them from time to time. There was noise everywhere and an annoying whistling above it all. The smell of metal. Every machine had someone checking the display and pressing buttons on the control panel in a regular rhythm. You wanted to look inside but, even on tiptoe, you couldn't reach high enough. One of the men operating the machines lifted you up and pointed at the movement inside the machine. He wanted you to press something, so he took your hand, placed it on a button, and told you to push a little.

But it didn't work. You tried with all your might, but nothing happened.

The man muttered something, laughed awkwardly, and quickly put you back down. You felt as though you'd failed an important test – now they'd never let you back in.

As you made your way through the hall, all you noticed were the metal filings on the floor. You clutched your mum's hand tightly. Now and again, she'd say hello to someone, pause and start explaining to you what each machine did. From the hall, you went through a narrow corridor with heavy plastic partitions into the adjacent building. There were lots of dark, twisting corridors, each leading to an endless number of rooms. They were all different, full of machines and tables with parts laid out on them, arranged so you could look at them. In one of the workshops, she made you try polishing a lens with a cotton bud. First, she dipped it into a glass bottle, and the sweet smell tickled your nose. You breathed in deeply and carefully rubbed the swab back and forth a few times. You dipped the swab in again and the world around you began to spin. On the way back, you bumped into a table, nearly knocking everything onto the floor.

She saved her own workshop till last. By now, you were almost completely alone in the corridors. It was a large, clean cube with several side rooms. The only way to peep into the room was through a window in the transfer chamber.

To get in there, you would've had to put on one of the overalls hanging up on a hook in the chamber. But Mum didn't want to lend you hers – "It'd be too big for you, Marek, and you'd end up breaking something." Instead, she wiped your nose and poured a glass of water in the kitchen area. She drank it, lifted you up and pointed out of the only window in the room to the roof of a nearby building.

"Look, that's our house."

You remember the light and Mum's breath. The surrounding air didn't smell of anything you could describe afterwards, and yet you could still smell it on your clothes at home – that same vague smell you'd always associated with your mother.

The two of you were alone in the room. You touched the glass and left a print on it with your damp hand.

"One day when I'm a worn-out old biddy," she said half-jokingly, "you'll report for duty. Just like I took over from Gran."

That idea used to appeal to you: walking through the gatehouse to the courtyard with the car park. There are people lined up in a row, applauding you. They know you. You walk all the way to the end, where Mum is standing under the only tree in the whole area. She's smiling as she reaches out her hand and passes you the sceptre. For a long time, that's how you thought it would be. One morning, you'd start working there instead of her. You'd put on her overalls and slip into them like a new skin.

You no longer remember when something snapped inside you and your plans changed. You remember the days when you and Marián spent the breaks discussing various scenarios, ways of escaping from the school and everything else. Forget technical college – you wanted to get as far away as possible, to another town. Only Marián understood something that no-one else knew – going to the same school as other boys from the class was out of the question. While he knew exactly where he wanted to go and put all his energy into persuading his mother, who had other plans for him too, – you didn't have the slightest idea where to go next.

You'd probably portrayed it in overly simple terms. You just wanted four more years. Four years during which you wouldn't have to think all the time. Mum couldn't understand it. She liked to have things well planned out in advance, needed to go through all the options in detail.

Out of desperation, you told Dad all about it.

"Mum always knew what was best for you," he said angrily, just as you'd expected. But you rolled your eyes anyway. You were leaning against the varnished worktop in the kitchen, twisting the cable of the landline around your neck, and when you started to get annoyed at all the crap he was coming out with, you made a noose and pretended Dad's words were strangling you. "I wish you'd finally get a mind of your own. She doesn't need to force you into everything all the time, dammit! So just wise up and put your foot down. We'll always find the money for it somehow."

Luckily, the very idea of a high-school diploma, something no-one in the family had achieved before, represented such a bright future to your mother, such a mark of success, that she didn't really care which school you went to.

But then, once you got into grammar school, the money Dad had spoken about – that same money he'd said could always be found – suddenly couldn't be found. "From now on, we'll have to watch every crown," Mum remarked and, ever since then, the voices on the TV have been repeating her words.

*We'll have to cut back.*

Whenever you browse the newspaper headlines these days, it strikes you that not much has really changed. "Even when the pandemic is over," you read in an interview with one of the richest Czechs, "the days of gluttony and excess are not coming back in a hurry."

Just as they had during the crisis of 2008–2009, the factory made more than four hundred people redundant in spring. During the first wave of the pandemic, they still had to go to work. The factory applied for financial help from the government. Some people got infected at work, but when it became obvious the company couldn't maintain regular growth, they started laying people off without a second thought. Not even Mum could be sure of her job. "We all have to start cutting back." Someone from management is standing in front of her, repeating this sentence. "It's time to make savings. Times are hard." She looked around and saw nothing but nervous faces. Everyone knew that times had been hard for way too long and it was impossible to tighten belts any more without tying the leather in knots. "Every death is terrible, but so is the demise of a company," concluded the man in the interview who had been speaking about the end of gluttony. "The economy mustn't shut down." For someone who loses their job, however, even the second option represents a certain kind of death. Words like those are really just a raw bundle of nerves.

If we are unable to understand experiences that are different to our own, we all too easily forget about other people and allow ourselves to be lulled into a false sense of security.

When you spoke to your dad about the money he'd promised that first year at grammar school, he just coughed nervously and pretended he didn't want to talk about it, before finally saying something along the lines of: "You'll need to talk it over with your mum."

The receiver crackled for a moment and then Dad piped up again, though in a completely different tone. "I mean about money. Things are pretty tight at the moment and I can't afford extra expenses. Listen – it's probably going to be bad for a while. I really need you to talk to your mum about it. I won't be able to send money for a bit, so you'll have to cut back, OK?"

It wasn't the first time he'd sent a message to Mum through you. She'd learned not to rely on money from him after having had to beg for it for several months. Somehow, Dad had found out that Martin was sleeping over regularly at yours. He went totally ballistic. Now he shouted down the phone at you as well and, in the end, he hung up and didn't get in touch for more than six months. "He still acts like he owns me," she said to no-one in particular, turning round and looking you up and down. "Just make sure you don't grow up to be like him."

You turn your gaze to the reflection in the window.

*Why didn't she just find something else?*

The guy's question seems ridiculous to you. Naïve. Though it wasn't the first or last time you'd heard it.

At work, that kind of talk makes you feel out of place. It's as if you're from a different world, one that those around you only have a vague, distorted idea of. You look at your reflection again, trying desperately to avoid making any mistakes that might reveal you don't belong there. So far, you haven't even been able to tell anyone you're gay. On your first day in the office, one of the owners made a casual remark about poofs, and you laughed along with the others.

An art gallery is about as distant a world as possible from the one you originally came from. All you have to do is mention politics at work and the owners start complaining about bureaucracy and paying taxes. They can't understand why anyone would vote for certain parties, why they'd overlook all the scandals and corruption, while forgetting that they do the same and there's no fundamental difference between them and the people they're talking about.

"The state has got no business butting in. There's no magic money tree," your boss said, leaning towards you and stabbing the air with her finger. "I really don't see why *I* should have to feed someone who has just frittered their life away."

Come the first days of quarantine, however, she was the one nervously seeking government support, and when the company wasn't awarded any, she nearly had a heart attack.

"Only a total idiot could vote for that Babiš[3]. It's because of him we're all dying here."

You opened your mouth, but before you could say anything, she'd changed the subject to another important matter that was troubling her. In her view, there were too few collectors in Czechia and not enough interest in art.

---

3     Andrej Babiš, former prime minister, leader of populist party ANO (Action for Dissatisfied Citizens) (translators' note)

You pictured the bailiffs' office in Přerov. The director is also an entrepreneur and recently set up a miniature gallery in one of the office's two front windows. *Window Gallery* on Komenský street is just two minutes away from Škodova street and, in that run-down building, the sculptures and pictures seem out of context, to say the least. Perhaps some of the passers-by will stop, you thought, and, like your mum, take a peek inside and leave with a warped painting. It's this kind of art that has forgotten about us. It's there for other people, for people who have time for it. Those who don't have time just shake their heads before going through the door into the office. Maybe those people – say, a woman in a similar situation to your mum – will have someone in their home raking through their things who then goes back to their own small art collection at home.

You can easily understand why your grandad and mum continued to vote for the Civic Democratic Party[4] so long after the revolution. The fairy tale of personal responsibility and freedom after years of having practically no control over your own life seemed like the only way forward to them. It only took a hint of socialist policies for them to label that person a Communist.

Did either of them realize that what they were feeling was akin to trauma? Was that even possible? Their memories were rooted beyond any conscious vocabulary.

---

4   Free-market party, founded in 1991 by Václav Klaus, who later became president (translators' note)

Later, Mum admitted to you: "I knew even then I wasn't going to have a good life under Klaus." Meanwhile Grandad declared, "We have to stand by someone like him. Even I'm a total blockhead compared to him." For Mum though, *the Professor*, as she'd always called him, embodied everything she despised about politics. Each time she talked about him, she adopted a high, sweet tone, that made the corner of her mouth twitch. You have no idea if she ever really believed her dreams, if she thought hard graft would really get her back on her feet and she'd earn decent money at the factory. In another moment of weakness, Grandad told you about his secret police records, brawls in pubs, and how he openly criticized the Communist Party. Gran also recalled the day when, because of Grandad's problems, she had to persuade the head of the trade school to let Mum attend any secondary school at all. Mum never found out why she wasn't accepted by the college she'd originally applied to, why she never became a hairdresser and instead spent the summer holidays in tears. On the first of September, she pulled herself together and made her way to the factory where she still works to this day.

When you were a child, you partly drew and partly wrote a story in a notebook after school. Right at the beginning, the mother of the main character (who, like you, was nine and had long dark hair, brown eyes and a name that began with M) dies. One day, you left the notebook out on the bedside table in your room. Mum found it and read the whole thing. The text was full of nonsense, dragons, magic and strange words, but she inevitably remembered one thing from it and one thing alone.

You came home and were barely through the door when she slapped you.

She was terrified by how easily these ordinary words were able to erase her from the world.

Neither your mother nor your grandad ever learned to ignore the media's contempt for the people they identified with. In 2010, the then leader of the Civic Democrats, Mirek Topolánek, was asked how he would describe the supporters of his opponent, Jiří Paroubek: "They're all just pork, dumplings and cabbage. We need to lock them all up. Give them a kick up the arse." Something similar could be heard from all sides during the last presidential elections. Everyone around you was trying to prove how much better they were as people just because of who they voted for. You pointed the finger at others as well and tried desperately to distance yourself from your family. Only riffraff could believe Zeman's[5] lies.

Mum got really mad then.

"You can't be serious!" She turned bright red and glared at you. "They won't leave him alone for a minute. Everything he does is wrong. You're happy to lay into someone just because he's a bit of a redneck."

5    Miloš Zeman, leader of the Social Democratic Party 1993-2001, president of Czech Republic 2013-2023 (translators' note)

You were surprised how easy it was for someone from the upper echelons of politics to appear to your mother as an outcast, as someone picked on by the elite. You don't think she voted for him because of his manifesto. You doubt that even interested her. Instead, she made her decision in defiance of those others, out of spite and distrust of a system that had never done anything for her.

"They all make lots of promises," she'd often say. "But, in the end, it all turns out differently and the only ones who are better off are those with their snouts in the trough."

These days, if anyone on TV refers to freedom or invokes the word democracy, Mum raises her voice, almost shouting in exasperation.

"And what use is fucking freedom to me, when I don't even have time for a bloody holiday or the money to save up for one?"

As soon as this dawned on her, she started voting for ANO. She was attracted by the notion that because their leader was so rich, he wouldn't be in a hurry to stick his snout in the *trough*. With the onset of the pandemic, she started to bristle at the slightest criticism of Prime Minister Babiš.

"I'd like to know what the rest of them would do in his place. No-one knows how things'll turn out."

But she wasn't speaking out of any deep conviction; it was more that she liked what Babiš said and how he said it. He spoke directly to her in her own language, in words that didn't try to erase her, that took her into account.

"He's on our side."

The train stops by a field just outside Přerov, with only yellow strips and a few randomly scattered buildings visible out of the window. The stench of rapeseed seeps through the cracks in the windows, filling the compartment and gradually making it difficult to breathe. You look out the window and a thin plume of smoke on the horizon indicates the chimneys of the Přerov chemical works. There's not a cloud in the sky, which looks flat as a result.

The man on the seat opposite has been asleep for a while now, and his head keeps slowly sliding down the headrest. Each time, he jerks a little, blinks in surprise and then closes his eyes again. A voice on the Tannoy announces that the train is delayed by about half an hour. You check your mobile nervously, but you've still got plenty of time. No messages, no missed calls. You put the phone down and, for the first time, it hits you that you'll never hear Grandad's voice again.

The thought of that isn't horrifying, doesn't fill you with regret. Nevertheless, you can't shake it off. For the last month, your phone had been ringing regularly at the same time. Grandad's name would inevitably pop up on the screen day after day. You never picked up. You were almost scared to look at the display, terrified of what you'd discover if you picked up the phone.

Mum filled you in on what was going on. *Don't worry,* she wrote early one morning just a few days before Grandad died. *He's just practising calling. He's got my old mobile.* She didn't know you were often scared to answer her calls as well. They reminded you too much of one particular evening fourteen years ago. The phone vibrates and your heart thumps, every movement awakening an uncomfortable feeling in the pit of your stomach.

It seems to you that the phone hasn't been capable of bringing any good news for some time now. For more than a year, each notification is just death, a series of numbers and violent acts. Each new message is a call for help. You open Instagram and the photographs seem at odds with what you know is happening in the world around you. Everything important happens here. Even memories seem to be plucked out of time; they're not real until you post them, until someone on the other side sets the story in motion. You let the photos of holidays and cafés flow freely until these snippets of other people's memories make your head spin. Each of them is just another filler, an image frozen in time that makes no sense on its own.

As proof that you have nothing to worry about, your mother sent you a photo of a mature tree in the grounds of the Kroměříž psychiatric hospital. You click on it and the permanence of the yellow leaves, firmly set in the branches, instils a sense of calm. In this photo, the world is still safe and orderly.

Grandad usually practised using the mobile at night; you'd be wakened by a buzzing under the pillow. You stared at the screen, which glowed more brightly in the darkness, filling the apartment with its artificial blue light.

Fourteen years. You still remember – back then, it all started with the phone ringing too. First, it was the landline at home that woke you up; then the next night, it was your mum's mobile phone. It bounced around on the glass-topped bedside table until she murmured something unintelligible into it in an exasperated voice, sat up and then stared into the darkness for a long time.

You still have an image of that night in front of you. You're standing in the bathroom in Marián's place, imagining how you'll finally escape the town some day soon. Is it really so strange for you to return there again? In every mirror, you still see your face framed by light and steam, just as it was then. Streaks of pinkish water trickle down from your wet hair, while around your nose the stream is darker, almost crimson. When your mobile goes off in the pocket of your shorts, dumped beside the washing machine, the sound doesn't even startle you. Without a second thought, you lean over and switch it off.

You don't really remember what you did after that. The rest of that evening vanishes into darkness. In some places, it's replaced by Mum's version from the end of September, when your arm was freshly in plaster and the skin on your wrist itched terribly. You forgot what you were doing for a moment and tried to scratch underneath the plaster with your pinkie. That annoyed Mum, so to get your attention, she banged her hand on the table.

A similar sound is shaking the window now too, only this time the impact is followed by silence instead of words. The train is waiting in a sea of rapeseed, while gusts of wind, sweeping through the shrivelled plants, crash into it. You can pinpoint the exact spot where an imaginary child has dropped a rock from the sky; the spot where the waves travel in circles all the way to the railway embankment, where they shatter against the side of the carriages.

The day it happened, the day everything fell apart and Mum nearly lost Grandad, the day she decided to forget once and for all, as only someone exhausted by a long struggle can forget, that was the day she was late for work. She'd only slept a couple of hours all night. The heat had transformed the bedroom into a red-hot oven, and she was afraid to touch the corner of the discarded duvet with even the tip of her foot. She sank deeper into the damp mattress, listening in the dim glow of the streetlamp as you talked in your sleep.

The night sounds drifted in and out of her consciousness. She tried not to focus on them, hoping that would finally allow her to get to sleep, but, in the end, she always failed and searched for hidden meanings in the sounds. You had argued that evening, though, by now, she'd forgotten why. She had talked while you avoided her gaze and then tried to leave the room. All day, she'd been trying unsuccessfully to call you. In the evening, she was waiting for you in the kitchen, full of fear and expecting the worst. When she eventually heard the door click, it was already dark outside. She ran into the hallway to be met by a younger version of your father. The same expression, hands buried in his pockets, back stooped. She had her hands on her hips and stopped mid-sentence. Suddenly, she was taller, more frightening. She wrinkled her nose – your nose – and, in the end, all she could do was raise a hand to you in desperation.

"Just like your dad," she said, her voice trembling with rage. "He only cared about himself as well."

You noticed Gran poke her head out of the door cautiously. As soon as she saw Mum's combative posture, she quickly made herself scarce.

"Tomorrow, you'll stay here." She raised her hand again. You ducked instinctively, but she was just hooking the chain on the door. "There'll be a list on the table and woe betide you if you don't get it all done."

She refused to speak to you for the rest of the evening. After dinner, she sent you straight to bed, thinking she was punishing you, but when she heard your calm, regular breathing, while she couldn't close her eyes for a moment, she began to regret it.

She lay there, wondering if it might help if she opened the window for a bit to let in some of the fresh night air.

But she couldn't stand the windows being open even the slightest crack. It made her imagine a stranger's hand in the darkness. A ghostly figure would appear to her out of the shadows and sounds of the room – just like that time years ago – and would climb through the window and step right onto her bed.

In the morning, she shuffled into the kitchen, completely shattered. She could feel the beginnings of a migraine on the left side of her head, so she swallowed a pill and checked the time.

All those years in the factory – an eternity spent poring over systems of mirrors and lenses – had taught Mum to be much more sensitive to the light around her. The daylight that filtered in through the blinds was dim, reflected off the windows and façades of the buildings opposite, though even this small amount was converted into warmth on the worktop.

"I'm a sunshine addict," she repeats at the end of every winter. As soon as the air warms up on the first hot day, Mum'll stand in the middle of the pavement, close her eyes and lift her head towards the sun. It takes all of eight minutes for the light to reach her, whereas it's capable of disappearing before she opens her eyes.

That morning, leaning against the kitchen worktop, she stared at the strip of light on the clock and had the feeling that more than eight minutes must have passed before it dawned on her what was wrong. Meanwhile, time was counting the intervals between the ticking of the clock. Two points where the light quietly falls, barely disturbing the surface. Before she'd had time to wake up properly, the hand had jumped forward again.

Later on, in the workshop, Mum's face breaks out in a rash from sheer concentration. She has trouble holding anything in her cold hands. As she tries to tighten a connection using brute force, the screwdriver slips from her hand and falls to the floor.

It's been a long time since she's had such a bad day. Since early morning, she's been trying to centre the same triplet of lenses, and she almost broke it as soon as she arrived – she put the collimator on automatic and forgot the machine doesn't stop by itself but keeps moving downwards. If she hadn't stopped it in time, it would've hit the glass.

*Defect*, the computer announces, and Mum slumps back down on her chair, *replace the lens*. At a loss, she stares at the screen, wondering whether she should ask the foreman for help.

She shakes her head to dispel the doubts.

She always manages in the end. Sometimes, she might have a bad day when the drill vibrates in her hand and she can't hold it steady. "The trick is not to take yourself too seriously," she was saying to someone on the phone the last time you visited. "I've always been more into the delicate work, 'cos if I think about something too much, it ends badly. Even a lens isn't perfect – there's always a compromise involved. I don't even have to know exactly what each piece does. I'm not interested in wavefront deformations. I just picture them as tiny little hollows. That's what the foreman told us in the workshop. He said we should picture them as mountains or forests – you have to take account of them in life too – and even the image you see through the lens is only an approximation. It just needs to resemble the real thing as much as possible. I measure things in thousandths, but actually that means it could always be better. Nothing's perfect. And my job is to find a way to get it as close to perfect as possible."

She's been trying to attain perfection her whole life. At times, she feels like giving up. She reaches out her hand to discover she's only just getting started.

In the adjustment room, she works alone. The centroscope shows her a reversed image. Like her eye, the machine perceives the world upside-down, and it's only from habit that her mind or the computer sets it right again. She aligns the tube and runs a series of checks on the entire system. Every ray of light that hits the mirror, the surface of Mum's eye, is reflected back at exactly the angle of incidence. The eye lets in light travelling through space until the rays meet at a certain point and are reflected back – but it could be said that light carries a memory with it. At the point where the rays meet, their memory creates a replica, assembling a reflection of the real object.

She turns the chair with a quiet click, bites the tip of her tongue and focuses on the screen. Her fingers tap the mouse. Everything's in alignment. Everything corresponds to the designs. She checks them once more and goes back to the computer.

Finally, she watches one point after another; with a slow, confident movement, they slide across the monitor, while graphs appear at the bottom and sides – she doesn't need to pay attention to those yet. More numbers and curves, then everything falls into place.

She lets out a cry of joy and then instantly regrets it.

She's been struggling with this unit for several weeks and almost managed to break one of the five main lenses, each of them the size of her hand. The day after Grandad called her about the television, she noticed a tiny speck on the edge of one of them. With a practised motion, she dipped a cotton bud into a bottle of ether-acetone and gently wiped the protective facet. She meant to put the lens back in place, but her attention wandered and she lost her concentration. One false move and she dropped the lens. At first, she thought it hadn't got chipped, but under the magnifying glass she discovered a tiny area where she'd damaged the UV layer.

She'd been lucky that time. A colleague from the optics factory had taken the lens, repaired it and brought it back the next day. It was a huge relief, because the time before she'd had to pay for the damage. She'd barely been working in development for a week, and she was trying to finish off a unit that had been returned when her hand slipped and the screwdriver chipped off a tiny piece of a large prism. The minute crack shattered the image into shapeless fragments. This was back when she was still paying off Dad's debts and desperately needed every crown. Gran was also in a bad way, lying in her room all day after the chemotherapy and refusing to let anyone in. Mum didn't know how to help her and, on top of that, she soon found herself having to cover the whole of the rent. "Hey, if something can go to shit, it will," Karolína joked as she lent her money. To make ends meet, she took on evening and weekend shifts behind the till at Hypernova.

"And, back then, everything really did go to shit," she says when something reminds her of it. "I didn't have two pennies to rub together," she says, automatically rubbing her thumb and forefinger together. "If I brought a banana back, I carried it home like it was a holy relic. A stupid bloody banana, can you believe it? And then I would watch you eating it and try not to be envious. And if you didn't finish it and there was a bit left over, that was like Christmas come early. Even my underwear was falling to bits. Your nursery school cost a fortune – it was just a nightmare, all those trips and everything. No amount of overtime could make up for that."

The people from the workshop used to go to Hypernova just to look at Mum. They'd point at her in her washed-out uniform and deliberately ask for things she'd have to leave the cash register to fetch, while the queue got longer and longer. Even now, after all these years, they still make fun of Mum – that's why she thinks there's something wrong with her and why she continually doubts herself. She and Marta, an older woman close to retirement age, were the only two women in the clean cell. The rest of the twelve-member team in the workshop were men. She could recite their comments by heart. *Not like that. Give it here.* The voices in her head can easily grow louder, sometimes frightening her. *Are you so incompetent you can't even put your make-up on in the morning and get here on time? Do you need help? You aren't cut out for this.*

Maybe she's wasted half her life in the factory, she thinks. Maybe they're right. She often lacks confidence and becomes unsure about what she's doing. At school, they taught her the same mechanical tasks. She knew how to set up various systems accurately and quickly, and she could probably still turn her own material on the lathe. For a while, she machined the tubes for telescopes in the production hall, and the memory of the noise of the machines and the smell of metal gives her a headache. She'd like to understand everything, but sometimes it's all too much. She wonders if the others really know what they're doing or if they're just putting up a front. "For God's sake, woman, are you completely stupid?" says the foreman every time she messes something up or doesn't understand something. "But what did I expect? Give it here." He picks up the screwdriver, tightens the nut – "there, now take a look" – but he fails to get an acceptable deviation either.

She's used to the stares of the men in the workshop, their stupid banter. She's used to the fact that, to them, she'll never be more than a pair of inept hands, a badly programmed machine. No matter what she does.

She came to fully appreciate this not long ago, when someone from Olomouc University joined them in the workshop.

"I'm just here to keep an eye on you," he joked on the first day, "and sort out anything you're doing wrong." Mum was proud of her apprenticeship certificate – she'd had a better education than her parents. She listened to the man's lectures in stony silence, letting his comments about what she was doing wrong go in one ear and out the other. She remembers how he grabbed her hand so tightly that she flinched but couldn't pull away from him. Slowly, as if speaking to a child, he started explaining to her what each component did. Meanwhile, he never took his eyes off her, not even when they were in the lift. They were alone there, and the man stepped towards her and put his arm around her waist. "We've got a lot of work ahead of us," he said, stroking her back and then moving his hand down lower. "But don't worry, we'll manage it together." She was afraid to move and froze completely. Before she could utter a word, the lift doors opened and some other people got in.

She lifts her eyes towards the flickering fluorescent light. *A week ahead of schedule.* The thought flashes through her mind: *I managed it a week ahead of schedule.*

She couldn't take a step without someone lecturing her on how to do things better, which sealant to use, how to clean lenses. As soon as the man from the university had left – she checked several times to make sure he was gone – she went back to doing things her way. It would have been difficult to prove it to him but, after all these years, she simply had a knack for some things. She knows that the best way to clean lenses is to pour alcohol instead of cleaning solution into the ultrasonic bath. She has to be very careful not to heat up the liquid too much and blow up the whole room, but the results are worth it. She also has a trick for measuring that the previous foreman passed on to her before he retired. He'd only revealed it to her: how the wheels of the cars driving along the main road make the building shake. She can't feel it herself, but the device senses the vibrations. That's why she comes in at night to do the final measurements, performs a series of tests and then hurries off home again.

At the end of her shift, Mum gets up from her chair, pulls off her overalls with relief, and the cloud that's been hanging over her head all day, threatening rain, suddenly dissipates. Although you can't say for certain, with hindsight you reckon it must have been a Friday. For you, summer always merged into one big blur, a stream with no end and no beginning. All you know is that Mum didn't have to go to work the next day and she invited Karolína over in the evening. Or, more likely, Karolína invited herself, as Mum would say, though there really wasn't much difference. Once in a while, a rotten mood would descend on her friend, and although Mum was the one Karolína vented her anger on when things got tough, Mum always stuck by her.

Daylight streams in through the small window in the kitchen area. She feels the warmth on her face, leans against the worktop and listens to the whistling of the kettle. Before she goes home, she has one last thing to do: when the cleaner comes in, she'll explain to her how to tidy around the finished piece. The afternoon shift is about to arrive, and Mum is in luck. Today it's the turn of the younger of the two women she regularly sees at the workshop. The older one can't speak Czech, so it's extremely difficult for my mother to explain what she wants her to do. Instead of words, she uses body language – she stretches out her arms and contorts her face, feeling ridiculous and, even then, she finds it hard to perceive the other woman as a human being. Instead, she feels as if she is speaking to a zoo animal through thick glass.

There's a wall separating them, and your mother imagines that, instead of specific words, she's just moving her mouth and making sounds that are incomprehensible to the other woman. The words are suddenly hollow and meaningless. Her language has ceased to be an instrument and becomes a memory.

She's not the only one who has problems with the older woman. There was a time when the most exotic language you'd hear in the factory was Slovak. But, for a number of years now, the cleaners, and also a sizeable proportion of the new labourers, had been recruited for the company by an agency. Rumour had it that, on top of their wages, the foreigners also got flats on the edge of town that they didn't have to pay for. What's more, she'd heard from the girls in quality control that they got a wage rise every year. She tried not to listen to any of the gossip, didn't want to believe it but, from time to time, doubt gnawed at her.

Then, quite recently, she overheard someone shouting in the kitchen area.

"I've got no bloody idea why they let you in here. You're useless."

She never got involved in these kinds of arguments, preferring to maintain a safe distance.

"Can you tell me what the fuck you're doing here?"

She actually felt sorry for the old woman. In the morning, she'd seen her leaning on her mop, exhausted and unable to catch her breath. Perhaps that was why the other cleaner would occasionally work two shifts in a row.

At least she can communicate with *her* without shouting or over-the-top gestures. A grimy flat face peeks out at your mother from the blue agency overalls. One time, Mum bumped into her in the kitchen just as she was sticking packets of dust-free cloths in her pockets. She winked conspiratorially at Mum and reached out her hand to give her a packet.

This time too, she nods at her, smiles, and Mum knows she will do everything she tells her.

It's a relief to leave the workshop. The air is thick outside – a wall of light, sound and the smells of summer, which allows Mum to think of nothing else. She feels like spreading out her arms and absorbing the heat and light all at once. She's done what she had to do and now she can look forward to time off, spread out over days when she doesn't have to do anything. The afternoon sunshine warms her bones, and the icy chill of the air-conditioning slowly leaves them. She breathes deeply and feels happy for the first time in ages.

This feeling lasts until the precise second that she opens the door and steps into the empty flat.

She tries calling out once. Then a second time, louder. She peeks into the bedroom only to find an unmade bed and the window wide open. She goes back to the hall, sits down on the shoe cabinet, and clumsily tries to take off her shoes while looking up your number with her free hand.

She doesn't know that by then you're far outside town and the sound of the phone ringing is muffled by the pannier bag on your bike. You don't notice a thing. You'll get three calls that day – one from Grandad, and then Mum will try again later in the evening.

You remember each of the missed calls because of the guilty feeling they left you with, the fear you felt from every vibration after that. Sometimes you wish you'd listened to her and not left the flat that morning as soon as you woke up.

She gets up from the shoe cabinet and walks down the hall. At this time of day, only a faint light comes in through the glass panel in the door. She searches in vain for the same feeling she had outside. But centuries have elapsed since then – at least that's how she feels, a storm raging inside your mother in this cold place without light. She would like to break something and scatter the shards across the empty flat; perhaps they would at least reflect some of the light onto her.

She drifts through the flat like a ghost, rearranging piles of laundry with trembling hands. "A good housewife never does the laundry at the weekend," was what Mum's gran used to say, and those words stuck with her, lodged deep in her subconscious. She couldn't help it. Every Friday, she had her work cut out making sure the laundry was folded and ready for the next week.

She clears away the dirty breakfast dishes from the kitchen table, opens the window and gathers in the towels from the washing line.

Did she have any idea who you were hanging out with every day? She would've had to be blind not to notice something, and last night's argument was further proof – she hadn't slept the night before either.

"What is it that's bothering you so much?" said Gran, asking her the very question you wanted to ask. "When you used to bring that Martin back here, you were always going on about how the child wasn't normal. *It's not normal* to just sit at home all the time." Mum lowered her eyes at the mention of Martin. After the break-up, she spent ages trying not to fall to pieces, trying to sweep that final image of him under the carpet. That was because her last memory was of him at the door, drunk again and talking – no, bawling. On the other side of the hall, she remembered raising her hands to cover her face. Through the gaps between her fingers, she saw for the first time how much Martin resembled Grandad.

"What kind of a man is he going to grow up to be?" he kept saying to Mum until she believed him.

"At his age, I hardly ever slept at home. Me and the guys were always off somewhere."

*What is it that's bothering you so much?* This time, she asks Gran's question herself, without even realizing there was more than one answer.

You don't know that Mum has seen the two of you. About a week earlier, she'd promised to help Gran in the allotment. On the way there, she made a quick stop at the Lagoon just to straighten up the stuff on her bike – since she crossed the footbridge, one of the bags had started to spill out of the basket. She swung her left leg over the frame and was about to get back on when a familiar figure flashed past.

She recognized your face in that blur of colour. You turned round. She thought you were waving at her until another movement ruffled her hair. You hadn't seen her at all. She lowered her hand and tried to hide her embarrassment. Later, she spotted you again on the way back from Grandad's and followed you at a distance till you arrived at the flats beside the embankment. There, you and Marián got off your bikes and he opened the door to let you in.

She probably wouldn't have admitted it to herself, but she wasn't that bothered about you hanging about the streets. If it had been anyone else, she might have worried about where it would lead. Her brother had had a child when he was just sixteen. Like you, he used to hang out with his friends in the evenings until, suddenly, one day, he was standing in Gran's kitchen. He'd got the whole family together and Mum was sitting in the room when he announced the news, watching as Grandad punched him and tried to throw him out of a flat he wasn't even living in. He and Gran shouted at each other for ages but, in the end, they both agreed that *the child definitely wasn't his, their little Jakub would never do that, and who knew who that slut had been hanging about with.* Your uncle and your aunt Kristýna moved out of town and, over time, he grew up to be a younger version of Grandad, as though the family trauma had come full circle for him.

In truth, Mum was more worried about Marián. She'd got a good look at him just before the front door closed. When he'd been transferred from another school, most of the parents had been up in arms. Even Mum didn't understand why Marián's parents didn't send him to a special school – somewhere they didn't have to pretend the boy was normal – but she kept quiet.

She knows troublemakers like that all too well. She can see it in their eyes. They run about town and, instead of making an effort at school, they harass decent folk. "I know fine well what they grow up to be," she fumed later on, sitting on Gran's couch. "Nothing good will come of it, you'll see." It didn't occur to her that she was just building a wall of prejudices and distorted memories around herself. She circles around the perimeter, and any time she peeks out, the world is altered through her memories, becoming exactly what she wants it to be. She remembers one of them who used to be in her class. This girl sat alone at the back of the room, saying nothing all day long, and refused to speak to anyone who didn't look like her. Mum laughed at her along with the others. She laughed at her because she couldn't read and had no exercise books and had turned up on the first day with a battered old satchel while all the other kids had brand-new stuff for school. All the kids apart from Mum.

No-one was really surprised when the girl eventually went crazy. After all, they had been driving her to it. One day, she returned to the class after the break and Karolína shouted an insult at her from her desk and that boy – she can no longer remember his name, just his messy black hair – raced towards her at the same time. He leapt forward just as she was sitting down and smacked the girl on the bottom.

Mum can clearly recall the moment when a muscle in the girl's face twitched. She can still see her launching herself across the desk and digging her nails into the boy's face.

After that, she never saw her again. What stayed with Mum were the screams and the blood and the ripped-out hair. Mum couldn't understand what had bothered her so much. After all, Karolína made fun of everyone, Mum included. And the boys, she told herself – well, boys were just like that. *I had to put up with it.* You just had to grit your teeth, hold your breath and stay strong.

Gran had warned her.

Each time they passed the train station, she kept her close. There were whole groups of people like that girl hanging around there. Her double pointed at Mum and shouted something.

"Keep a hold of your things or they'll rob you as well." She tried not to look round, took the stairs in threes. "Just stay close to me or they'll snatch you away to one of their hovels. And you don't want to know what a Gypsy would do to you."

From then on, Mum never liked walking past the station alone.

"None of them work, you can be sure of that!" Gran said angrily, dragging Mum across the concourse to the farthest corner of the platform. "No, no, it's us decent folk who have to work our fingers to the bone. I'd like to laze around too, but someone has to put food on the table."

She listened to Gran with a tense expression, looking suspiciously at the children, who weren't much younger than her. Some of them were throwing a ball around in front of the station. She and Gran walked past them. Mum thought they were calling out to her, but she couldn't understand them from that distance. She turned her head towards them.

"If you ever bring one of them home, I'll throttle you."

She admired Gran. They'd never try anything while she was by her side. The most they could do was shout and beg for cigarettes. Meanwhile, more and more of them were working in the factory. Not actually in the workshop but, lately, the people in the production hall were getting angry whenever someone new joined them.

"How am I supposed to work with that lot?" she heard the man standing in front of her in the lunch queue say. "She just babbles away and hasn't got a clue what she's doing."

The woman beside him perked up and gave the man an amused look.

"Come on, Ríša." Ríša twitched and stepped forward. "They're not as bad as all that. They're fast learners and, at least, they want to work, unlike the rest of their kind."

Mum knew the two of them by sight. When she worked in the same building, she used to sit beside the woman during breaks in the smokers' area, listening to her constant complaints.

Ríša scratched his chin, said nothing for a moment, then put his hand on the woman's shoulder.

"I just think some people are just born layabouts and stay that way forever."

Back in the kitchen, Mum feels like throwing something, taking the dirty mug out of the sink and seeing the broken pieces and the washing-up liquid dripping down the plaster. The thought makes her even angrier. She wonders if you and Marián are on something. She's seen that gang of boys hanging around the garages. Loitering there all day, crawling through the bushes at the entrance to the fallout shelter, smelling of solvents and booze.

She grips the edge of the worktop and digs her nails into it. She is eventually comforted by the thought that she'd have noticed something like that. She grabs her mobile and texts with wet fingers: *Fine then. We'll talk in the evening.*

You had no idea she'd been secretly reading the messages on your phone ever since the parents' evening in the spring. Until recently, though, she hadn't found anything in them. Every night, she'd wait until she was sure you were asleep. Then she'd creep out of bed and, to make sure she didn't trip up, quietly open the blinds, letting in the golden strips from the streetlamp, which formed a xylophone of light on the desk. She tiptoed over to it and, after yesterday's argument, she finally discovered what she had been expecting. She almost knocked the pile of books off your desk. They were lying everywhere, and she randomly picked one up and quickly leafed through it. Her bulging reflection blinked at her from the head of the metal lamp. She gave a start, and as she did so, a folded piece of paper fell out of the book. She unfolded it to discover Marián's drawing.

She immediately recognized it since she used to walk past the mosaic at your school every day as well, and she'd also see it whenever she was at a parents' meeting. Even in the dim light, she could picture the red sofa and the arm-chairs, the plants beside the stairwell.

But Marián's version was different. In it, the two fig-ures were closer to each other and their hands were touch-ing. Perhaps the darkness was playing tricks on her, but she could have sworn their fingers were intertwined.

In the half-light, she couldn't take her eyes off the piece of paper. She was aware it contained something impor-tant, something that was eluding her once again. It wasn't your work – she realized that at once. She had kept all your attempts at drawing in a box in the basement. Apart from the camel, she was particularly proud of a crooked figure drawn with a shaky hand – it was supposed to be her – with horns on its head instead of a bun.

She put the drawing back, thought for a moment, then grabbed your phone. She couldn't have understood the last message from Marián, but you reckon it was that night that she began to suspect the truth. She put the phone back on the table, went to bed and stared long and hard at the ceiling. As the darkness receded, she could make out the cracks in the plaster.

She never spoke to you about this, never said a word. It's only much later that you find out the truth. By then, you'll be at high school and you'll come home after a few days away, reeking of alcohol and smoke. During the ensuing argument, when she almost throws you out of the house – more as a form of revenge rather than out of desperation – you confess to your mum that you're gay.

She'll be silent, standing there for a long time and looking past you. But before she leaves, she'll turn round one last time, her eyes revealing nothing. She'll blink and eventually whisper: "I know."

When the doorbell rings, Mum is already sitting in the stiflingly hot room, grasping at any thought that is unconnected to you.

The late summer afternoon means that the blinds are closed throughout the flat, with the curtains half-drawn across them for good measure. Only a thin ribbon of light enters the room, aimed precisely at the glass panel in the door opposite. The reflection from the frosted glass spreads across the walls. White, blue and yellow spots. Whenever someone stamps about in the flat above, the spots dance as the old wall panels send vibrations all the way to the building's foundations. Laughter can be heard from the corridor. She frowns and moves her head to the cool part of the wall.

She's not in the mood to see Karolína and would prefer a few hours' peace and quiet after your argument and the problems with Grandad. She considers not opening the door, pretending not to have heard the bell.

The piercing sound stops and only its echo hangs in the air. Then it starts again.

"Is your doorbell broken or what?" asks Karolína reproachfully before Mum has even closed the door behind her. She throws her bag down on the shoe cabinet and then takes off her trainers without bothering to bend down.

Mum quickly gathers up the piles of clean laundry and hides them in Gran's room. In the kitchen, she takes out a bowl and fills it with nuts. She barely has time to put it on the table when she senses movement behind her.

Karolína's swinging a two-litre plastic bottle back and forth. She's always doing this to Mum. She knows Mum doesn't like to drink, and yet she forces her every time. *Have a drop at least* – she gets this all the time from Karolína, from the people at work... Even Martin was constantly making fun of her and trying to pour her another full glass. *You're not on the wagon, are you?*

"Where are Naděna and that boy of yours?" asks Karolína impatiently as soon as she's sat down at the table. She looks around the kitchen as though Mum could have

229

hidden her mother and son in the corner and they might jump out at Karolína any minute.

"Don't tell me it's just the two of us today?!"

Mum shrugs and takes down two of Gran's crystal wine glasses from the shelf above the sink. She places them in front of Karolína and slumps down on the bench across from her.

"Gran's in the allotment again and she'll probably stay the night there too," she explains. "She keeps banging on about starlings and how they're eating her bushes or something. And Marek..." She pauses. Karolína's rummaging in her bag for something. She brought the thing into the kitchen with her and now it's taking up half the bench. "Where did I..." she mutters, but then she sits up victoriously, holding a packet of cigarettes like a trump card. "Sorry, but if Naděna isn't here, we just have to."

Mum gets up and, from the same shelf as before, takes down a scratched tin mug Dad left behind. Gran hates anyone smoking in the flat, and she's made a scene about it more than once before. The last time, it was with Karolína. She'd come over to console Mum on the day she broke up with Martin. And although she did her best to block the gap in the door with a rag, Gran returned from the allotment around nine and almost broke the door as she burst into the kitchen.

You remember only too well what Gran did the next day. You got up slightly earlier in the morning to discover a huge piece of paper attached to your door with a note written in capital letters traced over several times. HOW MANY TIMES DO I HAVE TO I TELL YOU? NO FUCKING SMOKING! IN THE KITCHEN! You crumpled up the paper so Mum wouldn't find it. "I hate it," Gran explained to you later that day. "I hated it with your da'. The booze is one thing, but why should the kids have to breathe that stuff in too?"

"Hey, Dana..." The smoke traps Karolína's words in her throat. She coughs, bangs her chest with her fist, and starts again: "Do you never think about getting a place of your own?"

That moment when her voice breaks gives Mum a chance to think. The question doesn't surprise her as it's not the first time she's heard it. With half-closed eyes, Karolína takes another drag on her cigarette, tilts her head back and waits for Mum's reaction. Meanwhile, she blows the smoke out above her head and tosses her long red hair against the wall, hearing it rustle against the plaster. Mum reaches for the packet lying on the table and lights up too.

It's easier this way, she replies to Karolína. But you both know she has her dreams – and a folder with photos cut out of magazines, photos of rooms and houses and gardens. She'd look through them over and over again whenever she was alone or, at least, thought she was, while you watched her from the corner of your room, observing how she turned the pages with a moistened finger, as though each page transported her to a different room where she could afford to live a different life.

The truth was that the flat on Dvořakova wasn't big enough for all three of you. You kept on tripping over each other in the hall. There was nowhere to hide. That was why Gran slept in the allotment shed so often. Even Mum wasn't sure how much longer she could cope with it.

"You'll have to do it someday anyway," Martin pressed her, suggesting to Mum for the first time that she move in with him. He was careful not to mention you. But what would really change? She'd be moving from one cramped shoebox to another, ever so slightly bigger one. On top of that, she had money worries. She couldn't rely on any coming from Dad, and she'd only once had the courage to ask for a pay rise at work. Although her salary went up, the fact that she could no longer claim benefits meant she had a lot less at the end of the next month than she'd had the one before.

"Anyway, I can't risk it right now," she says into the silence as Karolína studies the bottle with narrowed eyes. "It's not just me I'm supporting."

They both flick their ash into the mug at the same time.

"That's what bloody Pavel is there for." Karolína hisses his name through clenched teeth. "He should start giving a shit about what's going on with that boy of his."

Mum nods. But she can't rely on Dad. She can't even remember when he last called.

"But the thing is, he never just hands over money – there are always strings attached. The last time, he wanted me to send him over."

Karolína knows what Mum's talking about.

A shadow crosses her face.

There's one thing she's not told Karolína yet. Until that evening, she hadn't told anyone as she was ashamed to even say it out loud.

She is scared of living alone.

Without the presence of another grown-up in the flat, she's scared it could happen again. Just thinking about it is enough to make her feel as if another day is running in parallel to this one, as if she is playing an old video tape and can make out the shadows of the original recording in the grey areas in the background. This is the reason why she can't sleep with the window open, why she locks the door twice, goes to bed and then gets up and locks it again, just to be on the safe side. And it's Grandad, her dad, who is to blame for all of this. And she could forgive him anything except that one night shortly before your dad left you and you moved in with Gran.

Karolína stubs out her cigarette and dusts off her hands, as though she's just finished a difficult and tedious task. She grabs the bottle of wine, unscrews the top and carefully pours them half a glass each.

"Here," she says, handing Mum her glass. Meanwhile, she swirls hers ostentatiously, no doubt something she saw in a film. "And don't say you don't want any. You do."

Your mother cautiously sniffs the wine and takes a small sip.

She can feel Karolína's eyes on her. Her friend smacks her lips in appreciation and stretches out the arm with the glass. She examines its contents admiringly, then nods to Mum. She knows Karolína wants to get her drunk. She tries this on every time she visits, but today it doesn't bother Mum as much. Not today. There's no harm in it once in a while, though she always makes sure not to drink in front of you. Besides, Karolína's the only one who knows how to handle Mum – she pours one glass after another, makes sure she's smiling. Your mother turns up the corners of her mouth carefully so her rotten teeth aren't visible. The skin alongside her nose forms two parallel furrows. Karolína smacks her lips again and starts talking. She complains for a while, talking about things she has lost and about a new job. All that time wasted on people who don't appreciate her. At one point, one of them asks: "What kind of a life is that?" They both grin – nothing is the way they'd wanted it to be. And yet neither of them has the feeling anything had turned out so dramatically different.

In hindsight, none of the years stretching out behind her seem real to Mum. To her, time is a reflection. She looks back and, like you, sees only numbers. You always pass them by without having time to notice what they really represent: A series of events, memories, glimpses of something real. What are they pointing to? To this current? To a river whose course you can't influence? You wonder when it happened. When did these days become mere memories stacked on top of one another, slotted together into fragmented stories which you can only recount? When did you both pass the point when life turns back on itself and everything new disappears beyond the last bend? All you can capture now is a smudge in a mirror.

She's sitting with her legs up on the bench, curled into a ball, her head resting on her knees. She reaches out and takes another cigarette from Karolína. Both women sip silently from their glasses.

Karolína is the first to break the silence.

"So I sent Dominik to the Vietnamese shop for bread and he said he saw Marek with some Gypsy. A weird kid, apparently. Has he started giving you trouble too?

She reaches for her glass, a malicious expression on her face.

"Aren't you worried about how he'll turn out if he's hanging around with people like that?"

Your mother doesn't say anything. She's looking at her reflection on the surface of the glass, so she doesn't see Karolína knocking back the rest of her wine and immediately pouring herself another.

"His dad's to blame," she adds decisively, checking to make sure Mum's glass is full. "He should be here. That's why you're having problems with him now. I'm always saying that – when was the last time any guy was worth a shit? All they care about is how they look. Like this guy I was just out on a date with. You might know him. He works over in the production hall."

She describes a tall man with dark hair, but there are lots of men who fit that description in the factory.

"He's only been living in the building for a few months. I was always bumping into him at the entrance and then I was taking the dog out and he comes after me and starts patting the dog. So he offered me a cigarette, we chat, and he says we should go for a glass of wine. He seemed like quite a nice guy and I said OK. He invited me to that wine bar on Žerotín square. I don't know though. I didn't have a good feeling about it, so I had to get drunk really quickly. I'm downing one glass after another while he's going on about his kids, his divorce, how his wife is deliberately causing trouble for him, how she wants to keep the youngest one to herself, how he has to send them money and that bitch is definitely just spending it on clothes. Can you tell me why I didn't just walk out, idiot that I am?

Mum finishes her cigarette and reaches for the packet. She holds the wine as far away from herself as possible – she can feel it slowly starting to make her head spin. She struggles with the lighter, her finger slips, then again, and once she's finally managed to light the cigarette, she pushes the packet towards Karolína.

"In the end, I stuck it out till closing time. He grabbed my hand and took me up to the town walls. I must have been a bit out of it. I dunno, it was all right. He seemed different to me. He didn't speak as much. He just held me around the waist, occasionally saying something about how his dad helped to build this or that house or façade. Fine, but what the hell's that got to do with me? He was really proud of it and I didn't want to spoil his fun. I didn't feel like going home, so we went to a bar for a dance and I guess I kissed him. Or he kissed me; it doesn't matter. I don't even know how I got home. I just remember him lying there next to me, groping me, and me telling him no, for God's sake, not now, the boys were sleeping next door, and to get off me; otherwise, they'd hear. Of course, I wanted to scream, but what good would that've done?" She looks through Mum to somewhere she can't see.

"And do you know the worst of it?" She lowers her head, tucks a loose strand of hair behind her ear and stares at the table. "He was so out of it he kept repeating her stupid name."

Mum swallows, the cigarette hanging from her lower lip. She opens her mouth and some smoke gets in her eyes. She tries to drive out the sharp pain with her knuckle, rubbing her eyelid until it starts to water. Karolína misinterprets her reaction.

"It's all right though. It's not that big a deal."

She sits up and waves a hand dismissively. She starts to pour wine out of the half-empty bottle for both of them, pausing by Mum's glass. She sees it's full, hesitates, then fills it to the brim.

"Why aren't you drinking?"

Mum sighs and rolls her eyes.

"It fucking annoys me that I always have to force you."

The last glimmers of orange light stream into the kitchen. Droplets of condensation form on the rim of the glass and Mum watches them slide down it. She looks up at Karolína and offers her a weak smile.

"They're all such sensitive souls now, you know? There was a time when a man was a real man." She nods without even knowing what Karolína was on about. "They don't have to stink like a Gypo. But these days they're more perfumed than a florist's. Men are no longer what they used to be. They should at least bloody well not cry to me about their wife leaving them. Why can't things be the way they were? Why can't people stay together till they die?"

Hearing these words, Mum digs her nails into the edge of the tablecloth. Several questions come to her at once. She gets up, goes over to the sink and pours a glass of water. The sudden movement makes her head spin. She has to lean against the wall, where she can hear her heart pounding against her chest. She sits back down on the bench, and the blood that's pumping from the centre of her body rushes to her head, stifling any thoughts. She tries to focus on a new fixed point, so she looks back.

*Why can't people stay together till they die?*

She mulls over Karolína's question but can't find an answer. She checks the time on the clock on the fridge. Nearly nine o'clock. The evening world outside casts a gloom over the rows of clothes lines. She could watch their movement without having to budge. She closes her eyes and lets the sparks of colour wander across the inside of her eyelids. Then she opens them, blinks and watches as the same shapes project a completely different image on the wall opposite.

Once again, Mum sees the house Grandad grew up in. It was in Blažovice, a village just outside of Brno. She sees the narrow, pointed roof and large windows, and the pink façade. When she was young, she used to go to her aunt and uncle's every year in the summer holidays. Gran would put her on the train, grateful to be rid of her for at least a while, and then wave tenaciously until Mum disappeared from view.

There was a long, narrow vineyard that came with the house. Uncle Jožka had been restoring it for years so that it would look exactly as her aunt remembered it from back in her father's day, before he was finally broken by the regime and burned down the entire vineyard out of fear. So Jožka had to start from scratch on the same ground. He built a wine cellar below the house, though Mum was scared to go down there as a child because the steps lined with porcelain figurines seemed endless. Your own memories of the house consist only of the smell of musty wood and a mixture of dust and food from the kitchen. You'd both turned your noses up at the stink, but now Mum would give anything to see the place again, to watch her aunt letting fresh air into the kitchen and observe the curtains lazily billowing back and forth.

Later, when you were older and had learned how to listen properly, Mum told you that all she'd ever wanted from life, all she'd ever longed for, was what those two had. What she thought they had.

"When we used to take you to visit my aunt, she would make a different meal for each of us," she said, talking about someone you can no longer remember. "She would even pop out from work to do it. It's true the station was really close and she'd just throw on a hat and jump on a train, but still. She was capable of baking three cakes within a couple of hours. She spent the whole day in the kitchen. Us kids would sit on the bench and watch her darting about from the stove to the sink and back again, talking to us and laughing all the while."

But she could only see these perfect images from the outside. She dreamt up their life, pieced it together from fragments and, from a distance, they seemed to make up a complete whole; but, in reality, her gaze described an arc around them, refracting the light so that Mum only saw what she wanted to see. You just needed to step a little closer and the image fell apart, revealing the shards of Mum's memory. It was only later that she learned from her uncle Jožka that they couldn't have children, that his wife Marcela had miscarried and spent most of her free time at the church after that. However, your mum can recall the day she had her first kiss in Blažovice much more clearly than those two combined. She still remembers the boy's name. She's standing with Petr in the middle of an old shooting range, so surprised that she forgets to close her eyes. Later, they're walking down the street past the church and hear her aunt behind them. Mum's still holding his hand, and even though she lets go of him, her aunt frowns at them both and walks on.

But Marcela told Grandad about it, and when Mum returned home, happy and suntanned, she entered the kitchen to be met by a slap instead of a greeting from Grandad.

"What the hell kind of family are you?" laughs Karolína. "So much shit all at once."

You occasionally ask yourself the same question. But Mum's not talking in order to be heard or to prove something. She wants to get it out of her system, to escape from the feeling she made a mistake somewhere.

With the passing years, she discovers the same thing you keep coming up against. While she can remember Petr's face quite clearly, the faces of her aunt and uncle are hidden behind a veil. She remembers everything except their faces. She vainly searches for them in her memory, and when she finally thinks she has them, they slip through her fingers.

"You know, Tonda – your dad – well, he and Marcela didn't have it easy either," said Jožka when they saw each other for the last time several years ago. This was the first she'd heard about the things he was telling her. Sitting in the armchair in your room, her uncle looked frail. His back was stooped and he fidgeted with the hem of his shirt. "Their dad lost everything apart from the house. He even set fire to the vineyard to stop *them* getting it. They would probably have lost the house too if half the village hadn't stood up for them. It got to him, though. A man like that had to make his presence felt in the village, not grovelling in front of people. It probably won't mean anything to you, but he started drinking heavily and taking it out on the children. Marcela told me how he beat her black and blue. But Tonda got the worst of it, cos his dad thought it was all his fault. The Communists had arrived the same year Tonda was born, so somehow he'd brought it all on and it was up to him to make things right."

This was news to Mum, who had only known Great-Grandad as a kind and good man and had never heard her own dad share a single story or memory from his childhood, aside from his lectures about excellent marks.

"So your dad had a hard time of it. He wasn't even allowed to play football with the boys. The only time he was let out was to fetch beer and cigarettes for him," continued Jožka. "Then those bastards wouldn't even let him go to school, sent him straight off to the chemical plant. And Kralupy was far away from our place and Tonda started slowly drinking himself to death there. He'd always been different – he read a fair bit and they didn't care for that there. They'd say Tonda was lording it over them all. I think that's where it all started. Marcela's mum had to go and get him. I can see him now, white as a sheet, with weird marks on his skin almost down to the flesh. When Marcela asked him what was going on there, he shouted at her about how they shovelled sulphur, just like that, with nothing to protect them, how when it rained on the way to his digs, the acid rain would eat away a hole in his jacket. That's probably why he started smoking so much as well. He must've had the feeling it helped him breathe, thought it was better to breathe in smoke than the air there."

"Even *you* must remember how badly Tonda took it when my Marcela died." She'll never forget the day Jožka came to visit them after Marcela died. She was living alone with Grandad by then. She opened the door, and her uncle threw his arms around her. It was the first time she'd seen a grown man cry. He was shaking all over and it took all her strength to lead him to the kitchen and sit him down.

"If your sister died – well, I know you don't get on. Tonda wasn't exactly a saint either, but I reckon that was what helped him the most to quit drinking."

But how is it possible you both remember everything apart from their faces?

She snaps out of her thoughts. Karolína is just putting down her mobile, and Mum knows she hasn't been listening to her. Neither of them says anything, waiting to see who'll be first to speak.

After several minutes, Karolína breaks the silence, indirectly confirming Mum's suspicions.

"That's all well and good, I know."

She hadn't heard a word Mum said.

"You already told me. But what Jožka and Marcela had, it doesn't just grow on trees. It takes work. And the way guys look today, I doubt anything like that would ever happen to us. Today, it's all me, me, me. No-one thinks about other people."

With those words, Karolína gets up and goes to the loo. Mum thinks about Grandad and you, about the drawing placed inside the book in your room. Karolína flushes the toilet, which is right next to the kitchen and, even over the noise from the street, she can hear the water rumbling through the pipes, making the walls shake and Mum's head throb. Karolína slumps heavily onto the bench, puts her finger to her mouth and mutters something. She remains like that for a moment and then launches in again.

"Anyway, it's awful. You just have to see Dominik putting gel in his hair. He styles that bird's nest of his and I have to fetch him all the crap he needs so badly. I'm telling you, *I* don't even slap that much stuff on myself. Half an hour – no, seriously, it takes him half an hour to get out of the bathroom. I think to myself, if only he was a poofter, it'd make sense. Not that I'd put up with that or anything. I've always said to the boys: I don't care who you bring home, as long as it's not some guy or, God forbid, a Gypo. But for Christ's sake, he's got all of these girls hanging around him and he never leaves the house. He's not interested in anything."

As it gets darker, it becomes impossible to distinguish between what Karolína's saying and what Mum's talking about. They both feel their words make up a shared melody, the tone of something different and something they have in common. They're comforted by the fact they have something to complain about.

*Men are no longer what they used to be*, repeats Karolína, and Mum thinks for a moment about what they did actually use to be. The things that Pavel, Martin and the other men in her life got up to seemed more like a swan song than anything else. Their anger was insecurity, a longing for lost certainties. The world as they knew it had ceased to exist and, suddenly, they saw people in it who were different from them. "They say a woman couldn't handle it," exclaims Karolína, waving her arms around furiously. "I don't want to sound like a feminist, right? I don't need some ditz in a skirt running the country. She'd just lie like all the rest do anyway. But for fuck's sake, anything men can do, I can do too – even when I'm bleeding at the same time."

At this point, Karolína stops talking and thinks for a moment. She looks at Mum seriously again before saying, "Isn't it weird? Marek grew up without his dad and you can see straight away he's different. Don't take this the wrong way, but he's a bit girly. Sensitive. Don't you think?"

In the silence that followed, you could hear the beating of Mum's heart. The air's becoming thick in the kitchen and she's not sure if it's from the cigarette smoke or the conversation Karolína's dragged her into in her drunken state. All it takes is one drink too many and it always ends up the same – she's nasty to Mum or tries to hurt her. Sometimes, their friendship seems more like a competition, where the other woman tries at all cost to demonstrate that she's better off.

"I know, I know, but my boys say the same thing. Don't take it personally. It's just that the lad doesn't have a male role model. No firm hand."

If Karolína had known what a firm hand Mum ruled with, she probably wouldn't have brought it up. Gran was a strong woman as well. She stayed with Grandad for years for the sake of the children and, after the chemotherapy, she would go home in secret, trying to avoid Mum, and lock herself in her room. She didn't want anyone to see her in a weakened state because she'd been taught since childhood never to show weakness.

And yet most of the time, all you need to do is go and ask for help. Mum would like to say to Karolína that there's nothing weak or fragile about it.

"Not that you can't handle him," she says, trying to dig herself out of a hole, but she's really just repeating what she once said to you before in this room. "I don't mean it in a bad way. But it must be hard for him to act like a guy when he lives with two women. Don't you ever have the feeling he should have been born a girl? He's so highly strung. Maybe you should tell your dad – he might be able to whip him into shape."

She straightens up. There's a metallic taste in her mouth and she swallows tentatively.

"My dad? He's whipped us into shape quite enough as it is."

She can see double, as though the world in front of her were reflected through an optical prism and she were seeing everything from someone else's perspective – perhaps a figure reflected on the surface of the wine or in the windowpane. Karolína sits there motionless, quiet at long last. The other Dana grips the edge of the table. She hears her take a breath in, about to say something, but before she opens her mouth, she becomes her old self again.

"Well, maybe he is a little bit effeminate, but I'd much rather have a boy who behaves like a girl than have a selfish drunk at home."

Together with the smoke, the silence spreads through the kitchen from floor to ceiling. Outside, grey fabric covers the space from the clothes lines to the windows of the building opposite. In the closest one, Mum spots a silhouette that reminds her of Grandad, moving and bending the same way. She blinks, the light at the window goes out, and the figure disappears.

"I didn't mean it like that..." mutters Karolína, sitting up a bit. She didn't expect such a reaction from Mum and suddenly feels small in the corner by the wall.

Later, Mum will swear to you – she'll take hold of your hand, and neither of you will be able to remember the last time she'd done so – that when the light across the street went out, she knew exactly what was coming next. She saw Karolína open her mouth, a trickle of foamy saliva in the corner, and she'd heard her words before too. She was able to pinpoint in advance the exact time her phone would spring to life. She had described the movement with her hand and fleetingly traced its axis a few seconds earlier. She knows she'll read Grandad's name on the screen before she turns the phone over, before she hangs up and puts the device back. And yet nothing's happened yet.

It will happen, and Mum will look around the room in confusion, burying her face in her hands.

"I can't do this any more."

She looks at Karolína through the gaps between her fingers, while time slips back to its well-established course and your mother speaks, in a whisper this time.

"I can't just play carer forever."

Her voice betrays her mid-sentence. Karolína extends a hand towards her, but when Mum shakes her head and continues to rub her temples, she quickly pulls it back again.

"You say he'd whip Marek into shape, but you've never lived with him. You weren't there when he had his episodes. He was always bloody careful not to drink and to behave himself before a visit. And I fell for it and believed things were going to get better. I'm also the only one stupid enough to fuss over him. If only he'd admit he needs help or, at least, thank me, but no – he's too proud for that and it annoys him if a woman tells him what to do. I just get on his nerves."

The darkness outside is advancing towards them, growing more dense and carrying with it shouts from the nearby street.

"I'll never forget it. I'll never get it out of my mind. I still can see that evening. Pavel and the rest of us were all living with him at U Tenisu. You know where that is, not far from your place. Pavel was at work that evening and I was stuck in on my own with Marek, who was still a baby at the time. I was getting ready for bed when Dad came home. From the commotion in the corridor, I could tell he was pissed. He was bumping into everything and bawling his head off."

She exhales, pauses briefly, then grabs the packet of cigarettes. She doesn't even ask Karolína. She just takes one and lights up.

"Except he wasn't alone," she continues, sweeping the ash the draught has blown onto the table into her hand. "He was trying to get in but couldn't. I said to myself, don't be stupid, Dana, don't let him in, but then he started kicking the door in. I had to open it or someone might have phoned the police. So picture this: you open the door and your dad's brought home some stinking lowlife with him. It must have been someone who'd bought shots for him in that dive of a pub and then Dad felt he owed him. I quickly shut myself in the room again, hoping he'd calm down and the guy would leave soon. But then little Marek started getting hungry, so I had to go into the kitchen."

She absent-mindedly runs her hand over the tablecloth, smoothing out a crease at the edge of the table, and feels her phone vibrating again. She looks away, back to that evening. She sees everything playing out in front of her all too clearly. It looks as if a bomb's gone off in the kitchen. Overturned chairs, the tablecloth pulled off the table and her father... her father's lying in a corner, holding his head and mumbling incomprehensibly. The room is filled with the stench of sweat and alcohol. It takes her a moment to notice the other man, who can't be much older than her. He's sitting on the worktop, fair hair falling into his eyes, smoking and laughing at the scene in front of him. They look at each other. Mum doesn't want to turn her back to him, but she can't think of anything better to do. As she turns, the man jumps down and grabs her from behind.

It would be ridiculous to say that it all happened quickly. She's gone over this memory so many times, prolonging every movement, and it was precisely this scene, this memory, that frightened her so much.

She doesn't know where she found the courage, but she turned round and, with one assured movement, rammed her elbow into his ribs. He hadn't been expecting any resistance, and before he knew what was going on, Mum was running out of the kitchen. But she hadn't got far when he caught up with her by the door to the hall, pulled her towards him and threw her to the floor. She tried to wriggle free. She could hear you making noises in the room at the end of the hall. You were too far away for the sounds to scare you, but too close for Mum not to be scared.

"He was too strong for me." She emerges from her memory back into the kitchen, far away from that man, to find Karolína staring directly at her. Her voice isn't shaky, it's still steady. "Down on the floor, I thought to myself: this is the end, Dana. Just don't move and stay calm. He was grabbing at me and I wanted to scream, but I'd forgotten how."

251

"And what about your dad?" Karolína asked, shaking her head in disbelief. At first, she has her arms folded across her chest, then in her lap – she doesn't know what to do with them. "Was he so far gone he didn't even know what was happening?"

"Well, that was the last straw. He started laughing and clapping like some daft kid. I don't even want to remember it, you know. I'd like to forget, but it always manages to float to the surface somehow. If Pavel hadn't come home then, I don't know what would have happened. The guy had me pinned down and was groping me, and I thought it would never end, but then Pavel came tearing in and started laying into him. I couldn't understand how Pavel had got there. He pulled him off me and I think he'd have killed him there and then, he was so furious. I reckon he thought I'd invited him over. But he managed to control himself. He threw him against the worktop, helped me up, and then we quickly packed our things and spent the next few nights at his parents' place. I never went back to Dad's after that."

The sound of voices from outside cuts through the air again. No doubt a group of people heading back from the pub. The sounds get louder, turning to chanting, but then gradually subside. They're so far away that neither woman shows the slightest interest.

The initial fury subsides inside your mother too, until only one feeling, one last memory remains. It has been folded and bent back in time for so long that it no longer makes sense.

"I must have told you before about that time a stranger came into our room one night."

Karolína nods. She wants to say something, but Mum doesn't let her get a word in.

"Pavel was still here, thank God. We were staying in one of those huge tower blocks in Předmost, though we were on the first floor. That was when I still left the windows open in summer."

Even back then, she had problems sleeping.

It was long past midnight. Dad was breathing loudly beside her. She was counting anything that might help her fall asleep. She was concentrating and, at first, she didn't hear the strange scratching noise, the unfamiliar breathing coming from the street into the room. At times, the sounds interrupted the series of numbers she was going through. Mum heard something but thought nothing of it. Then the scratching stopped and nothing happened for what seemed like an eternity. Or perhaps something happened without Mum being aware of it, because when she glanced at the window again, she saw the figure of a man standing there. To begin with, only the head peeked out, followed by first one leg, then the other. She was sure it was a man because of the shoulders and his long limbs, the deep voice. He was staggering as he balanced in the window. The contrast between the darkness in the room and the light from the streetlamps prevented Mum from making out more than just a rough, crouching silhouette. He lowered one leg and stepped on Pavel's stomach. All of Mum's initial shock spilled over into sheer terror. What came next was a series of quiet movements. She silently, carefully reached over to Dad and pinched him, causing him to leap out of bed with a start – she'd never seen him move so fast. Half asleep, he lashed out. From luck rather than careful aim, his random movement knocked the man back into the street. Silence inside, and outside the dull thud of impact and the snapping of bushes beneath the window. The man swore, got to his feet with difficulty and picked up a handful of dirt and stones.

She heard the clatter and then saw the broken glass scattered across the bed. She carefully wrapped it up in the duvet while Pavel went to turn on the light. The whole time, you had been sleeping motionless in the corner of the room.

"But that's not all. I never told you what happened next. It doesn't end there, you see."

Karolína no longer has to feign interest. She leans forward slightly, her elbows resting on the table, her chin on her hands. "Wait," she says, tilting her head to one side as something occurs to her. You can almost hear the cogs in motion. "What's this got to do with that first drunkard?"

Mum nods slowly and solemnly. Her eyes are unfocused, covered with a dull filter as if she wasn't quite there.

Karolína focuses on her, scratches her chin, and then with her free hand reaches for the bottle and pours out the rest of the wine.

"It was the same guy. After what happened at Grandad's, he started following me and even found out where I worked. He'd wait there for me by the gate every day, knowing he wouldn't run into Pavel there. I don't really know why I didn't tell you about it. I guess I was a bit embarrassed. I started taking the long way home, trying to shake him off. I never went out in the dark apart from to smoke and, even then, I was scared shitless as I always imagined he was waiting for me in the bushes round the corner. I could feel those disgusting eyes of his leering at me. To make me feel a bit safer, even though I was probably just kidding myself, I started walking everywhere with my keys like this…" She places her keys between her fingers to make spikes in her clenched fist, which she swings in the air. "And so, one day, he must have been totally off his face and just climbed through our window." She picks up her empty glass and goes over to the counter. She pretends to be washing something for a moment, removes some things from the draining board and attempts to polish them with a dish cloth. "And do you know what the worst thing is? The idea that my dad had sent him there. When I figured it out, put two and two together, I thought I couldn't take it any more and I was going to kill him. He'd crossed the line – I mean, our baby was in there. It could have turned out so horrendously."

She puts the dish towel down and forces a smile. She looks at Karolína, wishing she could conjure up some tears so she could feel anything other than this emptiness in her chest.

"I'm not even sure when Grandad let it slip. He was probably plastered again and came out with the whole thing. He'd sent him to our place because things weren't working out between me and Pavel, you know? Because Pavel was weird. And so Dad told him I was...that I was available."

She forces the last words out quickly, almost incomprehensibly.

"My own dad, can you believe it? He ruined my whole childhood and now..." She lifts up her mobile, which is vibrating again, presses the screen and angrily takes the call. "Even now, he can't leave me in peace." She finishes the sentence before putting the phone to her ear.

Some background noise can be heard from the receiver, as if someone was furiously pacing around the room, shuffling their feet.

"Grandad?" she asks hesitantly, while Karolína gestures that she has to go to the loo again. She hasn't even closed the door behind her when Grandpa shouts down the phone so loudly he almost deafens Mum.

"They're here!"

His voice is trembling, unnaturally deep. There's something wrong with it. The disjointed words are dished out slowly, in rounds, with enforced pauses between them – shots aimed in your mother's direction. She only understands some of what he's saying. The rest is gibberish – he might as well have been talking to someone else.

"Listen, they've come for me..." The receiver crackles and Mum can only make out Grandad's breathing and furniture being bumped into. "Can you hear them too? They're everywhere. Those bastards even know where I live now. They know. They've found me. But I locked them in the bathroom, they won't get out of there. They're finished."

Mum makes use of the next pause to try to talk to Grandad. Her voice seems to have a calming effect on him. She wants him to breathe deeply and listen to her voice. *At least, the last time it helped*, she thinks as she tries to keep talking.

She's interrupted as Karolína appears in the doorway, giving Mum a quizzical look. Grandad's not waiting for anything. He's pacing around to kill time. He seems to stumble, then gets up.

"Fuck it, Dana, I'm not giving them a thing, I'm not leaving them a fucking thing, I can tell you that. I'd rather kill myself than let them touch anything."

Mum keeps the phone to her ear. She wants to say something but isn't capable of forming a sound. Each time she takes a breath in to speak, Grandad starts talking about something else. She exhales and Grandad's off again, as though he knows what she's about to say.

"This is all your fault. I clearly told you not to give anyone a key. How else did they get in here? All of you are always hanging around here, not giving me a minute's peace."

He's talking faster and faster, the words merging into a single stream, a current where language conveys no meaning, only another torrent of words. Mum's had enough of them. They all reach her through a veil. She feels like her head is about to burst, something sharp is piercing her temples.

"This is all pointless, but I know what I'll do."

Grandad's voice breaks through. She opens her mouth again, manages to take a breath. She still remembers his last words and understands them clearly and distinctly. Before she can exhale, before she can answer, Grandad hangs up – a series of clipped tones, after which she hears nothing.

She's still holding the phone to her ear, but her body's getting ready to move. She places her free hand on the table and then draws it back again. Creases appear on Karolína's forehead and she reaches over to Mum.

"What's happened?" She doesn't even need to know the answer.

Mum blinks to rid herself of an intrusive thought. She gets up, makes her way past Karolína and runs to the hall.

Her eyes dart around the room, but she doesn't recognize the flat – the hall with the wallpaper, the linoleum and the furniture are all unfamiliar to her. Gran chose everything here and, at the very least, Mum would like to throw out the shoe cabinet. She sits on it, wondering why Gran was so annoyed by the idea of putting some wallpaper up on the empty, uneven wall.

She's struggling with her second shoe when Karolína comes over and squats down beside her.

"We'll take my car, OK? It'll be quicker."

She finally gets her shoe on, smooths her hair down with her fingertips and nods. She's grateful; otherwise, she'd have to ride her bike through Přerov alone at night, and she definitely wouldn't get there in time.

The houses on Dvořákova are only lit by a few street-lamps – the ones the children haven't smashed yet – and the cones of light reveal some grass and crooked paving stones. They drive beneath the lights towards the garages, neither woman saying anything. They continue along the dark lane between Hotel Fit and Hotel Jana down towards the school

In hindsight, you're fascinated by how narrowly you missed one another. You passed through the same place a short while before them. Before heading home, you rode your bike to Marián's, as far away as possible from the school, the garages and the streetlamps.

You tell yourself you couldn't have made up an evening like this one, and yet it remains shrouded and confused in your memory. You must have pieced it together a hundred times and, each time, you're confronted with another new version. You'd like to find the right one, one that would express everything at the same time, but, in the end, you always come up against the same problem. Every event happens at least twice. Once for you and once for those around you. They are separate sheets of paper.

You stare at them until a definite pattern emerges.

You turn on the lamp, place the two sheets on top of each other and hold them up to the light.

Now that the paper is translucent, where one word encounters another, you can trace several points of contact, points of intersection on the maps of images and sentences. That's how you know everything's heading in the same direction, everything's part of a problem that transcends you, Mum, and even Grandad.

We've built such solid enclosures for one another and for ourselves that we often have problems fitting into them.

*If I can't fit into them*, you ask yourself, *will I still be human?* You hope the enclosures will hold you, but more often than not, you fall out of them, get swept away by the current and are left to kick your legs hopelessly.

But it's only later that you'll learn to think about questions like these, only later that you'll realize all memories are linked and that if you exist here and now, there is another life being lived out somewhere else that's just as important as yours. You turn to another version and see Karolína's shabby blue car parked right next to number 8.

Karolína struggles with the ignition and it takes a few minutes before the engine starts. *It's too late*, Mum thinks, *what if I don't make it?* She squeezes the phone in her hand and accidentally dials your number instead of Grandad's. She only realizes her mistake the next morning but, for now, she's frozen to the seat. She forgets to put on her seat belt and nothing makes sense. She waits, and each ring means time, movement, followed by a pause on which her last hope rests. No-one answers the phone.

The car glides slowly through the town with Mum counting down the buildings. How many left? *Four*, she counts, *three, two*. She checks the time, five minutes have passed, six, Grandad hasn't called back. She could have been there ages ago if Karolína hadn't been driving so painfully slowly. She's surprised how few lights are on. It's not that late for the town to be plunged into darkness already. It makes each lit-up room all the more accessible – she'd like to peek inside to see if it's true that other families have to deal with things like this, or if she is all alone in the world.

Karolína slowly navigates the empty roundabout at the embankment, from where Mum can finally see Grandad's house. She's drawn to the windows of his flat, like a lighthouse in a brown sea of darkness. She doesn't see anything else. The car stops at the main road, her view blocked by one lorry and then another. She closes her eyes. Behind her eyelids, two spots are imprinted on her retina, the memory of his windows. She opens her eyes and, this time, she's close enough to see the scene in front of her clearly.

And it's this image that she will/she'll try to forget. She will forget. At least for a while, until the shadow in the top floor comes back to her again. Grandad dangling from the windowsill. From a distance, he looks like a spider, his hands groping for the walls of the building as he slowly moves down.

She leaps out of the car before Karolína's even come to a stop. She throws open the door, landing on all fours. Rolls on her side and is back on her feet in an instant. She can hear Grandad now as well. His words, if indeed they are words, have attracted a few passers-by. There are people watching from the buildings across the street too, except that none of them move, as though they've been waiting for her to arrive.

She stumbles on the way to the entrance, refusing to take her eyes off Grandad. She keeps calculating in her mind. How long will it take her to reach the top? The lift doors open and she senses Karolína's shadow behind her. They both squeeze inside and Mum presses a button. It doesn't even occur to her to leave Karolína downstairs to keep watch.

They step out into the dark, empty corridor. From the window at the other end, the light from outside flickers in the reflections of the tiles and washable walls. The corridor is silent – she can no longer hear Grandad. She reaches out to knock but stops mid-motion, takes the key out of her pocket, unlocks the door and turns the handle.

One step across the threshold is enough to send her back in time, dragging her back to the place she escaped from. The flat is in total disarray. She bumps into a chair leaning against the bathroom door. It only has three legs and she finds the fourth lying on the floor nearby. She steps on the cigarette stubs that cover the floor and stick to the soles of her shoes.

She quickly assesses the situation. Tattered advertising leaflets and pieces of clothing are scattered everywhere. The only thing Grandad hasn't touched is the TV, which has pride of place on an old chest of drawers.

First, she sees Grandad's legs, which are still in the flat. Then the rest of his body. The part from the waist up is hanging out of the window. Mum approaches cautiously. She doesn't want to frighten him – she can't afford to make a single mistake. She holds her breath on the last step, leaps forward and pulls Grandad back in. As she does so, she loses her balance, and her head just misses the kitchen worktop. She falls to the ground with Grandad on top of her.

She can feel every one of his bones, even the way they crack at the joints. She wraps her arms around his ribs as he thrashes around, trying to break free.

She strokes Grandad's hair. Some of the rough bristles are plastered to his skin with sweat, while the rest are sticking out. She breathes in and a strong, pungent stench fills her nostrils. She breathes out and whispers something into his ear.

Whatever it was will remain between them.

In the meantime, Karolína moves the chair away from the bathroom door, looks inside and closes the door. She shrugs her shoulders. Mum is frightened to move at all. Her body shakes with Grandad's fits of coughing and she continues to stroke his hair until the trembling in her body subsides. She can vaguely make out Karolína talking to someone in the hall, or so she thinks, until she finally hears a siren.

She tries to lift Grandad up but feels nothing in her left leg, while her right foot has gone numb. Grandad is making long wheezing noises. She thinks he's fallen asleep and puts the back of her hand on his forehead.

Later, when the paramedics arrived and took Grandad from her, she felt she hadn't been so alive in weeks. When she tells you about it, she'll mention their questions and how she answered them. She even laughed. They monitored Grandad's breathing. At first, he didn't want to leave Mum but, finally, he relented and they stood up together. He took a few steps and then allowed them to seat him in a wheelchair. In no time, they'd pushed him into the corridor and bundled him into the lift.

Suddenly, he was gone. He had disappeared, leaving Mum alone in the empty, smoke-stained flat.

Almost alone – she'd almost forgotten about Karolína. She only remembers when Karolína gently touches her shoulder. She glances around the flat once more, goes over to the window and looks out. The height makes her head hurt, so she closes one of the windows and looks out across Přerov through the nicotine-stained glass. The castle stands out in the darkness, its brightly lit tower contrasting with the windows of the tower blocks. Below, car headlights stretch out into long orange lines. Their reflections dance across the surface of the Bečva. Flickering waves, images carried far away to a foreign land, where perhaps one day, when all the light has faded from them, they'll forget what they have just seen.

What she sees now is a smoky room turned upside-down. Over the next few days, she will have to come back and tidy everything up. She follows Karolína out of the flat and pauses once more with the key half-turned in the lock, her forehead against the door.

"It shouldn't have ended like that," she'll admit to you later.

A couple of months later, it was obvious that Grandad would not be returning from the hospital any time soon. When you were moving his things from his flat to your cellar, Mum found an old black-and-white photograph of Grandad with Mum and your aunt. In it, he's wearing an ill-fitting suit while the sisters are in identical white dresses that Gran made for them. She probably took the photo as well. But for the life of her, Mum has no memory of that day.

"What kind of a person am I, Marek, if I only have the worst memories of my own dad?"

Outside the building, the silence is broken at short intervals by the hollow sounds of cars. Karolína turns the steering wheel and pulls out onto the road. They are both silent. Neither of them feels the need to say anything.

She tries to call you one more time from the car but, by then, you have your phone switched off. It's in your shorts beside the bed, and even if you heard it, you probably wouldn't have bothered to take your eyes off your reflection.

You wish you could describe the happiness, all of the feelings you had that summer by the water, the image of Marián wading through the current to the middle of the river, swinging his arm and throwing a near perfect skimming stone. Once more, you'd like to conjure up the field and the corncobs near the Bečva. You're lying down, wearing Marián's headphones, on a cleared patch of ground, with people cycling past just a few yards away. You close your eyes and listen to the music, the water and the rustling of the dried corncobs.

"But I've only got this stupid body," Marián said once, and that sentence has stayed with you ever since, even though you've been trying to forget it for years. Every time, you stumble over it and remember.

Memory bulldozes everything. It erases everything except our strongest recollections. You have to work hard to find the weaker ones, the happier ones. You dredge them up from the bottom, all covered in mud and algae. But why summon them up now? Why resurrect anything from memory? *Why are you always raking about in there?* Mum asks and, instead of giving an answer, you just open your mouth again and try to put a name to it, dig out the shards one by one, arrange them into words, into images, and perhaps prevent any of this from happening to someone else.

When your mum told you to stay at home that evening, you didn't care what she thought. In the morning, you waited in bed until Gran finally headed out to the allotment and then quietly – in case Mum could somehow hear it in the factory – closed the door behind you and went to the cellar for your bike.

Marián was already waiting behind the block of flats. He had a plan. The two of you cycled to an abandoned mill in Prosenice. Its old façade is peeling off and the only unbroken windows are on the top floors. You stood beside the mill race, not knowing what to do with your hands. You bent over, picked up a stone and chucked it at the highest window.

Some time later, you're at the pub beside the football pitch – gravel underfoot, holding plastic cups of Kofola. You swing up onto the railing beside Marián, hand him a plastic cup and turn towards the pitch, where a group of sweaty men are running after a ball. The loudest of them has no top on, his sweaty belly spilling out over the elastic waistband of his shorts. He misses twice, then a third time, and immediately collapses onto the sun-scorched ground, pounding the grass with his fists. Marián nudges you, points at him and grins.

A few minutes later, the other team score a goal at the other end of the pitch. A bunch of men press their sweaty faces together, their bodies close to one another. You could put your arm around Marián's shoulders – the way you did when you were alone by the river – after all, you wouldn't be doing anything they weren't. You could touch him and that movement would just be a reflection of theirs.

You decide to do it, but just then, as though to make up for their moment of weakness, the men start shouting at each other again.

"Pass it, you cunt," one of them shouts, waving his arms above his head. He just misses the ball by a fraction, takes a fresh air swipe and falls over.

"What the fuck are you playing at? Come on!"

The topless man jogs over to him and pulls him to his feet.

"He's a twat. He almost had it."

You're watching but you're not paying attention. Although you would never admit it to Marián, you'd like to identify with the men on the pitch. You'd like to belong somewhere. Learn the boundary between the right kind of touch and the wrong kind of touch, learn to mask uncertainty as aggression, stand up straight and go to a place where all the parts of your body fit together, where you can rid yourself of the shame of knowing you have a body at all.

But a stranger's voice wrenches you out of your thoughts.

"What are you gawking at?"

You realize you've been staring at a small group sitting on a bench nearby. A tattooed man with short hair gets up and slowly walks towards you, muttering something on the way. You can't understand him. He stops beside Marián and spits.

"Well, fuck me." Before continuing, he licks his sun-chapped lips and turns his head towards the two of you several times. "So now bloody Gypos are showing up here like a bad smell."

"Why do you think I don't like going to see my gran?"

When Marián first asked you this question, you still didn't get it. But at the football pitch, everything fell into place. "I really don't enjoy having to listen to how dirty I am, how unclean I am. Even to them. And I remember how you used to stare at me too."

You bend down, scoop up a handful of small stones and start sifting them through your fingers from the left hand to the right one.

"Always having to be on your guard in front of other people. Who would enjoy always having to listen to questions like why I am sitting like that or what on earth am I wearing?"

The gravel leaves a thin layer of dust on your hand. You absent-mindedly turn the stones over again and again, trying not to look at Marián.

"Aren't you worried about what'll happen once they figure it out at home?"

You clench your hand into a fist and then open it again. A couple of stones remain stuck to your skin. You pick at one with your fingernail, examine it, and the rest fall to the ground.

"I won't even be the first one in our family. Gran's always on about her brother – though only under her breath. She's got plastic mugs and plates hidden under the sink for him. She's all sweetness and light in front of everyone else, you know? She feeds him like everyone else, maybe even gives him extra, but as soon as my uncle leaves, she scrapes the leftovers into the bin and goes running around the house from room to room with bleach. It's like I can't even eat from a normal plate, I've got my own one as well, probably so she doesn't catch these spots off me. All I hear is how Mum's a witch and Dad died cos of her – which is why I'm weird and spotty. I'm not enough like them. I reckon…" He bends at the waist and picks up a handful of gravel just like you did a minute earlier. "I reckon she still thinks…" He draws back his arm and throws the whole handful towards the pitch, "these marks are a punishment. That it's some kind of a curse for being half gadjo."

There are small white indentations where the stones dug into his skin. You direct your gaze at them to avoid having to look him in the eye. The men on the nearby bench are laughing at something and, every time they swear, you turn your head towards them.

"There was a point when Gran was always shouting at Mum for that reason. The funny thing is, no-one else even cares, but just imagine going to visit someone and just as you're leaving, out of nowhere, someone starts yelling at you in front of the whole street, saying what a slut you are."

Disjointed images of s smashed-in door flash through your mind. You're walking through town with Mum and some stranger's shouting the same thing at her. You're about to say to Marián that you understand but, in the end, you decide to keep quiet.

"It's better now."

You finally lift your head and Marián's frowning. Even the skin on his nose is wrinkled up again.

"I guess she had a heart-to-heart with someone – that's what Mum says." He looks up and grins. "But how can you speak to someone's soul? Do you just lean over – " he says, leaning towards you, "and whisper it to them?"

His breath tickles your ear. You scratch and nudge him with your shoulder.

272

As soon as he pulls away, Marián straightens up a bit and his voice changes.

"I think she just got used to the fact that we're going to be in her life, one way or another. She can't do anything about it. I couldn't care less what she thinks, but Mum prays for me every evening because of her. But it's not my fault I've only got this stupid body."

The shouting from the pitch reaches you in waves. The few spectators watching the match alternately clap and boo. Marián turns towards the noise and when he looks back at you, the wrinkle in his nose is gone.

"I never asked for any of this, but I'm here. I've got no choice. So why should I always just hate myself?"

The journey to Výkleky takes almost an hour. One day, you'll look back to discover you remember everything. You'll see light and water in front of you. You spend the whole afternoon lazing around on the rocks on the only empty slope at the quarry, watching the distorted reflections of the clouds on the water's surface. You feel that some of them are repeating themselves, but they never remain the same for long.

Your legs are stretched out in front of you, and whenever you move, a few stones slide down the slope and roll into the water. There are a lot of people at Výkleky quarry, and a flat rock in the middle of the water has been occupied by a small group with blankets spread out and beer

273

bottles everywhere. Marián took you to a slope as far away from them as possible, close to trees and bushes, but still within reach of the water.

You block out the sun with the back of your hand and amuse yourself for a while spreading your fingers and looking at the translucent skin.

Marián is lying on his back on a blanket, chest rising and falling, eyes closed. The blanket' is made of some scratchy material, so you roll over and move closer to him, your arms by your side. The branches of the surrounding trees sway lazily in the wind, and the leaves let through light broken up into tiny fragments. One of them touches his eyelashes, slides down his face and disappears into the air.

You close your eyes and sleep for a while. When you awaken/wake up, Marián is leafing through the pages of a new comic book.

"What's that you're reading?"

"I'm not reading." He passes the book to you and points at a text bubble with some foreign characters. You squint at them, but he's turned the page before you can focus. "I'm just looking through it."

You try to imprint what you see on your memory. Marián's focused expression, his closed lips.

"Hey..." He puts the book down, shifts position. "When did you actually realize... When did it first hit you that you're...?"

You sit up slightly and try to put your finger on the exact time, the turning point. But the more you try, the more certain you are that *it* has always been with you.

"I really don't know," you finally say. "Always, I guess."

Marián stares ahead, his heel digging a small indentation in the stones beside the blanket.

All the memories of that particular summer are mixed up in your head. The days merge together, surfacing only in random fragments, probably floating to the top in a way that is totally different from what really happened.

Not counting the few days Mum had off, when you had to help her and Gran hoe the beds in the allotment, every day was spent with Marián. Never before had you felt so alive. Summer was coming to an end, the grass in front of the building was dried out and burned, with only a few lonely islands of green tufts around the clothes lines.

Most of the time, you were outside – either in the meadow behind the Lagoon or hidden on the roof of the garages just past the hospital. At first, you couldn't get up on the roof. You weren't strong enough to pull yourself up and scraped your knee on the roughcast, while Marián had no trouble climbing up. The sticky hot roofs smelled of asphalt, and puddles of glistening tar formed on the gravel-strewn areas. You poked at the bubbles with the tip of your shoe and, when one burst, you slowly moved on to the next.

One time, you stole fireworks from the old Prior department store. As soon as the assistant turned round to get something, you snatched the whole pack from the counter and stuffed it in your pocket, grabbed Marián's hand and dragged him outside.

Back at the Bečva – not far from the footbridge – you were throwing the fireworks into the river, one after another, and waiting anxiously to see what noise they'd make. If you timed your throw properly, water would spray up at the point of impact and ripple across the surface in gradually diminishing circles. You raised your hand again, but then someone from the opposite bank yelled something at you. The silhouette let go of a lead and a dog disappeared while the figure remained standing. It waved at you and shouted. The sounds seemed ridiculous. Marián managed to throw the last firework before running off, not stopping until he reached the BMX track.

You collapsed next to him on the kerb, but you didn't even have time to catch your breath. First, you felt a pain in your thigh – the fireworks were in your pocket – and then came the explosion.

Those two strikes form two points, marking the here and now. Now, in your mind, you're back on the blanket at Výkleky, and now your own sweat is stinging your thigh with every movement. While Marián continues to dig about among the stones with his heel, you're picking at a scab until a few drops of blood start to ooze. To clean it, you pour some cold tea onto your leg from the two-litre Mattoni mineral water bottle Marián's mum leaves for him in the fridge every morning. She pours the tea into it while it's still hot, the plastic warps and the tea smells of it. When it's lukewarm, it tastes a bit like pee. It even looks like urine – but when it's mixed with blood, it takes on a piercing rusty colour. You breathe in sharply from the pain, almost missing what Marián's saying.

"Me too probably. I've always known I was strange as well."

You look up at him. His shoulders are slumped. *Strange*, you repeat after him. You feel *strange* no matter where you go. You keep finding mirrors everywhere. You look into them, and although you'd like to recognize yourself, nothing looks quite like you. Nothing moves the same way in them. I can't even see you whole. I try to lean towards you out of every reflection, to stop and freeze you in time. Before, you reminded me of an empty space, a memory of someone I might have been. All that's left now is a world where the others expected clear answers from the two of us, without giving us the time to decide. Imagine what you could have achieved if they'd given you a real choice.

"Don't you find it hard to make sense of it all? Sometimes I... Sometimes I don't even know what's going on, what their problem is exactly and why the hell I should have to deal with it."

Marián brings his knees up to his chest and rests his chin on them. His head's turned towards the water and he only occasionally looks back at you. Slowly, it dawns on you that he's talking about something else entirely.

"If you look like this," he says, tapping his forehead, "you'll never seem normal. Spotty, a Gypsy, and a homo into the bargain. And yet I felt I was normal before we moved here with Mum."

He falls silent, takes the bottle you just rinsed your leg with, unscrews the cap and sips from it.

"It's just…" he swallows and screws the cap on again, "Before I ever looked in a mirror at nursery school and before I saw other people, before they started laughing at me, everything was normal. Don't you ever feel that if those pricks left us alone, you'd never know there was something wrong with you?"

You nod. There are two shadows on the ground, and when you wave a hand, the dark shapes come together. In reality, you doubt the shadow would detach itself from you, even if the others were to leave you alone.

"I remember when Mum got this great idea about signing me up for summer camp." Marián is speaking quietly and you can hear children shouting and splashing in the water nearby. "She didn't even ask me. She just thought I was spending too much time at home. Someone at work must have suggested it; otherwise, it would never have occurred to her. I dunno, maybe she really thought it was a good idea. Anyway, they were already all staring at me at the station as we were lugging the suitcase there.

You should have seen their dumb expressions. One woman took her kid aside, pointed at us and just... She didn't even try to keep her voice down. On the bus, one boy asked me if I'd been thrown into bleach by accident, or why else would I have all those spots. Everyone was like: Why am I so dirty? Why am I a darkie and yet I can't even be a proper one? *Just try fucking touching him. Christ, he stinks.* And when they let us tie-dye our T-shirts, that prick actually splashed bleach in my face. As if that'd make me clean at last."

The only one who spoke to him at all was the boy he shared a cabin with.

"The whole thing was weird. Sometimes, we'd be on our own and he'd behave pretty normally. But then he'd swear at me in front of the others – in fact, he was the loudest of them all." He scratches his calf, stretches his leg out and then draws it in again. He repeats this movement, still digging at the stones with his heel, both of you intently watching this movement. Then Marián continues: "During one of the group games, it ended up being just the two of us alone. We were supposed to find some stuff that was hidden in the forest, some treasure, but we managed to get lost. On the way down a hill, I tripped over a root and pulled him down with me."

You have to strain your ears to understand what he's saying. He practically whispers the last few words. "It only lasted about a second," he says, placing his hand on your knee.

They got up off the ground. The other boy looked at him in surprise but said nothing. He helped Marián stand up and brushed the dirt off his back. They even laughed about it on the way back to the camp but, in the evening, he dragged him out of bed and knelt on his chest till he could hardly breathe. "One word of this to anyone and I'll smash your face in." He started to get back up, changed his mind and spat in Marián's face.

You look at him closely, but he doesn't seem particularly sad. You search for a trace of a clear thought or movement that would tell you what's going through his mind. You know what you'd be thinking – you'd probably regret it all, feel sorry for yourself and try to figure out where you went wrong.

He soon starts talking again, and there's not the slightest hint of self-pity in his voice.

"The best thing to come out of what happened there is I have him to thank for this haircut." He runs his hand through his hair, which you remembered as being lank and greasy when he first joined your class. All that time, you thought his short hair was connected to his fall and the thin scar at the nape of his neck.

On the evening before going home, the whole camp sat round a fire, cooking sausages on sticks. All it took was a moment's inattention and a boy – Marián no longer remembers his name – came up to him and set his hair on fire with a burning stick.

When he came into the class after the summer holidays with his head shaved, the guys pointed and laughed at him. You don't remember where you were at the time – no doubt keeping yourself to yourself.

Your shadows are on the point of colliding just a short distance in front of you. Before they merge, they are separated by a thin strip of light. You move and it seems to you as if you have no boundaries. Out of the corner of your eye, you catch Marián's smile.

"You know, short hair doesn't burn so well," he says, shrugging.

Up close, his hair is shiny. "It looks better this way," you say, running your fingers through his hair. "You look a bit like Chester from Linkin Park."

On the way home, you don't feel great. It's late when the sun sets, everything is blurred and dull and it confuses you. You know there's going to be trouble. Mum will've been home for a while, and you didn't even think to phone her. You walk along, pushing your bike. The path along the Bečva is empty and you're both quiet. You're hot, the sweat's running down your back in long streams, your head's starting to hurt, and your T-shirt's sticking to you, weighing you down. The whole time, you want to hold Marián's hand, but you keep yours clenched in your pocket and can't work up the courage to do it.

Sometimes, you'd like to spend your whole life with your hand clenched into a fist.

You know only too well who you got this fear from – Mum is always afraid as well. She's always writing lists, sitting at the table, writing numbers on the edge of the calendar, frightened she might forget something. Then, after each evening cigarette, she locks the front door, forgets and then locks it again before going to bed. She makes sure all the windows in the flat are closed. The two of you are always looking for something more behind everything but, in reality, you might be longing to find out what exactly could go wrong.

As Gran says, things are never so bad that they can't get worse. You think she wants to comfort you, prepare you for the worst, but the idea only makes you even more afraid. The two of them forgot to prepare you for the possibility that things might get better. They never taught you what to do in similar situations – you just gasp for breath, trying to take the first step.

In the end, you don't even get the chance. Marián tugs at your sleeve. You take your hand out of your pocket and his fingers intertwine with yours.

He doesn't even turn round once. He keeps looking ahead, while each step is a leap somewhere – somewhere he can't possibly see. As you're thinking this, darkness begins to settle on the woods in front of you and it's increasingly difficult to make anything out.

You continue to push your bike with your free hand, gritting your teeth in the darkness. Now you know what it's like to become someone else. You push away all the usual feelings – the shame from the thought that someone might be able to see inside your mind and listen to all of your devious, foolish ideas. The things around you seem new and foreign, not of this world, as though someone has rearranged them and given them a new order.

But you wouldn't be you if you didn't trip over a root growing out of the asphalt. To keep your balance, you let go of your bike, which falls to the ground, and Marián bursts out laughing.

"You're an idiot."

You're standing by the footbridge and neither of you wants to go home.

"You sure you don't want to come back to mine? Just for a bit? Mum's on night shift, we could –" You say no straight out before he can finish the sentence.

You hadn't told Marián you were supposed to stay at home, and you avoided mentioning other things that Mum had said as well. You know you'll find her at home, arms folded across her chest, face burning. You can't tell him what you argue about at home – that you're arguing because of him. Then you'd have to admit you'd never found the courage to stand up to Mum, to stand up for him. You're in the middle of the path, trying to find the right words, imagining what it'd be like to be part of a normal family.

"Even if you phoned her now?"

Frantically, you search for your mobile in the pannier bag. "Sorry, I…"

Marián just waves his hand.

"OK, then, I'll see you tomorrow."

You nod and slowly get on your bike. But when you start pedalling, a loose shoelace gets caught up in the chain and you fall again. You pick yourself up and turn back round to Marián but he's long gone. You struggle with your shoe for a while, get off the bike and hop about frantically. Only when the lace finally comes loose are you able to get back on and head home.

Even from a distance, you recognize them. The plan had been to go up the hill by the hospital, but your path's been blocked by a group of people. Judging by the mixture of noises, fragments of voices and music, you can guess who it is. There are sounds and then there are sounds. Some of them don't bode at all well. Suddenly, you hear glass breaking as well as music.

*Tonight, I'm ready, been drinking like never before.*

By the time you spot Filip, it's too late. He's a lot smaller than the rest and is crouched in the middle of the pavement, bashing something against the ground.

*Tonight, I'll bring the cash* – you listen to the lyrics, which everyone repeats in unison, *I'll destroy the clubs, get out my way!*

You get off your bike. You don't know where you get the courage from but, this time, you decide not to back down.

"Give it here, for fuck's sake." You catch snippets of sentences as you push the bike forward like a shield, staring down at your feet. The air is thick with the smell of cigarettes, alcohol and something else. *Something stinks here, I don't know what,* continues the music. You hold your breath and wait for it to happen – for a stranger's hand to emerge from somewhere and knock you over.

But there's time for that yet.

"Hey!"

It's only Filip's voice that hits you from the darkness. You blink and his face is there in front of you, grinning with amusement. "It's that shithead from our class." You step forward, bump into someone – *shadows walking all around* – and someone else laughs. "And where's Spotty? Where's that piece of filth?"

You try to walk on, but Filip gets up and blocks your way.

"And where do you think... Where are you going, eh?" He hiccups halfway through the sentence and there's laughter behind him. This no doubt annoys Filip. He swallows, and when he next speaks, there's something new in his tone.

You try to push your way through again. Filip stands in front you. You move, and he does it again. "Oh, come on."

Someone shoves a bottle in his hand. He has a drink, then holds it out to you. "Here, gaylord, show us you're a man."

"I've got to go home," you say, pulling away. Nothing better springs to mind.

"To Mummy?" The laughter gradually subsides and another voice pipes up.

"She'll be fucking some guy now anyway." You take a quick count of how many there are.

"I swear, if mine brings home another Gypo, I'll strangle her."

"They probably wouldn't even pay to fuck her."

"This little poof gives it to them for free. He's got no problem with darkies."

Filip puts his hands on your shoulders and shakes you. His voice comes at you from all sides.

"But seriously, are you fucking each other?"

You almost fall and only regain your balance at the last minute.

"Do you shove it up each other's arses?"

You register movement out of the corner of your eye. The laughter's getting louder. You look towards the windows of the nearest tower block. There are lights on in most of them and, on the first floor, you see a motionless figure, a shadow that's been standing there for some time. You imagine they'll run down at any moment to save you, but then the figure draws the curtains.

"Does he even have a dick? And what about those spots, aren't you scared you'll catch something?" Filip lifts the bottle, drinks and wipes the drool from his chin with his T-shirt.

He passes it to you again.

"Come on, don't be a pussy. Take a drink." He thrusts the bottle in your face.

With your free hand, you gingerly wrap your fingers round it. For a moment, you stand there helplessly. Time is flowing backwards again. You bump into it with your body, trying to swim away, and the people on the embankment are watching you. Filip finally loses patience.

"Come on, only real poofs are scared."

Instead of tilting the bottle and drinking, you seem to drown in it. The glass clinks against your teeth and feels cold on your lips.

You tilt your head back and drink. Filip looks pleased.

"And now tell me..." He takes a step towards you, takes the bottle off you and smashes it on the ground. Even in the dim light, you can see the shards, the foam, the colours. Green and white against the dark pavement. "Now tell me, you wee fuck..." Filip towers above you. You'd never noticed how much taller he is or how broad his shoulders are. He pretends to be unzipping his fly. "If you do it with Gypos, then you can suck our cocks as well. And, this time, we're not at school, you've got no-one to help you. You can't get away from me today, you fucker."

The others form a tight circle around you. In the dim light, you can't make out their faces and you doubt they even have any. You try to run but can't find a single gap in the circle. In the nearest lit window in the building opposite, you notice a vague black figure, the edges of its outline blurred, and it seems as if it's waving to you, moving to help you. You let go of your bike and there's a clatter as you tumble to the ground after it. First the bike, then you. Someone's hands are pushing, pulling you down. Before hitting the ground, you touch the pavement and a sharp pain shoots through the palm of your hand, then you hit your head. The last thing you remember is the sound of your mum's voice.

"Maybe you'll get it clear in your mind."

There are strips of light, sparks and spots in front of your eyes. Then only darkness.

Sometimes, things are so clear in your mind that you remember everything: images, parts of strangers' faces, empty rooms, sounds and words, someone's voice. But the thing you remember most of all are the falls.

One Christmas, you are standing on tiptoe in the middle of the room, wearing pyjamas, with fairy lights wrapped around you. Gran and Mum are somewhere off to the side – they can't take their eyes off you and are both laughing. You try to reach the top of the tree, but each time you trip and fall to the floor.

"We'll have to make the tree come to you then," says Mum, lifting you into the air.

You remember the frozen Lagoon on Christmas Eve. Snow covering the ice, the three little islands, the bare tree branches. You stumble about on borrowed ice skates that are too big for you, holding onto Mum with one hand and Grandad with the other. The whole time, he's been smoking a cigarette, impatiently turning his head towards the pub behind you. You move carefully; it's more likely they have to push you along. Mum and Grandad release you at one point and you skate on. You can see an island ahead of you and head towards it. You move your leg.

And you're lying on the ground. You get up. And fall.

But each fall represents something new. You get back on your feet. One leads to another, and you lay them out before you. The falls attract each another. You line them up so close together that they collide and you skate over the small pieces to the island.

Later that evening, it was already dark outside. Mum even let Grandad stay for dinner for the first time. She sat you beside him at the table and poured you both Kofola in crystal glasses, while she and Gran had a small glass of wine. The lines etched in the glass cast broken reflections and spots of coloured light onto the table. You couldn't keep your eyes off them and tried to cut your meat without looking. And then, when you knocked over one of the glasses with your elbow, Grandad reached out to you, misjudged his strength and, in an instant, you and shards of glass lay under the chair, dripping with Kofola and blood.

You delve even deeper into the history of your falls. You couldn't have been more than five when Mum used to tell you the story of a cuddly toy squirrel every evening – the same bedside story Gran used to tell Mum, albeit featuring a different favourite cuddly toy. As a young girl, she also fell asleep night after night, curled up in a ball, letting herself be carried away by the story. You sat up against the headboard of Mum's bed with your chin resting on your knees. She closed her eyes and you hung on her every word. Habička – that was the squirrel's name – spent entire days hopping around among the trees, travelling across the world, and yet always returning home in the evening so that, through your mother, she could tell you all about her adventures.

In one of the stories, the squirrel travelled to a foreign land full of strange animals, tall castles and, above all, magic: a world where nothing looked the same as at home. Mum was able to describe everything vividly and in such colourful detail that you wanted to live there and never return to your cramped flat, to the shabby furniture in your room, beyond whose windows you could only see a factory and the walls of tower blocks lined up in a row. Maybe to bring that world even closer to you, at night you began to project different scenes from Habička's life in your mind. In your dreams, you flew across the branches with her, jumped from a tree –

And landed back in bed each time.

You thought other people would understand these dreams and that dreams were the only thing that really mattered. You talked about them constantly. Sometimes, you'd wake up at night on a soaked mattress, sweating from fear. If you occasionally misjudged your step and fell into the water, you'd wake up screaming.

Maybe that was why, one evening, Mum just turned out the light and left the room.

"Not today. I'm too tired."

You called after her, kicked off the duvet and ran into the hall.

"And you're too big for stories now anyway." You were so angry you could barely move and, in order to calm you down, she made you kneel in the corner of the dark hall long into the night.

The scene repeated itself the next day except, this time, Mum took the wooden spoon to you. You tried to escape, tripped and put your knee through the glass panel in the door. But nothing could stop you – not the blood, not Mum shouting, not the wounds, which she rubbed with a pungent green liquid. In order to get rid of the pain, you escaped into the squirrel's adventures, muttering them to yourself for days on end. They comforted you, even though all you really wanted was to hear at least some of them again and know you weren't alone in your imaginary world. You were constantly mumbling about the squirrel in your sleep, while eating or watching TV, until Mum finally lost all patience. One night, she set about Habička, angrily gripped her torso in her left hand and its head in her right, and with one single tug, ripped the squirrel in half right in front of you.

If I were to tell you now that all of this happened in a dream, you probably wouldn't believe me. The torso and head, two pieces of the same body; one without the other doesn't make sense. They fall separately to the ground and don't touch again until the morning. You talk and make things up until even a dream becomes a memory. At least, that's how it seems to you. In the morning, you shouted at Mum and she didn't understand why – after all, she'd found Habička lying under the bed. Why should she feel guilty about something she did in a dream?

Ever since Mum harmed the squirrel, you've been afraid to sleep. You toss and turn for hours on end. At night, you lie with your arms stretched out behind your head, boring holes into the ceiling through which you could escape, far from this tiny room, from the ever-shrinking walls of your flat. It's a pity that, in place of hope, only a penetrating dark colour flows through the crack in the ceiling into the room.

It was about a year after the scene with the squirrel that Martin first spent the night at yours. It was then that you discovered shadows in the corner of the room, along with strange sighs and shapes above Mum's bed. You thought they'd come to swallow her and Martin up, and you were afraid to move that night. But then a spasm ran through your body and you fell out of bed.

In the morning, there were no scars to be seen on anyone, nothing to confirm the existence of the shadows. However, by the afternoon, a battered rattan screen stood in front of your mum's bed. She'd brought it up from the cellar herself and, during the day, you poked holes in it with your finger so that at night you would be able to see if the shadows returned.

You remember each fall vividly and precisely.

You're six years old and Gran's invited you all to spend a few nights in Troják in the mountains during the summer holidays. There's only one bunk bed in the wooden chalet. You let Mum sleep in the bottom one, while you and Gran are on the top. You remember the darkness, the smell of smoke from a nearby camp, and the closed shutters that prevented even a chink of light from entering the room. You can't hear any of the sounds of the countryside inside the chalet. It takes you ages to fall asleep and you're hanging over the edge of the bed while Gran is sprawled on her back, snoring and grinding her teeth. You dream you're falling. You open your eyes and in front of you is real blackness. You're flying through the darkness and then you're winded from the fall.

Or a year later at the spa in Luhačovice – a building with a sign saying Radun, a room with a balcony, but they're afraid to let you out onto it. In the morning, you run down the stairs and fall. You run towards Mum and you fall. Halfway through the holiday, you catch scarlet fever and lie in a hospital bed next to a red-haired boy with an ice pack. Throughout the night, you suffer from coughing fits, and the sharp, harsh sounds waken everyone around you. By some miracle, the redhead manages to wriggle free from his ice pack, throws you out of the bed onto the floor and starts to smother you with a pillow.

When Mum started bringing Martin home, he bragged about the first time he'd shot something when he was in the army, no doubt hoping to impress you both.

"You can't say you're a man till you've fired a real gun," he said, winking at you from the kitchen door, before continuing, "Maybe I'll shoot you Daněks. You're just asking for it."

Mum burst out laughing by the sink in the kitchen.

"Don't say that to him. He'll be scared of you."

But you weren't afraid of him. Not even when, sometime in autumn, he brought some venison wrapped in a blue plastic bag. He placed the bag on the table, took the meat out, put it on his palm and held out his hand to you.

"Look," he said as he dug his finger into it, "it's still bloody." He squeezed the whole piece of meat, turned to Mum and added with a smile: "This is young meat, but you can put it in the freezer. It keeps a long time and it'll definitely be good for something."

It wasn't good for anything – it lay there for a few hours in the bag where Martin had left it, and as soon as he was gone, Mum chucked the meat in the bin.

That memory merges with another one. Something else ended up in that same bin. About a year after Martin began sleeping at the flat regularly, Grandad got you a gerbil for your birthday. Mum was angry to begin with – who was going to look after it and clean it? But that didn't worry you. You just put the plastic box on the table and stared lovingly at the animal all day long. The gerbil woke you at night. The first night, you secretly took him out of the box, pulled the duvet over you both and fell asleep. In the morning, Mum found it under the table, shivering from cold and fear.

"Did you know mice can swim?"

Martin came up to you just as you were getting out of the bath. There was still some water left as you never drained it completely till everyone had had a bath. He dashed off and came back carrying the gerbil.

"Let's see." The animal tried to wriggle out of his grasp. "What do you think? Will this one be able to as well?" He shook his hands as if holding a dice and threw the gerbil into the water. He stood over it, forcing you to watch the desperate animal – *not yet, wait a minute* – as it tried to scramble up the slippery sides of the bath. It couldn't. There was nothing to hold onto and it slid down each time. Finally, you couldn't bear to watch any longer, so you pushed Martin away, fished the gerbil out the bathtub, cradled it to your chest and ran down the hall.

But – just like that time at the Lagoon – suddenly, no-one was holding you. Your wet feet slipped on the floor. You tripped and crushed the animal beneath you.

A few days later, Grandad appeared at the flat and you tearfully told him everything.

"It doesn't matter."

He stood in the hall and slowly took off his cap. He bent down and put his hand on your shoulder, while wiping away your tears with a nicotine-stained thumb.

"Everything ends that way one day, Marek," he whispered, carefully seating you on his lap. "Nothing's here forever, not even us. You have to remember that, because what is up here –" he tapped you on the forehead, "– is the only thing that will stay with you in the end."

It took you a long time to understand. It seemed to you there were too many similar falls. Every one of them grows within you, opening a rift, and you're afraid they'll gradually replace you and, one day, you'll wake up and all that will be left of you will be an empty body, and finally even this hollow shell will collapse inwards.

Time after time, you sink into your recollections. You tumble into your memory. Each recollection is an abyss with a meaning all of its own. You lay it out before you and try to see what lies at the very bottom.

"You just have to learn how to fall."

It's spring and daisies are growing between the carpet hangers. You're sitting on your bike and can't even touch the ground with your tiptoes. Gran's at the side, holding onto the handlebars.

"It's normal to fall. You take something away from each fall and, next time, you'll do it better."

As soon as you learned to read, you discovered this from one of the few books Mum had on her shelf: It is only with the heart that one can see rightly; what is essential is invisible to the eye.

Early in the summer of 2007, you're standing at the door to Marián's flat. You've never gone further than the musty staircase before, so you're surprised when he lifts your bike by the handlebars, carries it to the entrance, blocks the door with it and gestures for you to go inside.

"No-one's home."

You don't have time to think about it properly. You go upstairs and close the door behind you. Marián takes off his shoes, stops at the end of the short hallway, disappears and then quickly peeks out again. You slowly follow him. He's waiting in a small kitchen – the same as yours, with similar cupboards, the same chipped tiles above the sink, only the table is a bit bigger. There are piles of paper lying on the worktop, envelopes with purple and green stripes, bank statements and, slightly to one side, Marián's sketchbooks. An old wooden cross hangs roughly at eye level on the wall above the table, alongside some faded pictures with nothing specific on them – just a blur and a couple of coloured spots that might once have been a person's face.

You pick up a book from the table and a piece of paper with Marián's drawing of the school mosaic falls out. The same red and blue colours, the same stupid wreaths around their heads, except they've been slightly improved on. And while the figures on the wall stretch out towards each other and barely touch hands, in his version they're much closer.

"Do you want something to drink?"

You shift your gaze from the drawing to him. Marián opens the fridge, takes out a crumpled plastic bottle and puts it on the worktop. It's only because of the dim light from the fridge that you realize how dark it is in the flat, as hardly any light makes its way through the small window. He pours the tea into two glasses and leads you through the hall to a room. You get the impression you could fit the whole thing into the palm of your hand – a wardrobe with a mirror, a shelf with a pile of clean clothes, a TV stand, a couch and a bed. Everything jammed together without any gaps. It's dark here too, the shadows from outside forming soft lines on the walls, occasionally dancing and setting the whole room in motion.

You remember the music. Marián at the doorway with his broad smile.

"Is everything OK?" he asks, and you realize you've been staring blankly at him for some time. "You look totally out of it."

"I *am* totally out of it," meaning from the heat and your sore head.

Marián comes up to you and suddenly he's so close, your noses are almost touching. He takes your hand and leads you to the middle of the room.

"No wonder. I'd probably be completely bowled over by it too."

Your legs are tingling and it feels slightly odd, almost improper, to be in someone else's flat. You're afraid there's something wrong with you both. You want to ask Marián if he's afraid too. But then you'd have to admit to yourself that you're afraid of what you're discovering inside yourself.

You take a breath and start again. You remember the music. He puts on a CD so loud it hurts your ears. You watch as he moves his hips. Marián had always been braver, freer. Even that time on the bank of the Bečva, he'd been the first to lean towards you. The floor shakes beneath him. He takes your hand, nods his head, motions to you to join him and let go of your fear – and yet every movement, every current of air is another obstacle. You step forward but something stops you and your feet are rooted to the floor. You're embarrassed cos you can't move like him. You want to pull him towards you, stop all the movement, but Marián jumps away, shakes his head and continues jumping around the room. You feel stupid standing in the middle of the room, waiting for him to get tired or bored. Only then will he fall onto the bed and say something like: *well, this isn't how I'd imagined it.*

You cautiously sit next to him, hesitating slightly before you finally put your hand on his chest. It rises and falls as he breathes. Through the material of his T-shirt, you can feel his hot, sweaty skin. The shapes on the walls of the room fade away and you feel as though neither of you belongs there.

You reach over. His breath is all over your face. It's warm and smells a bit, but that doesn't bother you. The waves that crash against your skin dissolve into the room. You're both silent. He moves his hand and you repeat the movement. You move your body towards him and lean towards the fabric of his T-shirt, which is rough and covered in dust. Marián shuts his eyes and, up close, you can see a map of thin veins across his eyelids.

A thought goes through your mind – what if you bit his tongue by accident? If you closed your jaw and jerked back your head. The idea takes over and you have a sudden violent urge to do it. You swallow and your teeth snap together.

You keep your eyes open and don't really know how to proceed. Your hand is buried in his trousers, rubbing against the elastic of his boxers. He takes off his shorts and you do the same.

Everything seems heightened and strange, and yet necessary. You hold it in your hand and think about what to do next. A trickle of sweat runs down your back. You touch Marián again and he grimaces as though something was hurting him. Maybe he was just pretending, you think, while the skin on his belly folds into several creases and his body tenses.

At the base of his penis, you stare at one large, irregular mark with white hairs growing out of it. Your palm twitches a little. You lift it up and sniff it. On the way home, it will still smell of smoke, skin and urine. You deliberately rub it against your stomach.

You remember the whole thing as more of a dream than a real memory. Heat and time fuse the image together, making you feel like you don't belong in your own body. Like you're not quite there. Your heart's pounding, unable to maintain a regular rhythm.

If you could choose to live something over again, it would be that day.

It would be your face on the couch near Marián, a thin layer of sweat between the fabric and the skin. It's hot both outside and inside. You listen to him breathing, focusing on the feel of another person's skin and how it smells. He's lying on his stomach, his shoulder blades rising and falling just slightly more slowly than yours. Something occurs to you, and you stick out the tip of your tongue and lick the bumps on his spine, right in the middle.

It would be this image: Marián bursts out laughing and falls to the floor.

All day, he was grinning *like an oaf, like an idiot* as Mum would say. He stood in the window and looked different, the light falling directly onto his back, creating a dull glow around him, a haze spreading from his face down to where the elastic of his boxers had left marks on his skin.

By evening, the sun was already low, filling the flat full of unfamiliar objects with light. You were afraid of all the strange sounds – what if one of them was followed by a door slamming, what if it was his mother leaning against the door instead of Marián? Every loud footstep signalled a threat, each vibration an idea: *Now* everything will end, *now* the door will open and someone will see...

*Now* Marián is cavorting about in the middle of the room, dressed only in his boxers, holding up a dress he took from the pile of ironing.

"I think they'd burst a blood vessel in class."

You see at once the dress is too big for him. He tries it on briefly, then has a better idea. He walks over and puts it over your head.

You straighten your back, and it falls down your shoulders. On the way to the mirror, you trip over the long fabric. You nearly break your knee on the edge of the wardrobe, but this time you manage to stay on your feet.

It was only then that you really saw yourself for the first time in the mirror, trembling as you looked at the curve of your back in the neckline. Marián's expression in the reflection conveyed your own feelings, which – even later – you couldn't put into words. You closed your eyes. Even today, you are both still spinning around, and you don't know if it's your laughter or his that you hear. The dress swirls out with each movement. The whole time, you were concentrating on not falling, on not killing the two of you. The truth was, though, that you felt you could suddenly do anything you wanted. There was nothing to be ashamed of any more – nothing about who you are is an insult and it never has been.

You remembered the words Gran once said to you. About a body in which everything is as it should be – as long as you can feel this way, she's right, as long as you close your eyes, open them and remain standing.

And sometimes, it may be your own choice to fall.

You could hardly breathe from laughing so hard and your sides were aching. You fell to the floor, dragging him down with you.

"Bloody hell," said Marián between gaps, "if they saw this at school, they'd kill us straight off."

Pain is felt from within, never from the outside. Outside there is anger, rage and strangers' hands shaking you and, from somewhere in the distance, you hear a voice.

"Get up."

You open your eyes. Above you is the night sky, dotted with holes made by stars and covered by murky, brownish clouds. They are dried blood, a scab on skin. Despite the surrounding darkness, the world has fairly clear outlines. The light from a nearby streetlamp displays the nearest shapes in a soft red hue, while things further away are shrouded in a green mist. Most of the hospital buildings are dark and you hear only a muffled hum. You try to get up and fall back onto the broken glass on the pavement. You bang your cut hand against the bike and the pain throbs through your arm. You swallow and rub your eyes. The bench by the football pitch is empty, as is the field. There are still lights on in the flats, though no-one's stood at the windows for a while.

"Come on, get up."

You look to see where the voice is coming from, and when you move your head, a series of stabs goes through your neck. You swallow some blood and phlegm, wiping the rest on your T-shirt. Nothing inside you is as it should be – there's a pressure on your side and ribs. Your face is wet, and you wipe it first with your hand and then on your T-shirt. You change your position slightly to see where the voice is coming from.

At first you only see legs. You look up. The guy towering above you looks both nervous and surprised. You feel you know him from somewhere – you remember the mark near his eye, his smoky breath, but you can't immediately place him. You blink and see several images at once. You're trembling.

You remember snippets of conversations and movements, but mostly Filip. The others formed a circle, the first impenetrable wall. Laughter is the second one. Insults the third. You count down the time in your mind. Now you'll try to run away. Now. But you remain where you are, eyes still open. You're holding your cut hand and no longer even try to get away.

"What the fuck are you doing? Are you trying to kill him?"

Someone grabs your legs, someone kicks you in the stomach and someone else aims for your head.

"Yes."

Later, you convince yourself: in the end, nothing happened to you. It could've been worse. Just another fall, another notch in your memory. What happened was just an everyday occurrence. It's your lot. It's another experience. You'll find it in that ugly part of your mind whenever someone comes near you and tries to touch you. At other times, it's an empty, shabby place at the edge of an image. Better to gloss over it instead of paying attention to it.

And yet you come across it everywhere.

Just like that time in the changing room after PE, you fall to the ground and bring your knees up to your chest, protecting your head with your hands. Nothing happened to you, you repeat, and it sounds more like a reproach – once more, you're lying on the ground, the events repeating themselves over and over without ever leading anywhere. How can you complain? You're still here. Then something cracks loudly inside you and that sound, that fracture, breaks up their circle as well as you yourself. Everyone disappears or, at least, you think it's everyone. I observe the scene like a ghost hovering above. I'm in every window reflection, every mirror.

"Stop gawking at me like that."

You realize you've been staring at the guy above you. You lower your eyes and wipe the mucus from your nose again. A dark smear of blood and snot stains your skin. You clench your fist and a sharp pain shoots through your whole arm.

One day, you'll want to describe it. One day, you'll get up and the things around you will stop making sense. Soon you'll discover that what you see on the outside is completely different from what's on the inside. You'll discover it's much easier to describe anger than pain, just as it's easier to observe other bodies than look inside your own head. You can't see yourself except in a reflection. And if the pain is hidden below the surface, it'll most likely never be seen. It can't be shared so easily.

All it would take would be for the guy to touch you and you'd jump up and start beating him with your fists. You imagine scratching his skin off, pounding everything out of him till there wasn't even a skeleton left.

Instead of moving, the guy just stands there in silence.

It goes on like this for several minutes. You lose control, scream and, once more, for the last time, kick out at him desperately. You end up breathless and on all fours; you spit, and try to stand up, but your knees buckle. The guy goes over to you and helps you up.

For a moment, you both sway from side to side. Blood's streaming out of your nose. You can taste it on your lips. You lick and swallow. The guy notices and gently moves you into the light of the nearest streetlamp and dusts off your knees.

"Tilt your head back," he whispers irritably. "Christ, come on. That's it."

He pulls off his T-shirt and carefully wipes the blood, mucus and spit from your face.

"Hold it like this."

He presses the crumpled material to your face. You squeeze the edges and squint into the darkness in front of you. Meanwhile, the guy stands to the side, eyes darting furtively from place to place.

"I told them not to mess around," he mumbles after a long pause. "But you shouldn't take it personally. Every one of them has been punched in the face before like that, some even worse. They don't mean it like that – it's just a game, get it?"

You continue holding the T-shirt to your nose. The guy wraps his left arm round his shoulder. He's skinny and, in the artificial light, his skin is dotted with yellow marks. You can see his ribs and a few hairs on his chest. When you take the T-shirt away from your face, the blood continues to flow.

"Keep holding it there."

Every movement in your direction frightens you. You step back and press the T-shirt to your face once more.

"Filip…" the guy continues, scratching his chest, "Filip's in your class, right? He's weird, if you want to know what I think. I said to him: Hey, that's enough. Leave him alone. But he never listens. He's just plain weird."

You're glad you can't speak properly through the T-shirt. *Filip's weird*, you repeat to yourself while the guy picks up your bike from the ground, examines it thoroughly, glancing back at you out of the corner of his eye. He eventually pats the saddle, signalling all's good. *Nothing awful happened* – it's as if you could hear him say it.

"What's your name anyway?"

You whisper something, but he can barely make out your name.

"OK, and where do you live?"

You point upwards.

"Come on then. I'll go with you."

He turns the bike in the right direction and starts pushing it uphill. He shuffles his feet as he walks. The sound of his soles is only disturbed by the quiet hum from the hospital complex and the occasional car on the nearby road. His bare shoulders are slumped, and it seems to you they're weighed down by a giant invisible burden.

Everything around you seems out of place. Parts of the world make no sense to you and if you lay them out before you, you see Mum's angry face. She wouldn't understand any of it, and you have no idea how to explain it to her. All you know is you can't go home the way you are. You don't even want to.

You stay where you are. After a few steps, the guy notices, stops and mutters something. A car drives along the road past the hospital to the garages. For the first time, you realize how close home is, how close other people are.

"I'll manage myself."

The words come out with a confidence that surprises even you. You walk slowly towards him. You're limping, a sharp intake of breath with each step. In and out.

The relief is obvious on his face. You take the bike and give him back his filthy, bloody T-shirt, but he turns his nose up at it and indicates you should keep it. He starts to head off but then stops.

"Hey, it really was just a joke."

You wait tensely to hear what else he has to say. You look him straight in the eye, recognizing the grey edges of his pupils, even though you still can't remember where you saw them for the first time.

"I don't even think you look like a poof. I reckon you're all right."

He pauses, waiting to see if you'll thank him for this. If you appreciate it, at least you've passed the test in his eyes.

"It'll be OK... Just be more careful. And put up more of a fight next time."

You're surprised by his certainty. Something similar *will* happen again. It'll happen soon and it's up to you to make sure you're prepared.

"You have to hit back. And if you keep staring like that, you'll just piss people off."

*The best means of defence is attack.* Martin or your dad or grandad would say something similar if they were standing in front of you instead of this guy. *You don't have to take it. Just get your act together,* they'd continue, and you'd stay in the same place and refuse to move.

But what are you defending if you then turn into the very thing you need protection from?

Imagine a circle and, inside it, place every fall and every memory of a fall. You keep running round and round in this circle, tripping over something. You lie there, then get up and angrily shove the figure in front of you. You trip over again, or you can't be sure who shoved you this time.

Before the guy disappears into the darkness, he reaches out and offers you his hand. You frown, not really understanding his gesture. You shake his hand ceremoniously. His palm is soft and moist. The whole thing seems ridiculous to you, and if it wasn't for the pain in your side and the tingling in your arm, you wouldn't have been able to keep a straight face.

As soon as he leaves, you fish out your mobile from the pannier bag. The cover's dented at the back and there's a crack across the screen. As you run your finger over it, you cut your thumb, but you're still able to make out the missed calls icon. You switch the phone to your other hand and put it in your pocket.

Another car passes the hospital. The headlights blind you. You blink and the car disappears around the bend.

You hesitate briefly – there's only one place you can go, and it's not home. You try not to think of anything – certainly not of the repercussions of what you're about to do. You slowly climb the hill till you get to the first garage door. You swing your leg over the crossbar, grip the handlebars tightly and feel a sharp pain in your cut hand.

Perhaps that's why the town is just a dark blur in front of you. Occasionally a flash of light. You let the warm waves of air pass over your face. You cycle blind, by memory, turning seemingly at random, following lines and coloured spots.

It seems to you that memory is red when you project it onto the screen inside your eyelids today. You'll remember everything this colour, even the precise second when Marián opened the front door. Several expressions crossed his face at once. He opened his mouth, closed it, opened it again. But before he could say anything, you slipped inside.

Inside the flat, it's dark and cool. You slide down trembling onto the shoe cabinet.

"What happened?" His question takes you by surprise. Not that you didn't expect it, but because you don't know the answer, and so it hangs in the air.

It occurs to you again that nothing happened. In the darkness, Marián's face merges with the wall. The bulbs in the hall don't work and you don't have your bearings.

Marián reaches out his hand to you but then lowers it again. It swings by the side of his waist for a moment, and you follow it, like a pendulum marking time. It keeps going and never stops. It only knows how to speed up so that, one day, it will suddenly come back and throw as many memories as possible in your face.

"Sorry" is the only word you are able to say. Images flash through your mind. You want to tell him everything, but your tongue slides over your gums, too heavy to bear the weight of the words.

All you can maintain is silence, distance.

Marián sighs, bends down and carefully takes the bloodstained T-shirt off you. You hadn't even realized you were still holding the T-shirt to your nose. He holds it as far away as possible on the way to the bathroom, pulling you behind him. He closes the door, throws the T-shirt on the floor and pulls back the shower curtain. He helps you into the bath, and you let the stream of hot water pour over your head. Marián crouches down to get soap and a flannel from the basket beside the bath.

In your mind, you return to a similar image. You remember how you and Mum – by this stage, Grandad was ill and could hardly walk – ran a bath for him at his place after a fight that had lasted several days. The water came right up to the edge. You helped Grandad out of his T-shirt. Mum had to turn her back, otherwise Grandad would have caused a scene.

"You're not taking my clothes off. You can't see me naked. My own daughter – who ever heard of such a thing?"

Eventually, despite Grandad's protests, you both took an arm and sat him down in the bath. He sank into the water up to his chin, breathing only through his nose, so the coughing fits stopped for at least a short while. Even in the water, he kept his underwear on, though he still covered his crotch with his hand. He muttered something under his breath, his teeth chattering while the water flowed into his half-open mouth. He was trembling all over. You see Mum's hand in front of you, holding a wet flannel. She wiped Grandad's back in careful, circular motions, washing away the soap bubbles. His skin was covered in dark spots and marks. He put up with it, even though he still cursed a little, and, at one point, he turned his head and some water got in his ear, causing him to kick his legs into the air and splash you both with soapy water. Mum put on her focused expression, a face without any emotion.

In contrast to this image, Marián looks quite helpless. You study him through the steam. His lips are pressed together and his eyes are fixed in front of him. It was the first time you realized you don't actually know what he's thinking. He's sitting carefully on the edge of the bath, pointing the shower head at your back. He has his back to the light, and behind him you see tiles covered in condensation. The skin on his ears is translucent, a pink membrane full of thin, twisted veins.

You don't know what colour a person is inside, what colour the distance inside and between us is. At school, they taught you that the sky is blue because of the atmosphere and that darkness is jet black because there is very little light. Even the sea is blue. You turn your hand over and carefully remove a small green splinter. It seems logical to you that everything would be red inside your body. You observe the blood, which has a light pink colour when diluted in the water. It's weaker when it leaves you than it was inside your body. You clench your fist.

Marián inhales sharply, throws the flannel over your head and then slides into the bath too. The water splashing around you reminds you of Grandad. It reminds you of how close you were to him. Marián sits up, his T-shirt now completely soaked. He looks annoyed, crosses his arms, but then you both burst out laughing, unable to stop.

Even the laughter finally fades into just an echo. Later, sometime in the early hours, you awaken, aching all over, and not even that trace is left – even the pins and needles in your body mean something else. It's hot and dark outside, though there is light in the room from the streetlamp and the glow of the TV. Marián looks different in the flashes of light – calmer. There are subtitles on the TV and you remember the first few minutes of Akira, the explosion in Tokyo, the motorbike chase, then just fragments, coloured streaks and sounds. You fell asleep so quickly. You want to store this image in your memory, but your body is an empty place once more.

You get up. Besides a vague pain – here one minute, there the next, your ribs cracking – you feel thirsty, your throat's burning and twisting. You carefully open the door and slip out into the hall.

The moon above the flats releases a new dose of loneliness as you walk back through the hall to the kitchen and the papers strewn across the table. Drawings and official envelopes. You take a dirty glass from the worktop, pour some water into it and hop up beside the piles of papers. The light from the streetlamp merely intensifies the distance. You insist on that distance, because only in retreat are you able to be yourself. A space between the lines. You listen to the sounds of the town, the car wheels and strange

315

voices bouncing off the walls and the cobblestones. Some men beneath the window seem to be banging their heads against the walls of the building. There are sounds and then there are sounds. You throw them at your face, at its reflection in the window, and wait for at least an indication of the pain in return. *Don't look at me like that.* And, in the meantime, you see only fragments and small snippets.

You think of light and its waves, which are similar to those in the nearby river. They crash against your feet, the edge of the table, anything that can be crashed into. In some places, the stream bursts its banks, a flood in a cutout from the lamp. Last year, the physics teacher told you about the rays from stars and how long they take to reach the Earth. The idea stuck in your mind – each dot in the sky is millions of years old, and the longer you look at the night sky, the more of them you see.

In reality, they are long gone.

What you are seeing are just more and more memories. Regardless of how far a ray travels, it will always contain an imprint, a memory of the point of reflection.

If time equals distance, how far must you go before someone notices you too? How much further?

You turn to the window and attempt to look out onto the street, but all you see is your own reflection. In the glass, your face looks unnaturally pale, framed by strands of black hair that blend into the surrounding darkness.

So many nights you've stared into the mirror, waiting for someone else to step out from it. You open your mouth, and it seems to you that the reflection is talking to you, that you're lagging behind it.

One morning, you'll wake up and forget about everything, you promise yourself. One morning, you'll wake up and find this reflection broken, with a total stranger behind it.

How can you forget and not lose part of yourself? You will ask yourself this question again many times without realizing it doesn't matter – even our memory is often capable of laying out everything except its own image.

Marián coughs in the next room. The sharp, dry sound transports you through time – at first, you pretend not to see the memory, but all that it takes is one movement for something to spill out.

In reality, you had never forgotten how badly they treated him. When you both started to hang out together later on, perhaps you had expected him to be grateful for your considerateness, for accepting him, for not minding. All you had to do was stand aside, you thought, and everything would pass you by. Just watch. Sit, locked in the toilet cubicle, and ignore the shouting and Marián's voice. Don't even move. Just listen to the body falling to the floor, the movement leading to a bang against the door, which shakes as you cover your ears. However, the ringing and more blows still reach you. Quiet. You wait, count to five, and only then do you go out.

He's lying beside the urinals, all wet, surrounded by either water or urine. You stand above him, looking at him, neither of you saying a word. In your mind, it lasts for hours as you wade through the memory and, as in every good mirror, you also see the image back to front. That's why you look so strange in photographs – you're used to seeing yourself from a better angle. Even in the window opposite, you are not able to capture anything other than your face, *your stupid mug*, as the voices inside your head keep reminding you.

Marián is sleeping with his mouth open, some foamy saliva forming in the corner. You watch him for what seems like an eternity. But what does eternity even mean? How long is it? You switch off the TV and walk across the room. You can't decide. What is eternity made up of? Memories? Maybe you are slightly ashamed of yourself, looking for some sense in it all, though there probably never was any. You are ashamed of yourself and even more ashamed of the fact you'd do it all again. You pull on your shorts and return to the hall, where you put on your shoes quietly so as not to wake him, then close the door behind you...

Now there's nothing but air where the windows to Grandad's flat used to be. All that's left of the former Chemik hostel is a scar, the outline of the foundations marked out by a strip of freshly mown grass. Even here, the town has been trying hard for years to force out those it has long refused to see. Maybe this was how it thought it'd get rid of them – in 2018, it gave the tenants of the more dilapidated of these two buildings less than a fortnight to move out. The building then remained empty until it was finally razed to the ground almost a year and a half later. In the photos of the demolition, the housing units look like exposed honeycomb filled with rubble and dust, while the other building, which is still there, stands out from the background with its new apricot façade. You're standing more or less where the entrance used to be. It's the first time you've been here since you and Mum moved Grandad's things out all those years ago. There's nothing here now. It makes sense that Grandad's home – or, at least, what was his home in your memories – disappeared along with him. You can still recall the trees, the birches and low conifers; they're gone now too, washed away along with the building by the current of the ever-shrinking Bečva.

On Google Maps, though, the view of Chemik hasn't changed one bit. If you open the view from the main road, you'll find the two buildings as they were. Behind them is a steel, cloud-darkened sky with small patches of light. Zoom in with your mouse and the picture changes again, going even further back in time to a day in May 2012. His windows are open in the right place, but no-one's leaning out of them. By then, Grandad was long gone, absorbed into the memory of that evening, the point when you and your reflection in the kitchen in Marián's house decided to get away from here.

You've got no idea if a town has a memory or if you're merely projecting your own experiences onto its streets. You used to think Přerov had no charm. It was full of shabby tower blocks, torn and crookedly pasted posters, and dusty windows with no reflections. You looked over the photos of New York sent by your dad and dreamed of any big city where you could get lost in the crowd.

Objectively, Přerov is like any other town. Here too, there are concrete car parks alternating with green spaces, all intersected by a network of pavements, paths and buildings lined up one after another, blindly resembling each other. It's true that since you left, a large part of the town has changed in appearance. The trees on the edges of the pavements struggle to survive in concrete squares that are too small for them. They're now twice the size and, in places, their roots are pushing through the concrete. The greyness has gradually been pushed out by a wide range of diverse colours – bright green, yellow and purple façades vie for attention with the renovated railway station and new bridges.

At first sight, it looks as though the town is consciously trying to shake off bad memories, remove places that resemble open wounds and hide the crooked limbs it's ashamed of. Instead of facing them head on, it has to pretend they don't exist. The Komuna cultural centre, the houses on Škodova, and now even Chemik – all demolished. What could be abandoned or forgotten was left to decay so that something else could be built in its place for different, *better* people. The town no longer cared so much about the evicted families and what would remain, because sometimes it's better if things disappear from sight and consequently apparently cease to exist. Every eyesore has to be razed to the ground, or at least covered in adverts, until it's just a place, another point in the memory, which you try in vain to overwrite with something else, which you walk around and pretend it isn't there.

Even this empty space is just another painful memory. You look away from the spot where his windows should be. A group of men are raking through the bins on a long cracked car park. You watch as they go through them, commenting on their new finds. One side of the Bečva is lined with trees scorched by the light, their tops allowing only fragments of this light onto the benches by the river, which are occupied by groups of children, heads back, listening to music on their mobiles, blowing out smoke without a care in the world. The river flows lazily over its bed and, judging by the broken branches on the surface, nothing will stop it and it will go on forever.

According to your mobile, you've got just enough time to walk over to Mum's to get changed for the funeral. You look around the deserted place one last time before heading towards the town centre.

"The most handsome guy in Přerov once waited for me here beneath this tree," Mum told you once as you were walking under a canopy of trees along the Bečva. But it could've been any tree – maybe one of the ones that will soon be gone. To allow the diggers access to the embankment and build anti-flood barriers, the whole avenue from the boatyard to the hospital has to be cut down. Most of the people in the town don't understand why. They protested in vain and even offered to dig the trees up by hand for free, but no-one listened.

There are also places in the area full of graffiti you don't understand. On every corner you come across strange messages. Perhaps they're nothing more than an attempt to fix the place in the memory. Lay it out across the whole town: *we were here*, names repeated on benches, messages scribbled onto façades. It doesn't matter how many buildings they demolish, how many trees they cut down, there will always be someone left who remembers. *I was here*, the thought occurs to you, and you walk on. You take a step forward and remember your mum, staring straight ahead with a slight smile.

"I knew straight away it wouldn't work out. He took me to the cinema to see some film that was full of sex and he was groping my thigh the whole time."

She lowered her head, returning to that evening in her memory, and when she spoke again, her head was still bowed.

"After I told him I had a wee boy, he never called again."

You walk along the condemned avenue by the Bečva all the way to the tennis courts. You'd normally take a different route, but, this time, you take a sharp turn at the newly rebuilt footbridge and head towards the school. You've avoided this place ever since that day at the end of the summer holidays when you finally spoke to Mum and she arranged for you to transfer to another school at the last minute.

With your fingers hooked around the fence, you stand there and try to see past the playground and inside. You hope the light is making its way slowly to you and that what you're seeing is a glimpse through time, that the school windows work in the same way as when you're observing the stars at night.

In one reflection, you can vaguely make out Filip. He's standing by the classroom door. The summer holidays are over, it's the start of September and you feel a rush of heat. Marián's not beside you or, at least, you don't remember him. Your heart starts beating so hard that the whole desk is shaking with you. The shaking lasts the entire lesson and returns on the second and third days. You thought the feeling would pass, that you could stand it, just as you could stand that final fall a few days later, when you were tripped at the edge of the stairs beside the mosaic.

This time, the arms of the two boys seem far apart. Filip says something to you, and you turn towards his voice and stumble. You don't even try to keep your balance; instead, you throw up your arms in resignation and take another step forward.

The impact is a sound reflected off a wall, the vibrations of the railings and the metal bars at the edge of the staircase. But you don't notice any of this. You hear other voices: Mum at home sitting at the table, you resting on it with your arm in plaster, and – for the first time in your life – you confiding in her. Filip pushed you down those stairs, you exaggerate, keeping some details to yourself; others you embellish until she has no choice but to believe you.

You never told her exactly what happened that evening when Grandad went crazy. She doesn't know where you spent the night when you came home early in the morning. You cleared your throat and went into the flat. The kitchen door was open, and Mum was lying curled up on the bench, the smell of cigarettes in the air. She lifted herself up and rubbed her swollen eyes with her knuckles. It seemed to you that through the slits of her eyelids she was transmitting a mixture of fury and sorrow, resentment and disappointment to you. Her expression twisted into a tired grimace, and she glanced at you again, probably not even registering Marián's T-shirt – you'd gotten rid of your own torn, bloodstained one – then got up and left the kitchen.

She never spoke the whole time. Only later did a few words slip out. Maybe she didn't even want to say them out loud and they reached you by chance. Karolína was standing in the doorway. She must've just missed you in the hall and was standing with her legs apart by the shoe cabinet, shouting something at Mum about the car in the street and the keys in the ignition. You slipped past them and fell into bed, where you mustered the courage to ask where they were going.

Through a gap in the door, you could see Mum as she checked the things she'd hurriedly thrown into a plastic bag. She didn't even bother to turn round, silently rearranging the bag's contents. With one foot out the door, she stopped and muttered something you didn't understand.

"We're going to see Grandad." The keys jangled in the lock. You sat up, gasped from the pain and almost missed the rest of the sentence. "You're not interested anyway; otherwise, you'd have been here. They had to take him to hospital yesterday."

You did tell her something, though. For effect, you appropriated and exaggerated the things that'd happened to Marián. You stole his story, and it all came to a head that evening. You lay it out on the table before Mum, asking her not to send you to that school any more.

Today, you barely recognize the buildings, and all the grounds have been done up. There's a new gym with a new playground in front of it, a new canteen and new plastic windows for the classrooms. From a distance, it looks empty, and you search within yourself for at least some evidence that the whole thing meant something more. Inevitably, though, all you can think of is Mum's question.

"Why didn't you tell me about it before?"

Even now, you don't know the answer to that. Maybe just... You never told anyone about it because it seemed normal to put up with it. *You have to grin and bear it.*

Mum's voice shook with anger as she pulled you up you for not being there for her, for not talking to her.

"You only look after yourself. Why should I help you?"

You dug your fingers into the holes in the upholstery and absent-mindedly pulled out the remaining threads, ripping and throwing away bits of foam onto the floor.

326

"What're you going to do about it?" You wanted to laugh at the idea that you could do anything at all. "And what do you want me to do about it?"

She eventually did what you wanted her to do. You couldn't go on pretending any more. You were tired and desperate, so you didn't really understand what you were doing. For you, running away represented the last glimmer of hope.

Within a month, you and Mum are in the headmaster's office at your new school, looking slightly perplexedly at a calendar by Pivrnec with smutty jokes. The room is small, as is the whole school. A single dirty ray of light falls through the dusty window onto piles of papers scattered across the desk. You check your reflection in the old glass cabinet and smooth down your hair with your hand. Mum brings out a plastic folder from her bag, opens it and places it in front of a small, grey-haired man. Before she can pull her hand back, the headmaster puts his on top of hers and the folder, leaving it there too long for the contact to be accidental.

Part of you was relieved and part of you was terrified at what you were leaving behind – mainly because Marián was unaware of the transfer as you hadn't told him a thing. You had been so out of it, you'd forgotten about him, and you were oddly relieved by the thought that you'd soon be far away from him, far away from everything.

Unlike Marián, you had a choice. During the long breaks and the free periods, you'd both gone over similar scenarios in the dusty corner beneath the staircase – the possibility of going to another school and starting over. Marián always had a slightly clearer idea about the future than you, but he came up against walls and barriers built of prejudice and incomprehension.

"No-one will want me." In the spring of 2007, you had first had the idea that you could transfer together. "And Mum wouldn't want it anyway. I just couldn't explain this to her. What would I tell her, that they beat me up? She already knows. I already tried, and believe me, no-one wants a Gypsy in their class, and I don't want to go to a place where they'll beat me up anyway." There was neither self-pity nor tiredness in his voice. Even years later, you admire how easily he always managed to find a gap and discover his own way out. "So we'll just muddle through this together somehow."

You're not at all proud of what you did. You sometimes think you took his dream away from him – you managed to escape, but he didn't. You were silent those last few days you spent together, withdrawn on your side of the desk once more, afraid even to look in his direction.

And one morning, all that remained of you was an empty chair.

You try unsuccessfully to remember when you last saw Marián. Everything's mixed up and confused in your mind. Just after transferring schools, there's an image in your mind where you bump into him at the library and duck behind a bookcase in fright. But that could well have been a dream. False and distorted memories, on the basis of which some unseen person creates misleading trails, rearranges images and mixes up faces. The only precise memories are of his text messages. The phone in your hand was a heavy, impersonal object, and the words on the screen were meaningless letters. You wrote a couple of your own but never sent them. You deleted them, only to receive a completely different message a few days later.

*I hate you.*

*I hate myself too*, you replied to yourself, reaching out of habit for the scissors in the tin at the edge of the table.

You tear yourself away from the fence. There's so much that you're ashamed of, that you regret, that you'd happily forget. The shame eats away at you from the inside, while the regret constantly brings you back to those ruins. After all these years, nothing remains except for the remorse and the knowledge that you used him, that the whole time you didn't stop to think about anyone but yourself. When you managed to find Marián on Instagram – or, rather, an algorithm recommended him to you – because, in this world, not even technology will let us forget – you opened his profile and saw his face smiling at you again amongst photographs of his drawings. Sometimes, he was alone, but more often with another guy.

Before you even realized what you were doing, you opened his photos one after another and put a heart icon on them. Marián had longer hair than before. His features were somewhat sharper, as though he'd taken off a mask and his true likeness was now looking at you. He looked happy. You'd almost forgotten about him, even though what you wanted to forget were the rows of buildings, all the windows with their reflections, the empty corridors and the mosaic on the first floor – two hands reaching out and never touching.

Your mobile goes off in the quiet of the funeral parlour room, giving you a start. You've been waiting quarter of an hour in complete silence, so the muffled sound of the vibrations echoes several times before the bare walls of the practically empty room manage to absorb it.

Mum elbows you in the ribs, but her gaze remains fixed on the entrance to the room. She still believes your aunt will show up as there's still time for her to appear, so she's determined to give her sister one last chance. Your uncle's sitting next to Mum, clutching her hand and staring at the floor. He looks like a younger, gentler version of your grandad.

Twenty minutes earlier, the three of you were standing in a small room with a dozen chairs, looking through glass at the open coffin. His hands were clasped to his chest, the suit yellowed from cigarettes, his face sunken, twisted and empty. Gran was waiting outside in the only occupied chair. Before going in, she gave you a hint of a smile, perhaps to support you, or perhaps she didn't know what else to do. Your uncle slouched and spread his legs to regain his footing and, after a long sigh, said quietly, as though to himself: "So they put them there after all. Look, Dana." He reached out and touched the glass partition between you and the corpse. "I wanted him to at least have some ciggies for the journey."

A new message from Jakub pops up on your display with a photo icon. *22 July*, it says on your phone, *you have a new memory*. It seems to you there are suddenly too many of these memories, so you don't even open the photo. You know what's there and it has nothing to do with the scene around you or how you feel.

Despite what others say and what you yourself once thought about them, photographs are not reminders of the past. Photographs are proof that what you see in them really happened. Which is why you take pictures of everything around you. You'll happily stop in the middle of the street and point the camera at an unusual feature or perhaps directly at yourself.

A photograph is proof for others – *I was here* – and, at the same time, a backup in case you forget. *Memories, here I come*, says one of the posters at Václav Havel Airport. You know this because you also took a photograph of it and the picture's still stored in your phone. This sign is telling you in advance that you're only living for the past.

You're counting on it beforehand and you know that every passing moment means another memory, and every photo that your phone won't let you forget is proof. You look at it and all the captured memories scatter from it like woodlice from an upturned stone. It's up to you whether you collect them and try to make at least some sense out of them.

*You have a new memory.*

Why do you have to remember everything, though? Every fall, every blow, even the light streaming in long rays through the windows on both sides of the hall, broken on the floor into coloured strips.

"You have to remember it all," you recall Grandad saying, "because that's what'll stay with you." It's for him that you're trying to hold on to everything. "For those who don't remember the past", said Grandad, reciting the well-known phrase, "are condemned to repeat it. Even a deer – and you've got a bit of that in you, you're my flesh and blood after all – isn't stupid and never returns to a place where a hunter took a shot at it."

You know now that Grandad was wrong – you, him and the deer will always return to well-known places, hoping to find them intact, just like those birds that time during the floods.

It's often more difficult to forget than to remember.

Early last spring, you were helping Mum clear out the cellar and, in a box of Grandad's things, you found four diaries from the psychiatric hospital. When you were sure Mum wasn't looking, you tucked them under your T-shirt and took them back to Prague with you. *I never feel more worthless than when I try controlled drinking*, he wrote in the first entry from the year you were born. *Whenever I try controlled drinking, I always think of those people I see in front of me, how I will never amount to anything compared to them. I see my family, who I was unable to look after. Controlled drinking offers me my own reflection, and that man inside me would like to grab myself by the throat and shake the coward he sees. Wherever I look, that's me. Which is why I lose control and end up comatose under a table. Only the drink can stay my hand, that uncontrolled, true drinking. I'm pouring my heart out here and I'm hungover, but I can't drive that image from my mind.*

As you read, you pause and recall all the situations where you felt the same. Your Grandad's handwriting was familiar to you – his tiny letters also slid down at the end of sentences, and it was hard work deciphering them.

*All because I couldn't handle it, and now I'm here, begging strangers for help. What would my dad say? I remember how he'd always stretch out his hand with the belt he'd forced me to remove from him. Did he recognize there was something wrong with me? He's calling to me again: a true Daněk doesn't behave like that. A Daněk doesn't whimper like that. Only a dog does that. If you were a Daněk, you'd hold your head up high. I don't want to go back to it, but I don't have much choice. I want to stick to the controlled drinking, but his voice and hand are still in my head. They don't want to leave me. It's only when I drink that the voices cease. Without the booze, I feel as though he's always standing over me. Even now, he's looking me up and down through the window. I'm still that lanky boy, standing in front of him in the kitchen, handing him his own belt. I'd rather drink, day after day, until the last remnant of me disappears, or until there's nothing left in me at all.*

The funeral assistant quietly closes the door and, head bowed, slowly makes his way to the podium. *We will never forget* is written on the ribbon tied to the funeral arrangement. But this is where you see the problem – clinging desperately to what was. Unlike your mother, you haven't forgiven anyone, least of all yourself. There are only four of you in the whole hall: your mum, uncle, gran and yourself. The pointed roof reminds you of a huge tent and makes the space that bit bigger and more deserted. You look at the beams, the wood panels and the light bulbs. They're on, even though there's daylight coming through the poorly blacked out windows.

There's no eulogy at the ceremony. Following a short, impersonal introduction, a nameless man descends from the podium and gloomily folds his arms.

"I couldn't bring myself to write one," whispers Mum. "What would I say? I don't even know that much about him."

You have to bite your tongue to stop yourself from laughing when, instead of a speech and memories of Grandad, they start to quietly play *Let It Be*. How many times had Grandad insisted that this song was to be played at his funeral? You keep coming back to the funeral arrangement and the writing on the ribbon. Mum doesn't speak English, so she wouldn't have got the irony – playing a song at a funeral that is literally asking you to forget.

The words of the song fade, and you can hear the irregular beating of your heart once more. The pounding doesn't even stop after the ceremony. You're standing in front of the building, and you can see Přerov cemetery, the trade school and even the factory building, beyond a low row of flats.

"Should we take a photo?"

Mum's got her phone ready and points the camera at you all. Gran's leaning on your shoulder while your uncle's to the side, looking at the pointed roof of the crematorium, his left hand casually tapping the ash from his cigarette.

The photograph has captured you like this: you're looking somewhere beyond the frame, your face flushed from a rush of blood and slightly blurred, as each heartbeat shakes you; Gran is looking straight at the camera, smiling; your uncle would have rather been anywhere else. You have no idea yet what this photo is evidence of. But you've saved it anyway and, perhaps, one day, you'll open it and find something hidden within it.

"In any case…" says Mum, leading you all out of the cemetery. "In any case, I'll never get used to it. I picked up the phone this morning to call him. I only realized how stupid I was when it was too late and it started ringing. They haven't even got round to disconnecting him."

On the way home, she tells you how she visited Grandad for the last time at Kroměříž psychiatric hospital. She carefully pushed the wheelchair in front of her, bumping it over the grass, and Grandad could barely hold the ice cream cone in his frail hands. It was melting fast in the hot afternoon air. Mum was holding a dirty hanky and the handle of the wheelchair in one hand, and her own cone in the other. She turned back when they got to the tree you're familiar with from the photo. It's spreading and has a crown whose leaves are already turning yellow, although it's also possible it was just a trick of the saturated light, which was shining down on them in tiny droplets. She stopped, looked up towards the light and then squinted back at Grandad.

He looked healthy and even seemed to recognize her. His ice cream was soon finished, and he began asking for another, but she refused.

"You'd get the shits, wouldn't you?" she said, laughing. But she did give him the rest of her own ice cream. Grandad parted his lips, exposing his blackened teeth. It seemed to her as though it was the first time she'd seen him happy. She bent down to wipe away some ice cream dripping down his chin and, as she was straightening up, he placed a hand on her shoulder and croaked out a barely comprehensible sentence.

"Forgive me."

You're at the crossing again, waiting for the lights to change. Mum interrupts her story, looks round, sees nothing's coming and crosses the road. The three of you follow her.

"I froze," she continues on the other side, taking a drag on her cigarette during the pauses. "This had never happened before. I'm daft, I should have known something was wrong – Grandad never apologised. And certainly not just like that, for no reason. But then I said something completely stupid to him. *But Grandad*, I said to him, *I forgave you a long time ago.*"

Gran grumbled discontentedly beside you.

"Well, I don't know – forgive him for all his drunken escapades?"

From somewhere in the distance, a flash of bright light hits you. You half-close your eyes and let the warm waves reflect off your face. Mum lowers her head and smiles slightly. Only then does she go on.

"I know, Mum. But it's better, isn't it, just to keep the nice days in your head. And the rest? You'll forget it one day anyway."

# Memory Burn – Translators' Notes

We were first introduced to Marek Torčík's novel *Memory Burn* when the Czech Literary Centre approached us to translate an extract from it last year. What immediately struck us was the stark language and intimacy of the narrator's voice, something that was also noted by the jury of the prestigious Magnesia Litera award, when *Rozložíš paměť*, to give it its Czech title, won the prize for literature in 2024 – no mean feat for a debut novel by a writer who had previously made a name for himself as a poet.

Without doubt, though, the greatest overall impact was made by the theme of the novel, which addresses issues long considered taboo in Czech society and rarely explored within the literary canon. The post-industrial peripheral Moravian town of Přerov will no doubt be an unfamiliar location to most readers and reveals a side of the Czech Republic that is far less well known than Prague or Brno, for instance. Here, Přerov could be representative of any small town. It may have its moments of beauty, but, fundamentally it is somewhere to be escaped from in order to avoid succumbing to its stultifying atmosphere. The schools, streets, river and nearby quarry provide a labyrinth-like backdrop to the harrowing story of a homosexual boy growing up surrounded by people who, at best, don't understand him and, at worst, lash out at him and his Romani schoolmate.

Intolerance and violence are shown here as generational scars, almost encoded into the DNA, as physical and verbal abuse is passed down from great-grandfather to grandfather to father, leaving our narrator to finally break the cycle. This is an act of heroism which the writer may not even be fully aware of, for he certainly does not present himself as being anyone exceptional. There is no self-pity expressed by the narrator; nor does he expect us always to empathize with him. Indeed, when another 'outsider' joins the class – in this case, a Romani boy – the narrator's initial feeling is one of relief that he is no longer the focus of attention and vitriol, and can escape the torments of his fellow pupils – albeit only temporarily.

And so the kaleidoscope of memories reveals the flaws in all the characters, not least in the narrator himself. Motifs of light and shadow, waves and currents, and reflected images abound in the novel, taking us from past to present and back again, all within the space of a few paragraphs. For the reader more used to traditional narrative styles, this can be slightly confusing initially, and it can take time for them to orientate themselves within the complex timeline of the novel. To challenge the reader further, we sometimes return to altered versions of the past, because our memories are notoriously unreliable and scenes can subtly change. Thus, versions of the past are interpreted differently by different people, in particular by the narrator's mother, until Marek (the narrator is also called Marek) finds himself asking where the truth lies in all this – *"What are memories but stories? I bring them up again in the belief that they belong to the same person you once were. You spin them into a web, sit within them as though they were the things keeping you afloat. But the truth is that with each re-telling they turn into something different, something distant."*

Which brings us to the title of the novel. Unlike the French and German titles, which have tended towards a more literal translation of the Czech *Rozložíš paměť* (literally, you lay out your memory) *Memory Burn* was the author's idea. When we asked him about the English title, his response was:

*When I was thinking about a title (way before I even thought this could be translated into any language), I wanted to keep the ambivalence of "Rozložíš paměť". The two meanings in the Czech title are a deconstruction of memory and also a laying out/spreading of memories in front of you, so that you can maybe make some sense of the mess they are. For me, this is the predicament of the story – destruction/understanding, whether it's better to destroy memories or try and make sense of them. I thought* Memory Burn *keeps this unclear duality. The idea of a memory that is burned into us and hence it's impossible to forget, but also that you can burn your memories away, turn them into ash.*

There is a great honesty in this novel which forces us to reflect on our own weaknesses and prejudices. Most importantly, though, as we struggle to shape our own identity, it makes us realize that the choices and decisions we make now not only have an impact on the present, but that they can come back either to haunt us or, conversely, to provide us with at least a modicum of comfort and consolation in the future.

Graeme and Suzanne Dibble, Letovice, 2025

# Acknowledgements

The text contains several borrowed passages. I first asked myself the question, "What am I to myself that must be remembered, insisted upon so often?" thanks to the poem *The Rain* by Robert Creeley. The idea of time as counter-movement and counter-current appeared in several poems by Viola Fischerová, in her collection *Domek na vinici*. "Let them lie, but where," and "Why hold onto all that? And I said, Where can I put it down?" are fairly loosely paraphrased lines from Anne Carson's *The Glass Essay*. And it was Roland Barthes who wrote first about photographs as proof in his *Camera Lucida*.

Every book grows and lives in conversation, and this one would not have been possible without a number of wonderful people. I would especially like to thank my Czech publisher Paseka, for their trust, hard work and everything they do for their books. To my editor Bára Klimtová, thank you for your care, advice, and support. Thanks to Lukáš Růžička and Nikola Janíčková. Thank you to my agent Pavlína Juračková, without whom you would not be reading this. To Bára Votavová, thank you for all our talks and for pushing me closer to finishing this book. Thanks to Dominika Papíková, Emma Kausc, Marta Nováková, Bára Voříšková and Sára Schejbalová.

I would also like to thank – if words are enough – Graeme and Suzanne Dibble, who translated this book to English. I do believe that translation is the closest and purest form of reading. And to everyone CEEOL Press, namely to Krisztina Kós. Thank you.

This book is dedicated to three very dear people. First and foremost, to my mother, the bravest person I know. Thank you for allowing me to talk about things that are difficult to talk about, let alone read about in a book. Thank you for everything. To my dad, who, apart from very vague outlines, has nothing in common with Pavel from the previous pages. And to my grandfather. His name was Antonín Daněk and I believe that despite all, he was a good man.

And finally, and as always, thanks to Jakub. For being, and for him and my cats Milo and Goya sticking up with the noise of my keyboard clacking until four in the morning for more than three years.

CEEOL**PRESS**

2025

www.ingramcontent.com/pod-product-compliance
Lightning Source LLC
LaVergne TN
LVHW051955271025
824392LV00014B/468